Praise for *Finding Mr. Write*

MW00618938

The idea of two writers falling ~~~~ ~~~~ ~~~~ ~~~~ has always intrigued me. (Hey, a novelist can dream, can't she?) Perhaps that's why I adored Carol Moncado's delightful new book, Finding Mr. Write. Jeremiah and Dorrie's individual stories hooked me right away and the merging of their lives offered twists and turns that kept me flipping the pages, wondering what would happen next. Highly recommended! ~ **Janice Thompson, author of the Weddings by Bella series**

Oh my goodness—if you've never been to a writer's conference before, this is the book for you! Light-hearted and fun, *Finding Mr. Write* captures the essence of a writer's journey on the road to publication and love, offering a fresh and frisky glimpse into a truly novel romance. ~ **Julie Lessman, award-winning author of The Daughters of Boston, Winds of Change, and Heart of San Francisco series.**

Finding Mr. Write is a mega-romantic story with amazing chemistry between the two characters, and Jeremiah is one of the most memorable and loveable heroes I've read in a long time. Carol Moncado's writing reeled me in and hooked me, and I was eager to see how Dorrie and Jeremiah would overcome their secrets and unusual circumstances to find true love. I loved this story! ~ **Melanie Dickerson, award winning author of *The Healer's Apprentice***

General Praise

Sharp-witted dialogue, clever plots and engaging characters - Carol Moncado is an author to watch and, more importantly, READ! - **Jennifer A. Davids, author of *Buckeye Dreams***

Author Carol Moncado's stories are truly irresistible! With endearing characters and make-your-heart-smile romance, you'll keep turning pages, never wanting to reach 'The End'... Go ahead and make room on your favorites' shelf, because this fresh voice in contemporary Christian fiction is here to stay. ~**Kristy Cambron, author of *The Butterfly and the Violin* and *A Sparrow in Terezin***

CANDID Romance

Finding Mr. Write
Finally Mr. Write
Falling for Mr. Write

Montevaro Monarchy

Good Enough for a Princess
Along Came a Prince
More Than a Princess

For Joe and Vicki -
For all the support you've given over
the years.
I appreciate you!

Chapter One

*A*nastasia Salome Keziah, Princess of Montevaro and her escort, Jonathan William Langley-Cranston the Fourth of the United States."

Ana tucked her hand inside Jonathan's elbow, knowing she would rather be with someone else, and pasted the best smile she could on her face as they walked through the ornate wooden doors into the palace ball room. A smattering of applause sounded from those assembled. Her slightly-older twin brother and his new girlfriend were announced about the time Ana and Jonathan reached the bottom of the steps. When Jonathan stopped next to their seats, the crier called again.

"Our guests of honor, Her Royal Highness, Crown Princess Adeline of Montevaro and her husband, Prince Charlemagne Brewer."

"I bet he hates that," she muttered to herself.

"What?"

She looked up to see Jonathan staring down at her, an amused look on his face. "I bet Charlie hates being introduced as Charlemagne all the time."

Jonathan chuckled. "I can imagine." He held her seat out for her as she sat down. Once he was seated next her, he leaned over to whisper in her ear. "You know, we both know you would rather be here with someone else, and we both know your mother would never allow you to attend with the escort you would have chosen, so can we just make the best of this?"

Ana scanned the ballroom until her eyes landed on the dark wavy locks and laughing blue eyes of Montevaro's most renowned pediatrician. When he looked her way, she broke eye contact and stared at the family crest on her plate.

"I'd guess he'd probably rather be here with you, too," Jonathan pointed out.

"It does not matter. You were correct when you said my mother would never permit it. Perhaps once Adeline is queen..."

"That's only two days away. Once all this pomp and circumstance is over, your mother will relax."

Ana watched Dr. Fontaine as he smiled at the woman sitting next to him, and her heart twisted, just a bit. She struggled through dinner, knowing her sister would point it out if she didn't eat well. Jonathan respected her space and did not try to draw her out in conversation.

When the dancing started, Addie and Charlie took the floor first. Partway through the dance, Rick - as the second in line for the throne - and Ellie joined them. The protocol secretary nodded at Ana, who allowed Jonathan to help her to her feet and join her brother and sister for the last third of the song.

Once the first dance was over, anyone could join in. She and Jonathan traded partners, and she found herself dancing with her brother.

"Why so glum, chum?" Rick's eyes twinkled at her.

"Don't get all psychological on me." If she wasn't careful, he'd dig and dig, until he figured it out. "How are things going with Ellie?"

"Ah. You're changing the subject, little sister. Are you not completely enamored with your date?"

"You know I'm not. Jonathan is a nice man, and I like him, but when it didn't work out between him and Addie, Mother decided she wanted him in the family anyway. That means me."

"And you would rather be here with the good doctor?"

Ana glared up at her brother but didn't reply.

"He was on the shortlist for Addie, so why not for you?" Rick twirled her out and back in. "That is your real question, is it not?"

How well he knew her. They had shared a womb. "Maybe."

Rick leaned down until there was no chance any of the other couples nearby would hear him. "I have it on good authority he's interested in my sister."

"Don't be silly, Rick. The man doesn't even know I'm alive except as the spare of the spare for the throne of Montevaro."

He held her hand to his chest and let his head fall back dramatically. "The spare? You wound me, sister."

If they hadn't been dancing at one of the most important balls of her lifetime, she would have smacked him right in the arm. The music began to wind down for this song, and she knew tradition dictated the third dance be with whoever was on the lady's right. She just hoped her brother wouldn't land her next to one of the stuffed shirts from Parliament. Instead, as he took a step back and bowed, she noted the glint in his eye.

She turned to her right and her heart stopped. The man bowed while she gave a slight curtsy. One hand rested on his shoulder while the other fit snugly inside his. "Dr. Fontaine, it is a pleasure."

Could she make it through this dance without embarrassing herself?

He smiled down at her. "Oh no, Princess Ana. The pleasure is all mine."

* * *

Dr. Jonah Fontaine could hardly believe his luck. He'd expected the princess to end up with her escort for this dance as well, but when he'd looked to his left and saw her standing there, his heart leapt in his chest. As Princess Anastasia tucked her hand in his, he reached for her waist, settling his other hand on her hip, the smooth satin of her gown cool beneath his fingertips. He led her through the first bars of the next song, and he needed to take this chance before it slipped away.

"Are you enjoying yourself, Princess Anastasia?"

"Ana, please."

She wouldn't look directly at him. "Princess Ana, then." He noted the Ah-na sound she used to pronounce it and did his best to replicate, though he wasn't sure he succeeded, not with his Texas twang. "Are you enjoying yourself?"

"So far it has been a lovely evening."

"The meal was delicious. I will have to mention to your sister what an excellent job they did with the choices."

Was it just his imagination or did Princess Ana stiffen at the mention of her sister?

"I am afraid it would be a waste of time to mention it to Adeline, sir. My brother organized this ball. The charity auction later this evening will benefit my sister's charities as a celebration of her coronation."

"Of course. I will have to mention it to Prince Richard then, if I have the chance." He had only met the prince once or twice, though he was on a first name basis with Addie. It made him uncomfortable, given her position, but she didn't let friends into her inner circle lightly, and he was grateful to be counted among them. He'd treated her new stepdaughter several months earlier when Charlie and Lindsey had flown to Montevaro less than two weeks after Lindsey's appendix burst.

The dance was passing much too quickly. He needed to find a way to spend more time with Ana. "We would love to have you tour the children's wing, Your Highness."

"I will see if I can work a visit into my schedule before the fall term begins."

Jonah felt his brow furrow. "I thought for certain I had heard you graduated this spring."

"I did. I am considering a Master's degree."

They continued to move around the floor, and Jonah tried his best to come up with something to say. Adeline got most of the attention because of her position, but Jonah had always thought Ana was the more beautiful of the two.

"May I call on you, Princess Ana?" The words were out of his mouth before he could think about it.

She finally looked up at him, long, dark lashes covering bright blue eyes as she blinked rapidly. "Pardon?"

He sucked in a deep breath. "May I call you? Take you to dinner sometime after all the hoopla has settled down a bit?"

Ana just looked into his eyes, searching for something. He didn't know what, but if she didn't answer soon the dance would be over. As the last notes soared through the room, she gave a single nod. "I will see that you have details on how to contact me before you leave this evening." She took a single step backward. "I do hope you have a lovely time."

Jonah bowed slightly from the waist. "Perhaps I can have another dance before the night ends?"

"I doubt I will have many openings, sir, but if the occasion presents itself..." She bit her lip then released it.

"Perhaps at the auction." Jonah could have kicked himself. If he didn't bid on her last dance, he'd look like a cad. If he did bid - and was outbid by a large amount as he suspected would be the case - she'd see the paltry sum he could afford and never agree to dinner.

Ana gave him a small smile, and a man stepped between them, cutting off his view of her. He turned to find Adeline standing there, smiling at him.

She smirked as the dance began, and Ana was twirled away. "You could ask me to dance, you know."

Jonah bowed at the waist, more deeply than he'd bowed to

her sister. "May I have the pleasure of this dance, Your Highness?"

"Of course." As he led her through the steps, she looked straight at him. "Do not give up, Jonah."

The truth of the matter burned in his core. "You know, Princess Adeline, I have only met your sister twice before this evening and only very briefly both times. An introduction during a receiving line. I doubt she has any idea who I am."

Adeline gave him a big smile. "Oh, she knows, Jonah."

He didn't contradict the woman who would be his queen in just a couple of days, but instead continued the dance with her.

"Bid for her last dance," Adeline told him. "Go as high as you need to, and I will see that you're reimbursed."

He shook his head. "Thank you, ma'am, but I couldn't win her dance that way." Jonah turned when he felt a tap on his shoulder.

"May I cut in?" Charlie stood next to them, a smile on his face. "I need to speak with my wife a moment."

Adeline's face colored at the sound of her husband's voice.

Jonah had no choice but to step away. "Of course, Your Highness."

This was going to be a long night.

The one thing Ana hated most about balls were her aching feet. She'd never liked heels much, but she had little choice in the matter. With a ball gown, you wear heels. Period.

She'd danced every dance and never with the same man twice, not even Jonathan. As her escort, he'd have the last dance before the auction.

"You look like you're about ready to get out of here." She turned to see Charlie standing there holding out his hand. "I haven't had the chance to dance with my favorite sister-in-law yet."

Ana shook her head slightly. "I'm your only sister-in-law."

"Beside the point."

She noticed how much he'd improved over the last few months. Her last dance with him had been after he'd been knighted and his parents awarded the titles of Marquis and Marchioness of Montago for service to the crown. And she told him so.

He grinned. "It's not much of a chore to practice with Addie. I'll dance with her any chance I get."

Ana smiled back. "I would imagine so." She giggled. "And you don't have to say good night anymore."

Charlie chuckled. "I can't say I'm disappointed we spend, ah, more time together."

"I know you had a hard time finding time for each other the last few months."

"And I know after the coronation things will still be busy but hopefully the extreme busyness will calm down some."

"How is Lindsey adapting to all of it?"

"She loves Addie. That's all that really matters to her. She gets to live at the palace now, instead of with my parents, and we should get to have family dinners soon. Addie has missed her, too." He spun her in a circle. "Now, how enamored are you with Jonathan? Is it a love match?"

Ana looked over to see Jonathan dancing with Christiana, queen of Ravenzario - one of Montevaro's two sister countries. "I don't believe so. He's a nice man, and I enjoy spending time with him, but I don't believe we will be a great love story like you and Adeline are." An ache had been building in her heart, and the conversation with Charlie caused it to spread. She wanted to rub her chest with the heel of her hand in the hopes it would dissipate.

"There's someone out there for you, Ana. I know there is."

"I'm certain you're right, Charlie. I hope, for Papa's sake, I find him soon. He was exceptionally glad to walk Addie down the aisle before..." She looked around. No one was too close, but the news of her father's Parkinson's Disease had not yet been made public.

"I know." Charlie squeezed her hand.

Tears pooled in her eyes as she thought of her father's deteriorating health. "If I don't find someone soon, Charlie, would you do me the honor of walking me down the aisle? If Papa can't?"

He let go of her and grasped her hand, headed for the balcony. Before they could escape, the music changed. Charlie groaned. "I'm sorry, Ana."

She nodded. "I know. Go find Addie." He squeezed her hand and walked off. Ana continued her walk to the balcony, breathing deeply of the cool night air.

"Are you okay?" Jonathan's voice reached her seconds before he did. Without asking he pulled her into his arms, and she rested her head on his chest, tears slowly seeping out of her eyes and into the shirt of his tuxedo. "What is it? Did Charlie upset you?"

"No. Not really. I just started wondering if my father would actually be well enough to walk me down the aisle when the time comes." She sniffled. "It could be years before I get married."

She sniffed again. Very unladylike, much less princess-y. But Jonathan tipped her head up to look at him.

"Then marry me."

Chapter Two

*J*onathan saw Princess Ana's eyes were still filled with unshed tears as she looked up at him. "What?" she whispered.

"Not right now," he backtracked. "But what if we dated? It would keep your mother off your back, and I like you. I think you like me. We're friends. And friendship is the best basis for a romantic relationship, isn't it?"

"You want to date me?" She started to pull away, but he wouldn't let her.

"I'm not saying we get engaged or anything. I'm saying give it a shot." He moved his finger from under her chin and wrapped his arm back around her waist. "Whaddya say?"

He felt her sniffles shudder through her. "I don't know, Jonathan. Getting my mother off my back doesn't seem like a very good reason to start a relationship."

Time to go for broke. "Then how about this?"

This time when he tipped her chin up, he lowered his lips to hers. Kissing her. His fingers finding their way into the strands of hair dangling around her neck. For the first milliseconds, she didn't respond, and he wondered if maybe the sparks he'd felt were one-sided, but then, with a soft moan, she melted further against him. Matching him beat for beat.

Jonathan had his share of experiences with girls in high school, many he wasn't proud of.

But this kiss.

It surprised him. In both its intensity and its impact.

He pulled away before he wanted to but probably after he should have.

Ana's eyes had gone wide, and she took a step back, her fingers covering her just-kissed lips.

"I won't apologize, Ana." Even though part of him felt he should.

"I know." Her whisper barely reached him. "But why?"

"There's something between us. You and I both know it. More than friendship. Is it long term?" He shrugged. "I don't know. But I want to find out."

"Why me?" She backed into the stone railing and turned to stare out over Lake Montevaro.

The palace, situated on an island in the middle of the Alpine lake, offered a view unrivaled in the rest of Europe, at least in Jonathan's perspective. He moved to stand next to her, leaning against the railing. He could hear small waves lapping against the rocks at the base of the island several stories below.

But he didn't know how to answer that question. "I don't know, Ana. Why are any two people attracted to each other? Why does anyone want to get to know another person better? I don't know, but I do know I'd like to know you better."

"Because my sister rejected you? I'll never be queen, you know. In fact, it won't be long before I don't even live at the palace anymore."

That made him laugh. "You think I care about that? Ana, my family has more money than any of us know what to do with. I have several cars, including one that's nearly as nice as your brother's new one. Both of my grandmothers' homes appear in magazines regularly, and when I moved to Serenity Landing for college, my father bought the second largest home in the area for me to live in. To this day, I have no idea why. I would have been happy in the dorms, but he didn't ask me. Believe me. A relationship isn't about the status for me. It never has been." Well, not since high school. When he knew dating him would increase any girl's status. And he used that knowledge to his advantage.

Izzy's face started to swim before his eyes, but he pushed it away. Now wasn't the time.

He rested a hand on Ana's lower back. "Just think about it?"

Finally, he got a nod. He slid his arm further around until he could pull her in to his side. She rested her head against his shoulder as clapping began in the other room.

"The ball is over for now," she murmured. "The auction will start in a few minutes."

Jonathan kissed the side of her head. "I'm planning on another dance with you."

"There's only one more dance, and you'd have to win it."

"If I don't, and I have every intention of winning, will you dance with me later?"

"Sure." She moved away. "But I need to go fix my face. My mother will have a fit if I show up looking like I've been crying."

He turned until he could get a better look at her and confirmed his suspicions. "You look beautiful."

What on earth was Jonathan thinking?

Ana hurried through a hidden door off the balcony and to a private bathroom. She wouldn't lie, even to herself, and try to say the kiss meant nothing to her.

After all, a girl's first kiss should be one for the record books. And it sure was.

At least to her. Ana puzzled over Jonathan's reaction to her fumbling attempt to kiss him back. Had she kissed right? Was there such a thing as "wrong"? How should she know?

Maybe it was time for a conversation with Addie.

Or maybe, she decided as she carefully applied eye makeup, it was time to forget the moment she shared with Jonathan and put her focus back on someone less intimidating, like Dr. Fontaine. Sure, she was a princess, but a sheltered one. She knew something of Jonathan's past from her older sister. He'd been a lady's man before *something* happened to change the course he traveled. What would someone as experienced as he want with someone so inexperienced? What could she hope to offer him?

Her phone beeped in her clutch and she took it out. Rick telling her she needed to get back from wherever she was sulking. It was nearly time to auction off her last dance. If only she could bid on her brother and dance with him instead.

Or run to the dock, hop in a speedboat and take off for the mainland, borrow her brother's car, and drive into the mountains with the wind tearing her hair out of its perfect coif.

But Ana had never done anything crazy in her life. Not showing up where she was expected two days before her sister's coronation definitely qualified as crazy. And so she tucked her makeup back into the drawer, scrutinized her appearance, decided it would have to do, and headed back to the ballroom.

She entered from the side, where few would notice her sudden appearance. Just in time, too. She'd been told her dance would be auctioned after one with Charlie. After her would be Rick. Then Adeline. Then the dance. And then she could kick off her shoes and drown her confusion in triple-Oreo-chunk ice cream. With chocolate syrup.

At the nod from the emcee, Ana made her way to the small stage.

"Ladies and gentlemen, the lovely Princess Anastasia's last dance is open for bids."

Numbers flew around her head. She couldn't begin to fathom that a dance was worth so much. The cause was a good one, sure, but three to five minutes of conversation wasn't worth nearly so much.

Jonathan's voice rang out above the crowd, doubling the last bid.

Silence fell over those assembled as Ana stared at him. His quick wink made her heart flutter. At least she wouldn't end up with the slimy Earl of Mevander. He'd tried to dance with her several times but fortunately, she managed to avoid it. The last time Adeline danced with him, she'd had to deal with his roaming hands.

And that had been at the wedding reception.

If he couldn't help but paw at the newly-married Crown Princess, how much harder would it be for Ana to fend him off?

There were no more bids, and before she could climb down the three steps to the floor, Jonathan was there, extending his hand. She took it and immediately felt safer.

"I wouldn't have let him win, you know." Jonathan's whispered words warmed her heart as they passed the glaring earl. "Addie told me what happened. I'd protect you from him at all costs."

"Thank you." They stood together near the dance floor waiting for the music to start.

His phone buzzed just as Adeline took Papa's hand, having "won" her dance - a tradition no one would have dared interfere with. Jonathan glanced at it, and a muttered curse slipped out.

"I'm sorry, Ana. I have to deal with this. Family emergency."

"Of course." Maybe she could sneak out. Before she could, her way was blocked.

The Earl of Mevander smiled down at her. If one could call the scheming, slimy look a smile. "You are free for this dance then? You've been abandoned by the young, impulsive American."

Before she could reply, Ana felt another hand on her elbow.

"Princess Ana, Jonathan asked me to accompany you."

She turned to see Dr. Fontaine standing next to her with Jonathan's paddle from the auction, a sign the two had spoken. Giving a barely polite smile to the earl, she excused herself.

"Thank you," she murmured as they walked to the dance floor.

"My pleasure."

They'd danced together just a few hours earlier, and he'd promised to win her last dance. Had she missed his bids?

She shoved the thought out of her mind as he tucked the paddle into his pocket and the music started.

Jonah didn't know what to expect from his dance with Princess Ana.

He'd heard Jonathan propose. Seen them kiss. Had he misinterpreted their moments together earlier when Jonah thought she might be interested in him?

There was no ring on her finger, though. It could mean she said no or not yet. But Jonathan had passed him the paddle and asked him to rescue Ana. The other man had looked furious as he punched at his phone with one finger.

But Jonathan's loss was Jonah's gain.

"I did get your number, darlin'. Your assistant gave it to me."

She smiled up at him, but the look in her eyes seemed more cautious than it had been earlier. "I'm glad."

"Can I take you to dinner, Princess Ana?" His boldness surprised him, especially after what he'd seen.

She hesitated.

Time to back it off a little bit. "If you and Jonathan have an understanding, then I withdraw the request."

Ana shook her head. "No. Jonathan and I are friends." That

kiss looked like they were much more than friends. "We have discussed dating but we have no claims of exclusivity."

So Jonathan had been trying to sway her. "Then let me take you to dinner. Next week. After the coronation."

"Of course." The music came to a stop, and she moved away, dropping into a small curtsy as he bowed. "Please call me to set it up?" For just a moment, she chewed on her bottom lip. "But I am exceptionally busy this week as I'm sure you can imagine. It might be easier to schedule with my assistant, and she'll let me know. Not my preference for how to schedule a date, but for this time only, it might work better."

Jonah didn't like the idea, but did see the wisdom given what he'd seen of the official schedule for the week. "I look forward to it."

Ana smiled at something behind him and Jonah turned to see Jonathan approaching. Of course.

Jonathan smiled what seemed to be a sincere smile and held out a hand. "Thanks for your help, Dr. Fontaine."

With a smile back, Jonah shook his hand. "My pleasure. I'm always happy to claim a dance with this lovely lady." He turned back to Ana and held out his hand. When she placed hers in it, he bowed. Bringing it to his lips, he kissed the soft skin gently. "If you ever need anything, you only need to call."

"Of course, Jonah." He smiled to himself as she blushed. "Thank you for a lovely dance."

When he released her hand, Jonathan moved to stand next to her. As her date for the night, he supposed it was appropriate, but couldn't resist a parting shot as he backed away. "I look forward to next week, Princess Ana. Good night."

"Next week?" Jonathan tucked Ana's hand into his elbow and walked with her toward the private section of the palace.

She didn't look at him. Not a good sign. "He asked me to dinner. Earlier I had implied I would like to go out with him. I didn't feel right saying no."

Ana keyed a pass code into a numbered pad next to a door and placed her thumb on the reader. The snick of the door allowed them to open it and pass through. As it closed behind them, Ana turned to him and took both of his hands in her own.

"I'm intrigued by your offer, Jonathan, but we made no claims of exclusivity, and I have hoped he would ask me out for some time." She ducked her head and blushed. "I don't know why. He was enamored with Addie, but Dr. Fontaine always intrigued me."

He took a step closer and let go of one hand. But then he turned and looked around, trying to figure out exactly where he was. He didn't want to do this here. "Come on." He led her down one hallway and then another, finding the exit he wanted. With a push against the heavy door leading to the garden, they walked into the cool night air.

He laced his fingers through hers, and they walked to the center of the garden where the wishing well stood. Jonathan turned to her, and his fingers found one of those bits of hair. He rubbed the soft silkiness, wondering what it would be like if her hair was down. "It doesn't surprise me Dr. Fontaine is interested. You're pretty incredible."

"Jonathan..."

With one knuckle, he tipped her face upward and leaned down to kiss her again. A soft brush of a kiss. Nothing intense. Sweet and simple. "It's fine, Ana. You're right. We've barely begun to see if we're anything. We'll be spending plenty of time together this week, but if you want to go out with him when you don't have anything else going on or after all the craziness ends, I don't have a problem with it."

"Are you sure?" She ducked her head again, refusing to look at him. "I've never been in a relationship. I am not quite sure how it works."

Jonathan chuckled and wrapped an arm around her shoulders, leading her to the iron bench nearby. "Well, if we decided neither of us wanted to see anyone else, and *then* you went out with him, we might have a problem. But we haven't." A sigh escaped from her as they sat down. "Are you all right?"

She leaned her head against his shoulder. "My feet hurt. According to my mother, a princess's feet are never supposed to hurt, but mine do."

A vision crossed Jonathan's mind. Him and Ana. Sitting in a living room.

Ana lay on the couch, already changed out of her gown and into a soft t-shirt and sweat shorts. Short sweat shorts. Jonathan followed the long, lean lines of tanned skin until he saw her feet. Toes tipped in soft pink. And likely killing her.

He tugged his tie loose and let the ends hang where they were before unbuttoning the top two buttons of his tuxedo shirt. Lifting her feet he sat down and rested them on his leg. With firm, gentle motions he massaged first one then the other, her sighs of relief causing him to smile.

"Is that better?" he asked shifting so he faced her and picking up one leg, beginning to do the same to her calf.

"Much."

His thumb ran from her Achilles to nearly her knee, over and over.

"If you don't stop soon, I won't be able to stand and you'll have to carry me to bed."

Bed? Jonathan blinked and glanced to the side. They weren't in a living room. They were in a bedroom. Hers? He didn't recognize it or...did he?

After another second, he realized it was his room in Serenity Landing, though redecorated. He continued to massage her calf but stopped when it caught his eye.

There.

On his left hand.

A wedding band.

All of that flashed through Jonathan's mind in less than a

blink. Could he really have just imagined himself married to Ana? He liked her and all, and they'd spent quite a bit of time together. He'd even proposed, sort of, earlier. But married? Really?

He had to clear his throat, twice, before he could speak. "Let's get you back to your apartment then."

There was no response. Jonathan turned his head to see that Ana had fallen asleep where she sat. He sighed. Great. How to get her back to her apartment? Rick was likely still taking Ellie back to her aunt and uncle's house. He didn't want to call Addie. She and Charlie should have been on their honeymoon. They'd be back in their apartment and he did *not* want to interrupt what little time they had together.

Except...

Hadn't she told him she wouldn't be going back to their apartment? She'd be headed to do... something. With the coronation only thirty-six hours away, her final preparations would begin.

Charlie. He could call Charlie.

Carefully, he shifted to the side, sliding his phone from his pocket. Another text from his sister confirmed what they'd feared during their brief conversation earlier. Philip was missing. The media would pick up on it before long.

He scrolled through his contacts until he found the right one and a few moments later, he waited outside the door, a sleeping princess in his arms. Charlie opened it from the other side, allowing Jonathan to get through. With just a few quiet words, Charlie led him to Ana's apartment, opening the doors both to it and to Ana's bedroom.

Jonathan was certain his face colored when he took her in there and laid her on the neatly-made bed. He covered her with a quilt from the chair at the side of the bed, then followed Charlie back into the main palace hallway.

Charlie shook his hand. "Thank you for taking care of her. I appreciate it, and I'm sure Addie will, too." Charlie rubbed the back of his neck. "When I see her to tell her."

They started down the hall. "It's not a problem. But you won't see Addie until the coronation, right? Married three days and now spending two nights apart?"

The new prince nodded. "Yep. We knew it when we set the schedule, but I never imagined how hard it would be."

Jonathan smacked Charlie on the back. "You'll make it, and you'll have a lifetime together."

"I know." Charlie's half smile seemed to be all he could muster. "Still, not fun being away from your wife of seventy-two hours for the next thirty-six. And by the time we make it back to our apartment after the coronation and ball and everything else, we probably won't have time to say good night before we both collapse."

They reached the top of the staircase where they would part ways. Jonathan gave Charlie a sympathetic smile and, after another minute of small talk, Jonathan trotted down the stairs, the scene from his mind scrolling in front of his eyes again.

Married?

To Ana?

He smiled to himself as he reached the docks where a boat would take him to the mainland and another car would take him to Lydia House. He might like that idea.

And his grandmothers would *love* it.

Chapter Three

*A*na blinked her eyes open and looked around. Her bedroom? How...

A slip of paper caught her eye, and she reached for it, realizing for the first time that she still wore her gown from the ball.

Ana -

You fell asleep while talking to Jonathan. He carried you up here with Charlie showing him the way. He covered you up but didn't want you to be disturbed until you had to be. Hope you slept well. If you aren't awake and getting ready by 8:30, I'll wake you. Otherwise, breakfast is at 7:30, but I'll make excuses for you. You must be in the chapel by 9:15.

Her assistant had signed it, and she read it twice before the implications sunk in. *Jonathan* had carried her to her room and laid her on the bed.

A glance at the clock told her she had precious little time to get ready. In one minute, her assistant would come through the door and wake her up. She sent a quick text then hurried to the bathroom, refusing to look at the mirror. In less than twenty minutes, she'd showered, dressed, and was working on her hair.

Her phone buzzed and she checked it, a smile crossing her face.

HOPE YOU SLEPT WELL. WILL SEE YOU TOMORROW.

Ana smiled and sent a quick text back thanking Jonathan for taking good care of her. *Is this what it's like to have a boyfriend?* No answer stared back at her in the mirror.

A knock on the door from her assistant meant it was time to go. With a quick application of lip gloss, Ana headed for what was sure to be a long rehearsal, sans Addie, and an even longer day.

It proved to be true and she still hadn't heard from Jonathan again when it came time for the coronation itself.

"Your Highness?"

Ana jumped, the butterflies in her stomach racing circles around her insides. And she wasn't even the one about to be crowned queen. An aide stood there, though one she didn't know. Jonathan hadn't arrived, and he was supposed to escort her inside the throne room in just a few minutes. Would she be forced to walk in alone?

"This arrived for you." He held out an envelope.

She took it from him, dread filling her. "Thank you." Turning and walking a few steps away, she slid a finger under the flap. Bold, confident handwriting filled the stationary from Lydia House.

> Dear Ana,
> I hate to do this to you, but I didn't want to text you, and I don't have time to see you. That family emergency from the other night has intensified, and I have to return to the States immediately. I took the liberty of making a phone call and arranging for someone else to fill in for me. I hope it's okay, and I really hope we get that dance when I get back. I don't know when that will be, but save one for me?

Affectionately,
JWLC IV

She slid the note into her clutch and looked around. Who could he have sent in his place? Surely not...

"Dr. Fontaine?"

The pediatrician gave her a tentative smile. "I hope you don't mind?"

Ana shook her head. "No. I pray Jonathan's family emergency resolves itself quickly, but I am always happy to spend some time with a kind gentleman."

Before anything else could be said, it was time to get into position.

Dr. Fontaine offered his arm and she took it. Ana breathed a prayer for this to go smoothly. For everyone to remember their lines. For no one to cause it to be anything less than the solemn, awesome occasion it was. For no one to ruin Addie's coronation.

Ten minutes later, tears streaked down her cheeks as she watched Addie raise her right hand, put her left on an ancient Bible, and take the solemn oath of office. She watched as her father, his hands showing only the slightest signs of shaking, as he took the crown off of his head and placed it on her sister's.

She watched as her father, king of Montevaro for decades, knelt before his daughter pledging his loyalty and fealty to her as the new queen. Her mother, now the former queen, did the same. Oh, how it had to irritate her! Mother was no longer the second most powerful person. Her mother's position on the council now belonged to her father as the retiring king. Soon it would belong to Charlie.

Rick followed their mother. Then her turn.

Ana knelt in front of Addie and promised the same thing as everyone else, but before she stood, she mouthed the words, "I'm proud of you. Love you."

She could see the tears in Addie's eyes as she nodded her

understanding. Ana returned to her seat as the members of Parliament and other officials each took their turns. Once the government officials were done, all the Montevarians in the building who had not already done so, including Dr. Fontaine, took a knee and swore their own oaths.

The bishop stood to the side as Addie, now Queen Adeline the First of Montevaro, took her place at the center of the stage. One hand held the scepter, now used only for ceremonial occasions such as this. The robe hung around her shoulders and trailed behind her as one last person came to the center aisle.

Charlie didn't climb the stairs to the stage, but knelt at the bottom of them. In a clear voice, he pledged his allegiance to Addie. Ana wondered if he would renounce his U.S. citizenship, but thought he had decided not to because of Lindsey. When he didn't, Ana knew the press office would release a statement saying why. It had been discussed *ad nauseum*, but it would need repeating.

The bishop's bellow brought her attention back to the present.

"Long live the queen!"

"Long live the queen!" the crowd replied.

Twice more he called out, and twice more the crowd responded. Addie descended the steps and walked up the aisle by herself. Charlie fell in behind her, followed by the now-former king and queen, then Rick, then Ana, leaving Dr. Fontaine behind. Once in the ante room, Ana saw the stress radiating off her older sister, and she went to her.

Addie let Ana hug her until the tension seemed to recede somewhat.

"You're going to do great," Ana whispered. "You've got this."

Queen Christiana of Ravenzario watched as the Montevarians filed out of the room where the coronation had been held. She had not planned to attend - she was not promising her loyalty to Adeline, after all. She had her own country to run. But their countries had a common history, ties that went back over a millennium. More recently, Adeline and Ana had been like sisters to her as she grew up. She'd spent many holidays with the Montevarian royal family and even lived with them for months at a time on several occasions.

"Your Majesty?" The low voice of her escort brought her back to the present.

"Yes, Alexander?"

"It's your turn, ma'am."

Of course. She stood and allowed Alexander to take her hand and tuck it into his elbow. She appreciated his presence but wished her preferred escort would have been there. But no. He insisted he was still not ready for their relationship to be made public.

She did not remember her own coronation. There had been one. She had seen the pictures, but Christiana refused to let them spring to mind. So young when she took the throne, only five, and only because her family - her father, the king, her mother, and younger brother with his nanny - had all died in a horrendous car accident.

One she survived only because she had been very ill and had not made the trip that morning.

"We don't have to stay, Queen Christiana." Alexander covered her hand with one of his own and tightened his elbow. "Queen Adeline would understand."

Addie would. Christiana knew she would, but Christiana was not ready to return to Ravenzario just yet either. Something was amiss at home, and she was uneasy every time she walked through the palace. What it could be? She had no idea.

Instead, she shook her head. "No. I need to talk with Prince

Richard and I believe King Antonio of Mevendia will be here as well. If not, Princes William and Malachi should be."

"Networking, Your Majesty? Among family members?"

She shook her head again. "No, Alexander. We do have a common lineage, but it has been more than a century since any member of the Ravenzarian royal family married into either of their families." Yes, the other two families joked about being distant cousins, but Christiana couldn't. Not when the Mevendian royal family was to have married into hers. Seeing Prince Richard and Prince Malachi stung when she thought about how they should have been her brothers-in-law in just a few years. Seeing their younger sister and knowing she was to have married Christiana's brother. That brought pain too deep to mention.

"They miss them, too, you know."

She looked up at Alexander. Way up. Had she ever noticed how tall he really was? "Who?"

"Kings Jedidiah and Antonio. They knew your father their whole lives. Queens Alexandra and Alicia knew them as well. Maybe it would be good for you to talk to them about your parents. To learn more about them."

Christiana shook her head. "It is too painful. My uncle tells me things from time to time. It is all I need for now."

Alexander's hand tightened on hers but a glance up showed strain on his face, not an attempt to comfort her.

It reminded her of the look Tony, her head of security, had worn all too often. Could Alexander be involved in whatever was going on? And when would they tell her? If they did not soon, she would demand answers.

Prince Richard walked their way and, after exchanging pleasantries, asked to talk with Alexander in private.

Christiana's eyes narrowed as they left her alone then were joined by Prince William, Prince Malachi, and, a moment later, their father.

What on earth could they be discussing?

And how could she find out?

* * *

"Does this count as dinner?" Ana smiled at him as he slid her chair in at the coronation banquet.

Jonah sat and picked up the napkin. "Nope. It's dinner, but our dinner date will be somewhere a bit less..." He looked around. "Public. And a little less fancy."

"Anywhere is less fancy than a coronation, Dr. Fontaine."

"Touché." Jonah stared into her eyes. "Please, Princess Ana, call me Jonah."

She held his gaze for several seconds. "Very well. Jonah."

"Now, do you own any denim?"

Ana nearly choked on her sip of water. "Pardon?"

He rubbed her back as she tried to catch her breath. "Denim. Blue jeans."

"Yes, I believe so. Why?"

"Because you'll need them next Tuesday."

"Tuesday?" she echoed.

"Yep. Your assistant and I set it up yesterday. You and I have a date. Tuesday. You'll need to wear blue jeans." He took a sip of his own water. "And cowgirl boots, if ya got 'em."

"Cowgirl boots?" she repeated again.

"You got it. You're goin' out with a Texas boy, ya know."

She raised one perfectly arched eyebrow. "Texas boy? I happen to *know* you are Montevarian."

"By birth, yes. But I was raised in Texas. Spent most of my life there. You've not seen me outside of a fancy occasion, I don't believe. Even at the hospital, if I'm not in scrubs, I'm in jeans, boots, and my cowboy hat."

"Oh."

Trumpets blared and chairs scraped back as everyone stood. Adeline entered, a sash and a much smaller tiara the only adornments to declare something was different. Charlie escorted her to the head table where she took her seat between Charlie and the head of Parliament. As soon as she was seated, a near-army of servers entered, trays piled high with the first course.

The evening passed quickly. The dinner and dancing didn't last as long as they had several other nights recently. Jonah said good night as they reached the family's private portion of the palace. He kissed her cheek and told her he looked forward to seeing her again soon.

By the time he made it to his apartment just blocks from the hospital, he was worn out. His tie hung loosely around his neck, and he wanted nothing more than to take a quick shower and collapse. As he walked in, his eyes sought out his favorite part of the apartment. The large picture windows overlooked portions of the city below and then across Lake Montevaro to the palace. As always, it was lit and looked like something out of a theme park in Orlando. He'd visited several times growing up and even then wanted to know more about the people, the real people, who lived inside.

He didn't turn on the lights, but stood, hands shoved deep in his pockets as he pondered those who lived behind the walls of the palace in front of him. Addie would be nearing sleep on her first night as queen. The responsibility would rest heavily on her shoulders. Charlie, now the prince consort, would attempt to help her relax and remind her God knew before she was born that she would be queen, and He had equipped her for it.

Princess Ana had looked very tired. She likely would head straight for bed, too, wouldn't she? Or would she spend time on the phone with Jonathan? She'd given no indication that she was disappointed with the change of escorts for the day, but also no indication she was excited either.

Before he could come to any conclusions, his phone buzzed. Pulling it out of his pocket, he sighed and his shoulders slumped. "Hello?"

"Dr. Fontaine, we need you to come as soon as you can."

"Who is it?" He feared he already knew the answer.

"It's Sara."

He closed his eyes and felt that same weight that threatened to crush the new queen bear down on his shoulders. She had the responsibility of a country. He tried to save the lives of children too young to understand the suffering. This little girl, a favorite of the queen's, had taken part in the wedding, but returned to the hospital the next day with a relapse. She'd deteriorated quickly, and he held out little hope for her recovery.

"I'll be there as soon as I can." He hung up the phone and turned. Without bothering to change, he headed for the hospital and prayed for comfort for the family.

It would take God's grace for all of them to get through the next few days.

Chapter Four

*A*na tucked the blouse into the blue jeans and studied herself from all sides. Did it belong tucked in? Or out? She pulled it out and decided to leave it out. A glance at the clock told her it was time to go. Jonah wouldn't be coming all the way to the palace, but she would meet him at the garrison on the other side of the lake.

She slid her feet into the brand-new boots and headed for the docks. When she reached the other side, she found Jonah sitting in a waiting room. He hadn't heard her approach, giving her a chance to watch him for a moment. His forearms rested on his knees and even from the back, he seemed weary.

"Jonah?" Ana didn't mean to startle him, but he jumped.

She'd been right. He looked tired as he stood. "Good evening, Ana."

Ana rested her hand on his arm. "Are you all right? We don't have to go this evening. You look exhausted."

He gave a small half-smile. "I want to go. I need to get out and do something fun, but you're right. It's been a long week."

They walked toward his car. She knew he'd been there at

least half an hour so it could be checked out, to make sure it hadn't been tampered with. Security would follow in a separate vehicle. When they pulled out of the garrison and onto the street, she turned to him. "Anything you want to talk about?"

Jonah rested on hand on the steering wheel as they sat at a stop light. "A patient. She's been doing so well, but..." He shook his head. "I can't really talk about it. Privacy laws and all."

"We don't have to go out," she reiterated softly. "If you'd rather go home, I won't be offended, and we can reschedule."

The light turned green, and he pulled forward. "Would you mind terribly if we went to my place? Nothing untoward, I promise. But you're right. I'm not sure I'm up to being seen out in public with the country's favorite princess."

It took her a second to realize her standard rebuttal of "No, that's Adeline" no longer applied. Addie was no longer a princess. Until Rick married Ellie, she was it. "Of course," she told him with a smile. "Your place is fine."

"We can make something or order in. Whatever you want." He flipped on the turn signal as she texted the security guards behind them. Marty would flip out, but Carrie would calm him down. And she would remain in the apartment while Marty stayed outside once they arrived.

"What's your preference?"

He leaned his head against the seat back. "You know what sounds good?"

"What?"

"Pizza. Loaded."

She grinned. "A man after my own heart. Pizza sounds great."

Five minutes later, she waited as he unlocked the door then stood aside to let her enter first. Ana gasped when she saw the view. "Jonah! It's gorgeous!" She'd never seen the palace quite like this.

"The view was a major selling point," he admitted. "The price was still a bit lower than I expected to pay, though, so I snapped it up."

"Can you actually see people?" She crossed the living room, barely noticing the open floor plan or the kitchen to the side.

"Not without help. A few 'ants' maybe, scurrying around the dock. I've never tried with binoculars or a telescope, but you probably could."

The door closed behind them. Ana glanced back to see Carrie wink at her and move to the side.

They stood there for a few minutes as she soaked it in, but then she turned to him. "Where do you usually order pizza from?"

"There's a little place just down the street. It's amazing. Mama Rossetti's."

Ana felt her eyes roll back in her head just a bit. "Mama Rossetti's is my favorite place in town to eat. Tell her I want my usual. You won't regret it."

Jonah gave her a tired but genuine smile. "Sounds like a plan." A minute later, he was on the phone asking for Mama Rossetti and ordering. She could tell Mama was excited. From the sound of things, the Italian woman might even deliver it herself.

He went to the kitchen and returned a minute later to stand next to her as she continued staring out the window toward the palace. "Drink?"

She looked over to see him holding a glass of red wine. "Thank you."

"Have you heard from Jonathan? How's his family emergency?"

Ana glanced over at him then turned, moving to sit on the couch. There was plenty of room next to her if he wanted to but instead he sat in the chair where she could see him. "I spoke with him briefly the day after the coronation. He said they could not find his brother. Apparently, he's had some difficulties recently. Addiction maybe? I am not certain, but Jonathan seemed upset and exhausted. His family relies on him quite a bit, I think."

"I'll keep them all in my prayers."

"I'm sure he would appreciate that."

Silence settled around them as they sipped the wine. Jonah's eyes closed and he nearly fell asleep before the knock sounded on the door. Carrie opened it, taking the pizza from Marty, and handing it to Jonah, who thanked her.

Ana took a paper plate from him as he flipped open the box and grinned .

"Looks great. Dig in."

If someone had told Jonah his first date with a princess would involve pizza on paper plates and red wine while they sat on the floor of his apartment, he would have dismissed them as crazy.

But here they sat. The fire crackled in the gas fireplace. He'd moved the coffee table to the side and they leaned back against the couch. Soft music played in the background. Remnants of pizza sat on plates on the coffee table. The bottle of wine was nearly gone.

They'd talked about his life growing up in Texas and his decision to move back to Montevaro. His parents still lived outside the small town of Splendora, Texas, where he'd grown up. He held dual citizenship since his father was a U.S. citizen who met his mother while backpacking across Europe.

Ana had shared a bit about her life growing up in the palace, but she seemed reticent to go into much detail, and he hadn't pressed her for more.

"So now that the coronation is over, what will you be doing?"

She shrugged and took a sip of the bit of wine remaining in her glass. "I am starting my Master's program this month. I'm taking a few classes online through Serenity Landing University. I may move into Addie's house there and take an eight-week class later this fall or possibly next year."

"What's your degree in?"

"Political science. It seemed logical." There was something in her voice as she said it that told him it wasn't her first choice.

Jonah shifted until he could see her better. "If you could do anything you wanted, family obligations aside, what would you want to be?"

Ana moved until she faced him and he could see her eyes. "I never really thought about it. I mean, I always knew I'd never have much choice. At least not until Addie has at least one baby. Maybe longer now that Papa has stepped down. Rick and Charlie will both help her with international relations and such, but I may be called on fairly often."

"Okay." He reached out and twirled a strand of her hair around his finger. "But if you could do anything, what would it be?"

She thought about it for a minute. "Something in marketing maybe? Public relations for a nonprofit. Help raise money for a good cause." Ana shrugged. "It's something I think I could be good at, plus I have a level of celebrity and that alone could help bring awareness to causes I believe in. What about you? If you weren't a pediatrician?"

He didn't need to think about it. "Well, what I already do, just probably in a different way. I already spend a few weeks a year working with kids in places like the Congo or Central America. I just wouldn't do doctor-y things. I'd probably spend more time building houses or churches or stuff like that instead of check-ups and vaccinations."

"And for your vocation? If you weren't a doctor?"

"A teacher maybe? I don't know. I always wanted to be a doctor, but I didn't decide on pediatrics until my senior year of college."

They talked for a few more minutes before Jonah decided to go for it. He leaned in and kissed her.

Soft, sweet. Tasting of wine and veggies from the pizza and something indefinably Ana.

She responded, kissing him back until he moved away a moment later.

"That was nice, Jonah," she whispered.

He nodded his agreement then gave her another quick kiss. "I should take you home. I have to be at work early in the morning, but I had a great time."

"Me, too."

"And thanks for understanding. This is just what I needed instead of going out." He stifled a yawn. "Sorry. It's been a long week."

She smiled, her eyes twinkling in the firelight. "And it's only Tuesday."

"It is only Tuesday." But if Sara didn't start getting better quickly, the week would just get longer and longer. "Can I see you again this weekend?"

Ana hesitated and he wondered what - or who - she was thinking about. But then she nodded. "That would be nice. Call me tomorrow after I check my schedule?"

"Sure." Another yawn.

Ana stood. "I can have Marty and Carrie take me home."

He stood with her and nodded in agreement. "I hate saying it's okay, but I'm pretty wiped out." With one palm he cupped her cheek then leaned in for another kiss.

Resting a hand on her back, he walked her to the door. "Good night."

"Good night." The door closed behind her, and Jonah headed back to the living room to clean up. A good night. If only there weren't another man out there vying for her attention. Or a little girl who may or may not survive the week.

If it weren't for those two things, the night would have been just about perfect.

Ana smiled as the text message popped up on the screen.

MISSING YOU. WISH I WAS THERE. TELL ADDIE I FINALLY SAW THE PICTURES AND I'M PROUD OF HER.

Jonathan had texted her at least once a day since he left. She still didn't know all the details but knew things weren't going terribly well. A glance at the time told her she had a few minutes to look it up.

A quick search of his name turned up a recent article about his younger brother, Philip. Ana's heart ached as she read. His car had been found, abandoned, not far from Jonathan's Serenity Landing home. One door stood open with his wallet and keys still inside. But he was gone. Without a trace.

They had no idea what had happened to him, and Jonathan had done the right thing. One of the pictures with the article was him and his mother as they stood on the side of the road near the vehicle. Jonathan's face was grim, and his arms held his mother tight as she cried. At least that's what it looked like.

Rather than text back, Ana slid her finger through her contacts until she found the right one. He answered after two rings.

"Jonathan." His voice sounded tired.

"Hello, Jonathan. It's Ana. I just got your text."

He seemed to perk up a bit. "Hey! I didn't expect to hear from you. I thought you'd be asleep already and you'd see the text in the morning."

How much to tell him? No. With everything else he was going through, he didn't deserve for her to prevaricate. "I had a date with Jonah tonight, but I was quite glad to hear from you. I finally had a chance to check the news sources and find out what's going on with your brother. I'm so sorry, Jonathan. Is there anything we can do from here?"

She could almost see him run a hand through his hair. "No. Nothing but pray. Believe me, my parents, my grandparents, my aunts and uncles - between all of them, they've done everything short of calling out the National Guard or maybe using CIA satellites to search the area. He's just gone."

"I'm so sorry." In that moment, she made a decision. She would leave for the States. Even if she couldn't do anything but stand next to him or bring him a cup of coffee when he needed it, he needed a friend. Someone who didn't ask anything from him, but who could be there for *him*. She had the impression everyone else asked and asked, and he took care of all of them but didn't take the time to care for himself.

She put him on speaker phone and sent a quick message to Addie and then the travel secretary. By morning she'd have an itinerary and by noon, she'd likely be on her way out.

"So how'd your date go?" Jonathan's voice seemed light, but she could tell it was more than mere curiosity.

"It went fine. Jonah's had a rough week at work so we ordered pizza at his place."

"Did he kiss you?"

Ana hesitated. "Jonathan, do you really want the details of my date with another man?"

He sighed. "No. Not really. I do miss you, though."

Her phone vibrated slightly in her hand and she looked at it. "Jonathan, I hate to do this, but I have to go. I'll call you tomorrow?"

"Of course."

"We're all praying for you. Let us know if there's anything we can do." The door to her apartment opened and three aides walked in, heading for her room. They'd have her packed in no time. And since it turned out the flight would leave in less than an hour, that was a very good thing.

"I will." A noise came through the phone, and he said something to whoever was around. "I'll talk to you later, Ana." And he hung up.

She wondered what had come up. Had someone found information? Before she could wonder further, the door opened again and Rick walked in.

"What's up, sis? Why are you headed to Serenity Landing?"

She told him what she'd found out and he nodded. "Jonathan's a good man. I'm glad you decided now and not in two hours. Ellie and her folks are headed back home for a quick trip. I was planning to go with them, but I'm headed to Mevendia tomorrow afternoon. I have a meeting with the king and William about Ravenzario."

He followed her into her room. "What is going on there? Christiana seems okay in general, and there's a new man in her life who she really seems to like. She was extra quiet the other day. From what you said, there's some odd stuff going on with their foreign policy, too."

"I can't say more. Addie was just brought completely up to speed Sunday. I'm *still* not. Hopefully, soon."

"And Addie's letting you send the family plane to Serenity Landing anyway?"

"Yeah. I don't need it to get to Erres." True. The Mevendian capital was less than four hours by car. Or he might be able to catch a commuter flight.

"Well, keep me posted. I'm worried about her."

"I think she's missing her parents a lot right now. With the wedding and coronation and all of us together at the different gatherings, it just drives home that she has no immediate family. I got the impression she doesn't like dealing with any of the Mevendian family because it reminds her that Yvette was supposed to marry her brother."

"Arranged marriages?" Ana shook her head. "I can't believe they still have those."

"William and Malachi won't, at least that's the way it looks right now." He flopped onto her bed. "Malachi told me there are no plans for actual arranged marriages for either of them, at least not until they find someone they *want* to arrange a marriage with. But Yvette was betrothed to Nicklaus not long after she was born. Technically, the contract doesn't expire until two weeks after her eighteenth birthday, a week after the wedding was supposed to take place."

Ana had heard all that at some point, though she didn't know when, but it still seemed hard to swallow. "They were really going to get married as soon as she turned eighteen? What were her parents thinking?"

"That it's a chance to renew ties with Ravenzario. And Nicklaus would have been king. Technically, they still have the old rules of primogeniture in Ravenzario, but since her brother died at the same time, she became queen. He would have been..." Rick thought before continuing. "Twenty or twenty-one at the wedding if he'd lived."

Ana directed one of the aides to make sure she had clothes she could be comfortable outside in. Tennis shoes, blue jeans, and the like. "She needs something happy in her life."

Rick's phone rang and by the time he finished, Ana was packed and ready to head out.

At the airport, Rick kissed his girlfriend good-bye as Ana made small talk with Ellie's parents. Her eyes closed, and she began to doze off as the plane taxied to the runway. Just a few hours and she'd be able to support Jonathan in a more tangible way. Prayers were good and needed, but nothing quite beat a good hug whenever possible.

Chapter Five

"Sir?"

Jonathan looked up from the map spread across the dining room table. "Yes?"

"There's someone here to see you. She says you're friends and would want to see her."

He glanced at the clock over the mantle. Nearly two in the morning. "Who is it?"

The security guard shifted. "Um, she says she's a princess. Anastasia?"

Jonathan straightened and started for the door. "Ana?" He increased his pace to a trot as he crossed the living area toward the foyer. "Where is she?"

"At the front gate, sir."

Jonathan went into the security office off the foyer and looked at the screen. Sure enough, the camera showed Montevaro's princess. "Let her in."

It only took a couple minutes for her to get up the drive, but he waited at the bottom of the stairs leading to the front door. Before her driver could get out, he had her door open. "What are you doing here?"

Before she answered, she wrapped her arms around his waist. "I had to see you. To make sure *you're* okay."

"I'm not the one missing." He kept an arm around her shoulders as they went into the house.

"No. But if I'm not mistaken, you're the one taking care of everyone else. Who's looking after you?"

He conceded her point but didn't actually respond.

"You weren't kidding when you said you had a big house. Second biggest in the area?"

"Yeah. An acquaintance has the biggest. Or his former mother-in-law, I guess. Josh married their daughter but his wife and her father, Bo Jamison, were killed in a car accident around the first of the year." He frowned. When had he last seen Josh? After Bo's funeral? "I know Bo did business with Montevaro and Mevendia. I should check on Josh. See how he's doing." Josh had remarried and...that was the extent of Jonathan's knowledge.

Ana turned and placed her hands on his shoulders. "Jonathan, you need to take care of yourself. I'm sure Josh has people taking care of him. His mother-in-law, his own parents, his friends. I'm worried about you."

He closed his eyes as gentle fingers brushed across his brows. She was right. He was tired. So tired.

"You need to rest. I'm guessing you won't actually go to bed, so how about you sit here with me for a bit and tell me what's happened. When did your brother go missing?"

Jonathan sat on the couch, his arm finding its way around her shoulder as Ana curled next to him. "The day of the ball. I found out when I had to take that call instead of dancing with you. They hadn't located the car yet, but my sister was pretty sure something was going on. No one wanted to tell me until after the coronation, but they decided they didn't have a choice. Did you have a nice time with Jonah?"

Ana said something but her words didn't register. He felt his eyes close and his consciousness slip away. No matter how he struggled to open them, to resume the conversation, to continue looking for new spots to search for his brother, he couldn't convince them to do anything but remain closed.

When they blinked open again, the first thing he noticed was the head full of brown hair on his chest. The second was sunlight beginning to stream in the window. The third was his mother glaring at him.

"Good morning," he whispered to her and tried to shift Ana so she could stay asleep.

"Who's the floozy?" His mom's voice grated through the room.

"Mother!" He laid Ana's head on the pillow and grabbed Mom's arm. "Don't go there."

She held up the glass, already filled with amber liquid. "Your brother is missing, and you bring a floozy back to the house."

He pulled her into the other room. "You will *not* talk about her like that. Ana is *not* a floozy."

"Then who is she?"

This wasn't how he wanted to get into this. "She's Princess Anastasia from Montevaro. She came to see what she might be able to do to help."

"What can she do?"

"I don't know, but I'm not about to turn her down or make her feel like she shouldn't be here." And she was the only one who'd taken care of *him*. "Mom, you need to put the alcohol down."

"You needed to spend more time figuring out where to look next."

"No. He needed to sleep."

Jonathan and his mother turned to see a very poised, put together, Ana standing there. With her arms crossed in front of her, she looked more formidable than he'd ever seen her.

And more beautiful.

"Jonathan has been working tirelessly to find your son, Mrs.

Langley-Cranston, to find his brother. But if he doesn't take care of himself, he won't be able to take care of anyone else either. Multiple studies have shown that driving tired is just as bad if not worse than driving under the influence of alcohol. No one can think clearly when they're so exhausted they can hardly stand. With a few hours of sleep, Jonathan will be better able to help everyone."

Maybe we should make her the spokesperson for the family. The thought flew through Jonathan's mind. None of them could handle his mother that well. And his father refused to hire an actual spokesperson.

He turned to his mother. "Mom, why don't you go lay down? Ana and I are going to look over the map some more and see if we can come up with anything."

She downed the little bit of liquid left in her glass. "Very well." Tears, real ones, began to stream down her cheeks. "I just want my son home."

With both arms wrapped around her, he let her cry. "I know, Mom. I know."

"I can't do this, Jonathan." Ana held a hand to her stomach, willing the butterflies to slow down.

"You can. And you can't know how much I appreciate it."

He'd asked her to make a statement for the family. His father had made the first one before Jonathan arrived from Montevaro, but Jonathan had been responsible since, and Ana knew it wore on him. She had volunteered but didn't think he'd take her up on it. Together, they'd written and revised. And now she was about to appear before dozens of cameras from news crews around the country and in front of millions around the world.

Two minutes.

Jonathan thought she could do this, but what would his

father, who had been adamantly opposed to anyone outside the family talking for them, say? What would *her* father say?

The Highway Patrol spokesman motioned to her. She turned for last minute reassurance from Jonathan, hating that she needed it from him when everyone else needed so much. Someone must have called because he'd turned and spoke quietly into his phone. Ana turned back and followed the uniformed man out the door. She stood to the side at the bank of microphones and waited to be summoned. After the Highway Patrol spokesman made a statement and took a few questions, he turned to her.

"A representative of the family will make a statement."

Ana moved to stand in front of the microphones, papers in hand. She set them on the podium and took a deep breath. "Good morning. My name is Ana and I am a friend of the Langley-Cranston family. I will make a brief statement on their behalf."

She made it through without her voice trembling too much. The questions shouted at her ranged from "Who are you?" and "What's your last name?" to "Do you think he's dead?" She answered none of them. When she returned to the house, the first person she saw was Jonathan's father. He was livid. The second person was Jonathan. He looked relieved.

"Don't start, Dad." Jonathan's first words weren't directed Ana's way, but he walked straight to her. Wrapping his arms around her, he whispered, "Thank you."

"I'm glad to do it."

Jonathan kept his arm around her shoulders as they walked back into the dining room to look at the map again. "I think we're going to try to look over in this area later. The Highway Patrol agreed. It's the next logical place to look."

"Are there plenty of searchers?"

"I think so."

Jonathan's father continued to glare while he spoke into his phone.

"Is he all right with me speaking to the press?"

"I don't care." He ran a hand through his hair. "I appreciate you doing it. I'm glad to when there's no one else, but I don't mind having someone else do it."

"It won't be long until they know who I am. Will that shift the focus?" Something they should have thought about earlier.

"Hopefully, it'll bring more attention and more searchers. Or maybe someone who knows something will see it if the spotlight increases."

They spent another hour at the table, going over the map with others.

And then her phone rang.

Ana looked at the screen and sighed.

"Who is it?" Jonathan looked up at her from the other side of the table.

"My sister."

"If you have any information about Philip Langley-Cranston, please call the number on your screen. If you are in the Serenity Landing area and would like to help with the search, please report to the Serenity Landing police station. The family asks that you keep them, and especially Philip, in your thoughts and prayers. Thank you."

Jonah watched as Ana spoke. When had she gone to Serenity Landing?

The face of a local news anchor replaced hers on the screen. *"Princess Anastasia has gone to the States to be by the side of family friend Jonathan Langley-Cranston. She appears to have taken over the role of spokesperson for the family, hoping to bring more international attention. Though there is no indication that Philip Langley-Cranston has traveled overseas, it is possible that, with his family resources, he is able to travel outside of the United States without leaving a trail."*

Jonah rolled his eyes. He felt for the family. Really. But what they needed was boots on the ground. More people looking near where the car was found. Not international attention for someone who, sadly, was likely already dead. He hated even thinking the thought, knew how petty it made him sound, but it was the truth. The buzz of his phone drew his attention away from the television. He clicked it off and headed for the front door.

He needed to focus on work. There were patients who needed him. Including Sara. Pocketing his keys, he left the apartment. Less than fifteen minutes later, he pulled into the parking garage and then went into the hospital.

"Dr. Fontaine?" Before he even made it to his office, he was stopped. "They need to see you on the third floor. ASAP."

Third floor. Administration. He thanked the receptionist for the seventh floor and went back to the elevator. Before he even pushed the button, he decided four flights of stairs would help burn off some of his excess energy.

Hours later, he ran back up the same four flights. After washing up, he took a deep breath and tried to slow his rapidly beating heart. He kept a smile on his face, but tried to keep it from showing his true feelings. As he hoped, both of Sara's parents were with her. They usually were about this time.

"Dr. Jonah!" A giant smile lit Sara's face. How could she be so happy when her situation was so dire? Granted, the smile wasn't as big as it had been a few weeks ago or even the week before, when she'd been well enough to be the flower girl in Addie's wedding.

"How are you today, sweet girl?"

She gave half a shrug. "I feel okay."

"Well, I have some news that should help you feel a bit better." He glanced at her parents. "There's still a long way to go, but we found a bone marrow donor."

Gasps from the other side of the bed made Jonah turn to her

parents. Tears streamed down her mother's face and her father seemed to be holding back some of his own.

Her father stood. "Can I speak with you outside for a minute, Dr. Jonah?"

"Of course." He patted Sara's blanket covered leg. "Hang in there, kiddo. We'll beat this thing yet."

Out in the hallway, her father struggled to maintain his composure. "Dr. Jonah, you know I'd do anything for Sara, but..." He dragged a hand over his mouth. "We have no money. We're mortgaged as far as we can go. We've maxed out the credit cards. Borrowed as much as we can from our families. I work three jobs. My wife works two part-time jobs online. We can't pay for this."

Jonah put an arm around the other man's shoulders. "It's taken care of. When Princess Addie sent you here, she told me she'd make sure the Wishes and Prayers Foundation would take care of everything, even compensating you for the bills already paid so you can pay off those credit cards. She told me it might be a few weeks after the coronation before she could get the paperwork through, but promised everything would be taken care of. There's nothing for you to worry about on that front. Just concentrate on getting your daughter well." He made a mental note to follow up with the new queen. Given everything else going on in her life, it would be easy for that to slip through the cracks.

The hoarse words, the raw emotion, cut Jonah to the core. "Thank you."

"I need to get some paperwork started. I'll be back to check on Sara in a bit, and as we know more about the timing and exactly how this is going to happen, I'll make sure you're kept up to date on everything."

"Thank you." The other man turned around and went back into the hospital room. Jonah felt a small smile cross his face as he watched the husband and father put an arm around his wife and reach for his little girl.

Jonah pulled out his phone as he headed to his office. He'd missed several calls and texts while in the meeting, but if it had been something truly urgent, they would have come to get him. Instead, he saw a missed call from Ana and a text message.

I'M IN THE STATES. DON'T KNOW HOW LONG I'LL BE HERE. WILL HAVE TO POSTPONE A NIGHT OUT.

Right. Because she was there with Jonathan. Jonah knew Jonathan needed her there, as a friend if nothing else. But he still wished he could take her on a real date. And soon. He only had a couple of weeks before he headed out on the first of several trips he'd take during the fall. One was a medical missions trip. Another was to an orphanage in Ravenzario to help with care there for a couple weeks. If the passport situation got sorted out. If not, the trip might have to be postponed.

As he prepared to call Addie, he wondered if she might be able to talk to Queen Christiana. The orphanage there had lost most of its government funding over the last few years.

He dialed. Time to see if the queen would help him do some good.

"What are you talking about, Addie?" Christiana leaned forward in the wingback chair.

"No one from Montevaro or Mevendia can travel to Ravenzario without meeting these ridiculous requirements. We have never been so stringent with our borders. None of us. The people are wondering why Ravenzario is suddenly being so difficult to get into. Two of my personal staff members had to cancel family holidays because of the timing. They didn't have enough time to get the visas they needed."

Christiana stood and paced around the sitting room of the cottage. "I have no idea what you're talking about. I haven't authorized any changes to policies regarding travel between our countries."

"Your uncle told Rick about them when he was there earlier in the summer."

An uneasy feeling spread through Christiana's belly. "I did not know Rick would be here until after he was gone. I never would have approved those things. You should know that. So should Rick and your father." Something her uncle said tried to worm its way to the forefront. Changes to travel requirements had been mentioned but he had implied the changes had come from the other countries.

She heard Addie's sigh. "I know. We were not sure what to think so we decided to wait until we could talk to you directly. With everything else with my father, he did not have the opportunity. I have been queen for a week and here we are."

"I will see what I can find out and get back to you in the next few days." They talked about mundane matters for several minutes. As they talked, Christiana tried to decide the best way to find out what her uncle had been up to without raising his suspicions.

"Wait a minute," she muttered to herself. "You're the queen. Just ask for the records of the meetings."

"What?" Addie interrupted whatever she'd been saying to respond.

"Um, nothing," Christiana told her. If she were truly honest, she was afraid of her uncle. Technically, she had gained control when she turned eighteen, but she had been content to let him continue to run things until she felt better prepared. He'd promised to keep her up to date, but more and more, she wondered if he ever planned to relinquish his hold. And it came back to her. She *had* asked. There had been no notes of the meeting with Rick.

She tried to pay attention to Adeline, but a knock on the door distracted her. "Just a minute, Addie. Someone's here."

When she opened the door, Christiana found a very serious looking Alexander Bayfield. Long a friend of her family's, he had been especially tight with Tony of late. "Can I help you?" she asked, curious.

"Your Majesty, I need you to come with me. Right now. No questions asked."

"What?"

"Tony said to tell you he's '2 Cool 4 School.'"

Christiana nearly dropped her phone. "All right. Let me grab..."

"No. Leave your phone. There's no time."

"But..."

"Please, Christiana." His blue eyes conveyed his urgency. And he hadn't called her *just* Christiana since he found out who she was.

"All right." She set her phone on the table next to the door. "Where to?"

Alexander took a hold of her arm and led her outside. Her little cottage, on the palace's outer wall, had been her sanctuary since she returned to Ravenzario permanently. They walked quickly along the wall to a seldom used pedestrian gate. She was sure it was never so heavily guarded.

About the time Alexander ushered her into a waiting vehicle, Christiana realized she'd left Adeline waiting for her on the phone. Before she had time to say anything to Alexander, the car peeled away from the gate. In no time, they were at the dock and on board a boat. Alexander made sure she was below decks but didn't stay with her on the ride to a nearby island where his family owned property.

Once there, she was whisked away in another sedan with heavily tinted windows. When the door of a guest cottage closed behind him and they were alone in the living room, she turned to Alexander. "It is past time you tell me what is going on."

Alexander took a deep breath. "Tony is arresting your uncle, and he wanted you somewhere safe."

Chapter Six

"What is it, Rick?" Ana's eyes refused to stay open any longer. She had been asleep for mere minutes when her brother's call came in.

"Uncle Henry's been arrested."

Ana sat up and blinked. "Is Christiana all right?" Could he have gone after the queen of Ravenzario?

"We think she was taken somewhere safe before it all went down, but we haven't heard from her yet."

"Then how do you know?"

"She was on the phone with Addie. She answered a knock on the door and Addie overheard the conversation but the phone was left behind. Whoever it was used the code phrase '2 Cool 4 School.'"

"What on earth does that mean?"

"Remember that teen show from the States with Chris something and his twin brother?"

"The one Christiana and Addie loved so much?" She had too, but she wouldn't admit that to her brother.

"Yeah. That was the code phrase. Addie thinks it was Alexander Bayfield who used it to get her out of the cottage. We got another coded message about the arrest. It'll likely hit late news cycles tonight and in the morning. We wanted you to know before you heard it from somewhere else."

"Thanks." He was right. Christiana had been her second sister at times.

Rick changed the subject. "Any word on Philip besides what's public?"

Ana closed her eyes and breathed a prayer for Jonathan and his family. "No. Nothing new that I'm aware of."

"How's being the spokesperson?"

She thought about how to answer that. "I like it. I think I'm good at it. I think, once it got out who I was, the additional publicity seems to have helped some."

"Good." He hesitated. "You're good at it, sis. I've been watching and I'm proud of you."

"Thanks, Ricky."

Her brother chuckled. "Get some sleep, sis. Love you."

"I love you, too." The phone clicked off, and she closed her eyes again. This time it was harder to drift off. She knew the others were concerned about Christiana, but they had never brought her into the circle of information. She didn't know why. William and Malachi from Mevendia probably knew more than she did. But she was third in line. Everyone thought she was too young and too sheltered to do much of anything.

And she was only four minutes younger than Rick. One of these days, she was going to prove to them that she really could be strong and capable. That she was more than *just* a princess. But that day wouldn't be this one. She rolled over again and finally convinced herself it was time to sleep.

When she woke up, it was time to work on the next statement from Jonathan's family. It would likely be the last statement unless something dramatically changed. The police had done all they could in the area. Woods and lakes had been searched. Leads had been chased down. All that could be done had been done. The size of the investigative team would decrease significantly. Private investigators would be hired. No stone would be left unturned, but the immediacy was dying down. She would need to return to Montevaro in a couple of days. If she wasn't careful, she would fall behind in her online classes. She'd had little time to work on them. Jonathan would understand.

Ana finished getting ready and went downstairs to find Jonathan nowhere to be seen. Instead, his mother and father were in the kitchen, almost like they were waiting for her. Before either of them could say anything, something she was certain wouldn't be friendly, he walked in and put his arm around her shoulders.

"Good morning." His parents both turned away. "I'm sorry about them." He pressed a kiss to the side of her head.

"I understand. This is difficult for them."

"That's no excuse for them to be rude."

She turned to look more directly at him. "I need to head home, Jonathan."

"I know."

"It's more than that." She explained the developments in Ravenzario.

"Are you going to see the queen?"

"I thought about it, but haven't decided yet. I may. She could probably use a friend who isn't connected to her uncle at all. She and Addie were closer growing up, though."

"Go. I've got this here. Every thing's winding down, at least as far as the publicity side of things is concerned. The daily updates are stopping. I'll probably be back in Montevaro before long, anyway. There's not much more I can do here either." He gave her another long hug. "Thank you for just being here. Even if you hadn't been the spokesperson, I would have been extremely grateful you're here."

"I am glad I could come."

He tipped her head up with his finger. "Can I take you out

again when I get to Montevaro?"

"Of course." Her eyes fluttered closed as he moved to kiss her. The kiss was different than the first one. Soft and gentle and over almost before it began.

"I have to go out of state for a couple of days before heading back to Montevaro. You can come with me, if you'd like."

She shook her head. "No. I think I should head back to Europe. Rick is heading this way right now to meet up with Ellie and her family. They won't leave for a few days so I may see if I can take the plane back. I could fly commercial, but my father would be livid. And Marty and Carrie would never let me if there was any other way."

His phone buzzed. "Be safe, Ana. I'll see you soon." Another kiss to her forehead and he was gone, phone to his ear.

Ana turned and went back up the stairs. Time to pack and go home.

Jonah looked up at the knock on his office door. "Come in." A genuine smile crossed his face when the door opened. "Princess Ana!" He pushed back from his desk. "When did you get back to town?"

"Late last night."

He leaned over and kissed her cheek. "I've had too much going on here to follow the news. Did they find Jonathan's brother?"

"No. They have not been able to figure out anything about what happened to him. The day-to-day searching has slowed down, though. I'm only here for a few hours then I'm going to Ravenzario to be with Christiana for a few days."

Jonah motioned to a chair across from his desk. He sat next to her rather than in his own chair. "How is she? I did see that her uncle had been arrested, but that's about it."

"She's safe. That's about all I know. I don't know if she was ever in any real danger."

"Good." The television in the corner of the office was muted but on a news station. Jonah reached for the remote as the Ravenzarian palace appeared on the screen.

"Moments ago, Alexander Bayfield, a close friend of the queen's, released a statement on behalf of the palace. It reads, in part, 'Queen Christiana was taken to a secure, undisclosed location prior to the arrest to ensure her safety. The revelation of Henry Eit's betrayal has shocked her as much or more than it has the people of Ravenzario. Please keep the queen in your thoughts and prayers as she, and the rest of Ravenzario, struggle to come to terms with the betrayal by such a trusted relative.'"

The reporter said something else about the people of Ravenzario, but Jonah clicked the power button, turning it off. "I'm glad she's safe." He leaned back in his chair as something occurred to him. "I wonder if her uncle is behind the funding for the orphanage?"

"Pardon?"

He explained about the lack of government funding for an orphanage run by a friend of his and how he and a group of volunteers would be there in a few weeks to work on updating one of the buildings and bringing it up to code. "I wonder if she'll lift the travel restrictions, too." Maybe this was a good thing on many levels and not just because her uncle clearly wasn't a good guy.

"I have no idea, but I would imagine so."

Jonah reached for her hand. "I thought about you a lot while you were gone. I missed you. Can I take you to dinner when you get back?"

For all her confidence, Ana suddenly turned shy. "I would like that. I missed you as well."

"And Jonathan?" Did he really want to know the answer to that question?

Ana pulled back. "I am not sure that's an appropriate

question, Jonah. We spent our time looking for his brother."

He leaned away from her. "You were both out looking?"

She glared at him. "No. We were at the house, trying to find new places to search, writing statements from the family, things of that nature. Hundreds of others were searching. We were trying to make sure they were looking in the right place."

Right. As much as he did like her, she didn't seem like the kind who would actually get in and get dirty. Hiking through the woods to look for a missing person was more Prince Richard's thing. Someone needed to write statements and stuff, but boots on the ground were much more necessary. Getting in there and getting things done.

Speaking of boots on the ground... Jonah stood. "I'm sorry to run off, but I need to go see a patient."

Ana walked toward the door with him. "I will let you know when I get back."

He grinned. "I can't wait." Another kiss on her cheek and they left his office. Her bodyguards fell in behind them. Her shoes clicked while his boots clunked. When they reached the elevator, he reached for her hand and gave it a slight squeeze. "Be safe."

"I will."

He waited until she and the bodyguards left then turned and headed toward the patient rooms. Time to check on Sara.

The plane rolled to a stop on an island off the coast of Ravenzario.

"Where are we?" Ana asked Carrie.

"The Bayfield family property. The queen was brought here immediately before the arrest."

Ana nodded and waited for the stairs to be lowered. Cool weather greeted her, and she pulled her coat a bit tighter. Though she couldn't see the water, the breeze had a definite cool, Mediterranean feel to it. On the ground, a chauffeured electric cart waited to whisk her away. A few minutes later, it pulled up to a secluded guest cottage, and the driver told her to go on in.

Before she made it to the door, it opened and a man she thought was Alexander Bayfield stood there.

He inclined his head and bowed slightly at the waist. "Princess Anastasia, thank you for coming."

"Of course. How is Christiana?"

"I am fine." Ana turned to see her friend standing there.

She looked tired, but otherwise all right. Ana went to her and gave her a hug. They'd never been huggers in her family, but if any time called for a hug, it was this one. After one of the longest hugs Ana had ever been a part of, they moved back and Christiana led the way further into the living room. A fire burned brightly in the stone fireplace, and they took seats on the couch in front of it. Ana took her coat off but was grateful for the crackling flames.

"You're really all right?"

"Yes. Alexander came to get me before my uncle was arrested."

Ana glanced at the man as he walked into the kitchen. "I am so glad. Addie thought it was something like that. You hadn't hung up on her when he came to the door, and she heard the conversation."

Christiana leaned back on the sofa. "I realized about the time we got to Alexander's boat that I hadn't hung up with her. Apologize to her for me?"

With a laugh, Ana shook her head. "Addie was glad you hadn't. She knew the code phrase was the one you had worked out with security." She turned and sat cross legged, facing Christiana. "*2 Cool 4 School*? Really? I know you and Addie loved that show."

Something crossed her friend's face, but she didn't explain.

"Yes. We both enjoyed the show. In fact, I remember you watching it with us on more than one occasion."

Ana blushed as she giggled. "We did watch it together often, didn't we? All three of us had crushes on Alex and Chris."

Before Christiana could answer, Alexander returned with two steaming mugs in his hands. He handed the first one to the other woman. "Ma'am. Hot chocolate, just like you like it."

She smiled up at him and Ana saw the weight of the world slide off Christiana's shoulders. "Thank you, Alexander."

Alexander nodded to her and held the other cup out to Ana. She smiled and thanked him before he left them alone.

"He takes good care of you." Ana looked at Christiana over the top of her mug as she took a sip.

Christiana didn't answer for a moment, but stared at the marshmallows in her mug. "He does. Alexander is a good man, but I already have someone in my life. I haven't been able to talk to him since I got here."

"They won't let you call?"

A quick shake of the queen's head was her only answer for a full two minutes. "I cannot talk with anyone outside of a very few people. They are trying to ascertain how far Henry's tentacles reached. Tony knew he could trust Alexander, but very few others for certain. He met with Rick on the sly and sent coded messages to your father and Addie hidden on board the Montevarian plane. The intelligence teams in both Montevaro and Mevendia helped Tony get the information he needed to make the arrest."

Ana took another sip of the chocolatey goodness. "What are the charges?"

"Treason, I would imagine, but I've not been told yet. I am supposed to be briefed tomorrow or the next day." With a shake of her head, she changed the subject. "What about you? You've been in the States with Jonathan for a week."

With a prayer whispered heavenward for her friend and his

family, Ana filled Christiana in on what had happened and what they knew. Not much of anything.

Christiana's blue eyes twinkled over the top of her mug. "He kissed you?"

Ana's jaw dropped and she tried to deny it, but the words wouldn't come. "Fine. Yes. He's kissed me. A couple of times."

In that moment, Christiana seemed more like the carefree almost-21-year-old she should be. "Do you love him?"

"I don't know." Jonathan's clean cut good looks, marred only by scruff when he didn't shave, swirled with a vision of Jonah's white lab coat, green scrubs, and black cowboy boots.

"You don't know?"

"He kissed me at the fundraiser ball," she admitted. "And it was incredible. We decided to see what happens between us. He had to leave before the coronation because of everything with his brother."

"And?"

"And Jonah asked me out to dinner." The words tumbled out in a rush.

Barely concealed glee crossed Christiana's face. "Jonah? The cute cowboy doctor?"

Heat rose in Ana's face. "Yes."

Her friend's voice went squeaky. "Did *he* kiss you?!"

"Maybe."

"He took you out to dinner and kissed you?" She threw back her head and laughed before her voice took on a sing-song tone. "Ana and Jonah, sittin' in a tree..."

Ana tossed a throw pillow at her. "Stop it!"

Christiana easily swatted it aside. "So who's the better kisser?"

Melted marshmallows had never been so fascinating. "I don't know," she finally answered. "I like both of them. Jonah and I ended up ordering pizza at his apartment. He had a patient who wasn't doing well and was worn out. That kiss was..." She struggled to find the words. "Sweet. He kissed me on the cheek a couple of other times, but that's not the same. Jonathan and I haven't been out on a real date at all. He's gone with me to several balls, but only because my mother set it up."

"But you've talked about it and you spent a lot of time together, right?"

"Yes."

"That's almost better than a real date, then, isn't it?"

Ana hadn't thought about it that way. "Maybe."

"So who's the better kisser?"

Ana tipped her mug up until the last bit of hot chocolate flowed down her throat. "The kisses with Jonathan were different. The first one was intense."

Christiana turned serious. "So which one is the one for you?"

Chapter Seven

Christiana struggled to keep her feelings of jealousy at bay. She was happy for her friend. Truly. Several people, including Ana, knew she had someone special, but none of them knew how close they were. How close they were to being engaged. In a year or less, she'd be married.

"I don't know, Christiana. I like both of them, a lot. And I think Jonathan probably understands me better." A smile reached all the way to Ana's eyes. "Did you see that I was their spokesperson? I wrote a lot of it with Jonathan's help. I know his family is practically royalty in the States, but I think my position helped some. Brought more attention and help to the search."

"You really enjoyed it?"

"I did. And I think I was good at it, too."

"I'm sure you were." Christiana only saw one of the statements by Ana, but her friend had seemed poised and confident. And as the third child, she didn't have the same expectations Christiana or Addie did. Ana could choose what she wanted to do with her life. If she wanted to be a society girl who *only* sponsored charities and did other kinds of philanthropic work, she could. If she wanted to have an actual paying job doing just about anything she wanted, she could do that, too.

Christiana had been queen since the accident killed her parents when she was five. Addie had planned to work closely with her father until the time came for her to take over, but that time had come much sooner than anyone expected. The early onset of Parkinson's and a major skiing accident had seen to that. Prince William, but not *that* Prince William as he liked to say, knew he'd eventually take over for King Antonio in Mevendia. The three of them had few choices.

William and, to a lesser extent Addie, had plenty of time to learn from their parents.

Christiana had been looking to Henry to help teach her what she needed to know. That plan was obviously out the window.

"Jonathan understands that." Ana's voice brought her attention back to the present.

Something seemed off in her friend's voice. "But?" Christiana prompted.

Ana sighed. "I don't know. There's something about Jonah that draws me to him. Maybe it's the doctor thing."

"Or the cowboy boots?" Christiana smiled as she sipped on the remains of her hot chocolate.

That brought a small grin. "Maybe."

"So what are you going to do?"

Ana shrugged. "Date both of them, I guess. See what happens. But enough about me. What about this man in your life? What's his name?"

Christiana hesitated. "He is exceptionally private, Ana. No one knows about us just yet."

"No one?"

She stared into the empty mug. "Just Uncle Henry."

With a clunk, Ana's mug landed on the side table. "Don't you think that's a bit odd? I mean, I get not being in public.

Charlie's holding his breath that Lindsey's mom doesn't show up out of the blue and want something from them now that he's the prince consort. She terminated her parental rights when Lindsey was a baby. But to not even hang out with you and your friends or with us here or to invite us over for dinner once you're back home or before now. That doesn't strike you as odd?"

Christiana hadn't thought about it quite that way before. "Perhaps," she finally conceded. "But for the moment, he has asked that we keep our relationship very quiet, and I promised him I would."

Skepticism continued to shade Ana's face. "If you say so."

Alexander chose that moment to return and stepped between her and the fireplace. "Ma'am, you have a call. You can take it in the office."

He was so irritatingly formal all the time. Christiana stood.

Ana stood as well. "I am going to rest for a bit."

Christiana gave her a quick hug before Ana left for another cottage. She walked into the other room, picking the handset up from the base. "Yes?"

"Hello, darling." The dulcet tones of his voice sent chills through her.

"Hello," she whispered. "I did not think they would let you call me."

"I convinced Tony I needed to talk to you about business." His voice lowered an octave. "If I am to marry you, I need to be able reach you. To be able to talk to you even if they still won't let me see you."

She wound the cord around her finger as she leaned forward in the desk chair. "I have missed you..."

Before she could say his name, he admonished her not to. "You never know who could be listening in."

"This is a secure line," she reminded him.

"I would prefer not to take the chance. Now, tell me how you're enjoying your stay wherever you are."

She looked around. "It is fine. It's not home." It wasn't her cottage. But would she still live in her cottage when she returned?

"Are they treating you well? Can you see the sea like you can from the palace?"

"No, I can't see it, but they are taking very good care of me. Alexander..."

She could hear the frown in his voice and practically see his clenched teeth. "Alexander is with you, but I can barely convince them to let me talk to you and even then I have to be in the security office of the palace."

"He is the one who made certain I was taken somewhere safe while Tony took care of the arrest."

"You're at his family's facility aren't you? I know someone who was supposed to get married there this weekend, but they were told the facility was suddenly unavailable. They're paying for everything to be moved elsewhere and covering everything, but my friend is very annoyed. She'd always wanted to get married there."

Christiana uncrossed then recrossed her legs the other direction. "I am sure I don't have any idea what you're talking about." Bile churned in her gut as she knew she'd revealed her location, but it would be all right. He wouldn't do anything to hurt her. If anything, maybe he would sneak in to see her.

A cleared throat caught her attention, and she looked up to see Alexander standing there. He tapped his watch and Christiana nodded. "I need to go. I'll talk to you soon. I love you."

"I know you do. I just wish..." Before he could finish, the line went dead.

Christiana stared at the handset before replacing it in the

cradle.

"You implied where you are, Your Majesty." Alexander spoke before she could.

"I know. I didn't mean to." She sat back in her chair. "Besides, you have nothing to worry about from him. Surely you know that."

Alexander didn't reply, just shook his head sadly as he walked away.

Seeing his disappointment tore at Christiana. He had become a trusted friend and adviser. She did not like the idea she had let him down. Rather than spending more time with Ana, she turned to her computer to get some work done.

With the betrayal by her uncle, Christiana realized she had much to get caught up on.

Visions of Ana laughing with Jonah at the coronation clouded her vision. How long until she spent special occasions with the love of her life?

Two words came to mind.

Too long.

With a deep breath to calm his nerves, Jonathan entered the room.

"Jonathan?" Ana stood in the living room of the guest cottage he'd just entered. "What are you doing here?"

He crossed the room in three giant steps and wrapped his arms around her waist, burying his head in her shoulder as her slender arms tightened around his neck. They stood there for long minutes as he breathed in the scent of lavender and something else he couldn't define. Slowly, the tension eased away and he loosened his grip.

"What is it?" she whispered. "Did they find something?"

He blew out a breath into her shoulder. "No. That's the problem. They didn't find anything, and they're calling off the official search. We've looked everywhere. My father refuses to give up, but the reality is that the clues are drying up."

Her hold tightened again. "I am so sorry." He could feel her tears on his own cheek. "I cannot imagine..."

Jonathan held her closer until he finally felt able to let his shoulders relax. "I know." He put an arm around her shoulder and steered her to the couch. When he settled into the corner, she situated herself next to him, with her head resting against him and his arm still around her. "I know I said it already, but I can't tell you how much it means that you came to be with me."

"I am glad I could help."

He turned his head slightly until he could press a kiss on her head. "It means so much to me." Had anyone ever dropped anything and come to be with him during a tough time? Not really. Not even...

No. He wasn't going there. Never again.

"Ana, there's something I need to tell you."

She twisted her head until he could see her eyes. "Yes?"

With his free hand he reached across to take one of hers. "I like you a lot, and I know we're kind of seeing what happens, and I know you aren't sure about Jonah. Or me. Or how you feel about either of us, but I need to tell you something about my past that could affect your decision making process."

Would she reject him? Addie hadn't when he told her. They'd decided to see if something could develop between them despite the fact that she was in love with Charlie already. Her parents had practically forbidden her to even think about him at that point. But would Addie have been able to live with his past, if they had actually reached the point of being ready for marriage?

"What is it, Jonathan?" He could see the beginnings of tears in her eyes. "You're starting to scare me."

He squeezed her hand. "Nothing like that." An empty feeling filled the pit of his stomach as he rubbed his thumb along her knuckles. "I sowed some wild oats in high school." Without taking his eyes off his thumb, he told her about the drinking and the girls. How he'd used his family name and status to get them into his bed - or the back of his truck - or pretty much anywhere else.

"In the giant scheme of the world, or even the high school, it probably wasn't *that* many girls, but way too many. Too many parties. Too many mornings waking up with a hangover. I haven't had a drink in years. I haven't been with a woman in just as long. But you need to know that my past isn't pristine. I've been washed clean by the blood of the Lamb, just like all believers, but decisions have consequences. I know that. And I know there's a chance you'll decide it's something you're not prepared to deal with, and I wanted to have this conversation before our relationship got too serious."

And because he knew she had another suitor who likely didn't have his baggage. He hadn't even mentioned Izzy and the scandal surrounding the two of them. His parents had paid out the nose to keep that out of the tabloids. He'd sworn not to risk his heart with Addie, and they hadn't been serious enough for him to get too hurt when she chose Charlie. Charlie had been her choice all along. It wasn't until the other man's parents were awarded a March and the titles of Marquis and Marchioness to go along with it, and Charlie knighted for service to the crown, that her parents and Parliament would approve.

He'd gone out with Ellie a time or two before she and Rick worked things out. He'd always known there was no chance they'd develop into anything more, though he'd convinced himself it was possible and had even kissed her once.

But Ana...he liked her. A lot. Much more than he could have

imagined. And not just because she'd been there for *him* and helped him stay strong for the rest of his family. No. He liked her for herself. This time, despite his intentions to never get his heart involved again, there seemed to be a pretty good chance he would get his heart broken if she chose Jonah. Better to find out now if his past was the deal breaker.

Unless he was very mistaken, she held herself more stiffly than she had moments earlier, and she didn't look at him. A telling sign.

"I don't know, Jonathan." She took her hand out of his and delicately wiped under her eyes with one finger. "I've led a very sheltered life, you know that. And I know of the redemptive power of the cross, but I always thought I would end up with someone who had a past similar to myself, if I ever thought about it at all. I never thought my parents would approve of someone who didn't, but they obviously approve of you."

And her mother had pushed Addie toward the awful Count Bladvile earlier in the year. That man was doing significant time in a Montevarian prison for what he tried to do to the then-Crown Princess.

Her shoulders shuddered under his arm as she inhaled deeply. "I just don't know how I feel about it." She looked up at him and it tore at his heart to see the pain in her eyes. "Can I take some time to think about it?"

"Of course." He wanted to kiss her, to try to convince her without words that he'd changed. His past was in the past, where it belonged. But sometimes it reared its ugly head, and he wished more than anything he could change it. That Izzy...no. He couldn't go there. God had even managed to use that situation for good, for His glory. Something Jonathan never would have believed possible. In the here and now, he needed to let Ana make up her own mind without trying to sway it with what he believed would be a stellar kiss.

In fact, just such a thing could backfire - remind her of his experience. And he wouldn't do anything to jeopardize his chances. She squeezed his kneecap and stood, walking into the kitchen to collect her thoughts he presumed.

"Take all the time you need," he whispered after her. "But if you could still choose me, my heart would appreciate it."

* * *

Ana stared out the window in the kitchen nook. In the distance, she could see the guest cottage where Christiana remained. Beyond that she could see dark gray in the distance. Likely the Mediterranean. The incoming clouds and wind moving the trees told her the water would be choppy, much like her emotions.

If she really thought about it, Jonathan's past should not have surprised her. He was deliciously good looking and incredibly rich on top of that. What girl wouldn't have wanted to spend time with him? She couldn't be certain she would have said no if she had dated him during that time period. Or that she would have had the strength to say no even now. Not when his kisses left her so weak in the knees.

But today, he wouldn't ask her.

And maybe that made all the difference. He wasn't the same person anymore. Could she live with his past? Yes. Could she, someday, marry him knowing he'd been with any number of other women? She was less sure of that answer, but she thought she would be able to pray her way through it.

Help me to make the right choice, God. Jonathan. Jonah. Both are wonderful men. I don't know how I'm supposed to choose between them. Show me the right way to go?

A movement in the trees on the other side of the nearly empty hay field caught her eye. She squinted trying to get a better look. There shouldn't be anyone over there, especially not that close to Christiana's temporary home.

Was that a person-shaped shadow? "Jonathan!"

He was by her side in seconds. "What is it?"

She pointed to the tree line and told him what she'd seen. In a few seconds, the movement caught her eye again, and he saw it, too.

A grim look settled on his face. "Stay here. Tell Carrie and Marty." Without waiting to hear from her security team, he took off out the back door of her cottage.

She called for her bodyguards as she watched Jonathan skirt along the outside of the field. Marty followed him while Carrie put out a call on the secure communications system and stayed behind to protect Ana.

"I'm going to Christiana as soon as this over," she informed the smaller, tougher woman.

"We'll see," was the only answer.

Yes, her safety was their main priority, but if someone was after Christiana, she would need a friend when the time came.

"Bring her here if you need to."

No answer.

For several heart pounding moments, she watched though she couldn't actually see what was going on.

She jumped at a scraping sound behind her. Ana turned to see the fireplace in the living room moving.

"It's all right." Carrie kept the binoculars to her eyes as Ana clutched her own stomach.

Movement in what must be a secret passage kept her attention. Light from a flashlight appeared, followed by a serious Alexander and a frightened Christiana. Ana hurried to her friend's side as Alexander closed the fireplace, complete with its brightly burning fire.

Christiana clung to her for a moment before pushing back, a determined look settling on her delicate features. "What is going on?"

Ana explained what happened on her end. "I have no idea what they might have found."

The earwig wire coming out of Alexander's ear made Ana

wonder if he might have joined Christiana's security team at some point. "We'll talk about it later. For now, we need to get both of you somewhere safer. This way."

He pressed against a spot on the wall and the fireplace opened again. Ana just gaped at him as he took Christiana's hand and led her back into what appeared to be a steep staircase.

"Let's go, Ana."

Carrie's words jolted Ana to action. The woman *never* called her by her name. She followed behind Ana down the staircase.

"I'll close it from down here," Alexander called.

"I'm in." Carrie took her first steps down behind Ana.

With another scrape, the wall moved and darkness enveloped them. A light came from behind her to show her the way. Carrie must have brought a flashlight of her own.

"Go to the right at the bottom," Alexander told them.

Christiana reached back and took Ana's hand, but she still had not said a word.

They walked along a narrow passage for what seemed like an eternity but eventually, they came to a blank wall.

"Hang on." Alexander held the small flashlight in his mouth while he typed in a code on a very modern looking keypad. With a creak, the wall swung open and she blinked rapidly as they walked into what appeared to be a high security war room.

"What is this place?" Christiana turned in a circle, taking in the televisions, computers, and high tech phones just like Ana was.

"The reason you were brought to the Bayfield property, ma'am." Carrie answered the question.

Christiana turned to look at her. "What?"

Alexander answered. "Tony knew about the tunnels and helped us put this room in. We made sure it's as secure as it can be from anything short of a direct explosion."

"Why are there tunnels?" Ana lowered her shaky self into one of the chairs.

"This was a place where Jewish people and other 'undesirables' could come during World War II. Allied forces lost behind enemy lines were also able to get here from time to time."

Christiana expanded. "Ravenzario was officially neutral in the war, but did what we could to help the persecuted."

"Exactly. This property has been in my father's family for generations. Tony had this room built as a safe place you could come in case of emergency when you needed to not be in the palace. We didn't feel the need for you to be here unless there was a direct threat."

Yes. He had to be on the security detail. Ana wondered if Christiana had realized it.

"What is the threat?" Ana couldn't take the waiting. "Is Jonathan all right?"

"To the best of my knowledge he is, ma'am." Alexander held a seat for Christiana. Was he also in love with her? Ana determined to keep a close eye on their interactions. Could he be Christiana's secret boyfriend? "The early indication is someone lurking in the trees where they caught your eye. We haven't determined if it's local kids wanting to hunt on the property, someone associated with Mr. Eit, or some other group wanting to hurt the queen. For the moment, we're taking no chances."

Ana tilted her head as she stared at him. "But no one knows she's here."

She noticed his glance slide over to Christiana, but his mouth remained set and determined until she spoke. "No one is supposed to." Immediately, the mask slid back into place. Whatever he truly felt was hidden.

Christiana's face had turned pink. Had she told someone where she was without permission? Had that person tried to get to her? Was it a good thing? Or not?

Given they were in a secret underground bunker, probably not.

Chapter Eight

*J*onathan blinked his eyes open, his pupils contracting at the sudden influx of light. He shut them again and opened them more slowly. Sunlight filtered through the trees, dust and other particles dancing on the breeze.

So this is how Jack must have felt after Flight 815 crashed.

Where was he? And why did his head hurt so much? Something must have happened if he started thinking about the main character of *LOST*. Jonathan glanced to one side then the other. Nope. Not on a tropical island. No yellow lab bounding past. No white Ked hanging from a tree.

You need to watch less television.

But when he'd stopped drinking, he'd stopped going out. He hardly ever went out to just hang out with friends. And his television viewing had gone up significantly. *LOST* was his favorite. The cerebral nature of the show. The philosophy connections. The religious connotations of Mr. Eko and his Jesus stick. He'd bought the entire set on Blu-ray and rewatched it when he needed to escape into something besides his own life.

Focus.

He was in the middle of trees. A splitting headache. And a vague reason to believe he shouldn't be. That something had happened. That he was supposed to be protecting...

Ana!

With a groan, all of his willpower went into making himself roll and stagger to his feet. One foot stumbled in front of the other until he reached the tree line. Before walking out into the open, he stopped. No beach. No smoldering airplane wreckage. Good signs. But were there bad guys lurking?

"Sir?"

He nearly collapsed in shock. Strong hands held him up and he saw Marty at his side.

"Let's get you seated, sir." Marty helped him sit back down. "Where's it hurt?"

"My head."

The bodyguard's face betrayed nothing, but something wasn't right.

"Are Ana and Christiana safe?"

"Yes." Jonathan knew it was the only answer he'd get. Marty knelt at his side, firearm safely in its newly-exposed holster. Usually only Jonathan's familiarity with concealed weapons allowed him to spot Marty's gun. "Let me look."

"The guys in the trees?" *Please let them be some local kids who didn't realize they were trespassing.*

"You'll be briefed on what you need to know later, sir."

So not locals. "But both women are safe?"

"Yes, sir." Marty pulled gloves from the pouch at his waist and put them on. "Tell me if this hurts too badly."

Despite the other man's attempts to be gentle, Jonathan winced as soon as his fingers reached the affected area. "It hurts."

"There's a doctor on the property. You're likely not in his area of expertise, but we'll have him look at you in a few minutes." The sound of gloves snapping off was recognizable even with his eyes closed.

"Thanks, Marty."

"You're welcome, sir. Let's get you on your feet." Marty gripped Jonathan's upper arm and his hand.

Jonathan couldn't hold the groan in as he managed to get upright. His arm went around the bodyguard's shoulders, and he leaned heavily on the other man as they made their way out of the woods. To one side he could see several men on the ground. Face down, their hands were bound behind their backs and their feet were as far apart as they could be. A guard Jonathan didn't recognize stood over them with... He squinted. An AR-15? Something along those lines. They weren't kidding around. This was serious.

He reached back to feel the warm, sticky substance on the back of his head. Not surprising. Neither was the bright red all over his fingers when he looked at them.

Before he could analyze the situation further, a fancy golf cart pulled up. Marty helped him into the front seat next to a grim looking driver.

"Tony, Dr. Fontaine needs to take a look at him and see if he needs further medical attention."

Tony nodded. "I'm headed to find the queen and the princess. Dr. Fontaine is on the property and will be going to the same place once he passes through security." Without waiting for a reply, he drove off.

"Security?" Jonathan hadn't been subjected to any pat-downs or anything of the like.

"Protocols have changed in the last half hour, sir." Another security guard. Something in the way he spoke made Jonathan believe this guy was important in the security world.

"I would imagine so." The name *Dr. Fontaine* whispered around the edges of his brain. If only he didn't feel so foggy, he'd be able to figure it out.

The drive didn't last long, but the road wasn't freshly paved. In fact, it wasn't paved at all. At times, it wasn't even a road, but just a relatively clear patch of land cutting off a curved section of the dirt track. Tony didn't even pretend to be driving carefully out of concern for the patient.

Jonathan couldn't help but cry out as they bounced over a particularly large bump.

"Sorry, sir." There was no remorse in the man's tone.

"It's all right," Jonathan answered, his teeth grinding together to keep from giving in to the desire to cry like a little girl from the pain.

In a few minutes, they pulled up to the main administrative building. An aide of some sort came out and helped him into the reception room. Carefully, he lowered himself into the chair. "Is there a towel or something so I don't bleed over this chair?"

Someone else hurried toward him with a first aid kit and a baggie of ice. Once it was wrapped in a pristine white kitchen dishcloth, Jonathan took it and held it gingerly to the back of his head. It hurt at first, but as the cold started to seep in, he began to relax.

"Where's the patient?" The voice reminded Jonathan how he knew the name Dr. Fontaine.

He turned his torso, careful not to move his head much. "Jonah. Good to see you."

The man didn't smile. "Same here." His gloves snapped into place. "Let's look at your head."

The last thing Jonah wanted to be doing was tending to a wound on the back of his main rival's head. But he was a doctor and he'd taken an oath. He forced himself to be as gentle as he could while he felt the injury. He could feel Jonathan tense under his fingers. "Sorry," he muttered.

"Not your fault," came the reply.

After a thorough exploration, he moved back. "I think you're all right. Someone will need to stay with you, make sure you don't start feeling weird, but I don't think you have a concussion."

"We have another doctor coming out soon." A large man walked into the room, his presence commanding everyone's attention. "We thank you for looking after our injured men, but we also know this isn't your area. We sent for him before we knew what you thought, just in case we needed him."

Jonah nodded. "Good plan." He looked around. "Where's Ana?" He had no clue what was going on, just that his plane landed, and he'd planned to take the ferry to this island. But when he walked into the terminal, someone stood there with his name on a sign. He figured Ana had found out he was coming and arranged for him to be picked up. Instead, he'd been whisked to another part of the airport and taken to a helipad. The trip to the island had been a quick one, the pilot obviously in a hurry.

But when he'd landed, Jonah was ushered into a room where he was patted down, his belongings searched, and practically interrogated. Reaching the administration building, he quickly realized something big was going on. Jonathan with the knot welling up on the back of his head. The security guards who appeared to be on a hair trigger.

None of that told him where Ana was. Or Queen Christiana for that matter. If something too serious had happened to either one of them surely there would be even more urgency on the part of the security teams.

"Mr. Langley-Cranston? Dr. Fontaine? If you could come with me?" A man Jonah recognized stood in the entry to a hallway. Another man - one of Ana's security? - helped Jonathan up, though Jonathan waved him off once he was on his feet. Jonah grudgingly admitted the man was tough. He doubted he'd be walking so well after taking such a knock on the noggin.

Jonah fell in behind Jonathan. No sense in letting the man fall if he passed out.

The three of them entered an elevator with Jonathan leaning in the far corner. Jonah turned in time to see the door slide shut. The motion of the car was so smooth he couldn't be sure if they were going up or down.

This time the door opened into a high tech room full of every surveillance gadget imaginable but the only thing he cared about...

"Jonah?"

There she was. Jonah walked toward Ana, loving the smile on her face, but before he could get to her, she gasped.

"Jonathan?!"

Jonah came to a stop as she brushed past him.

"What happened?"

He closed his eyes and whispered a prayer. Jonathan needed the attention worse than he did. Deserved it even. The murmurs Jonah heard on the way to the administration building let him know Jonathan had been hurt during whatever melee had taken place.

"I'm not sure," the other man said.

Jonah made himself turn to see Ana cradling Jonathan's face in her hand.

Then she turned away to pull out a chair. "Sit down." She looked at him, pleading in her eyes. "Jonah, can you..."

"I already did," he interrupted. "He should be fine, though his noggin will be sore for a while."

She didn't even thank him, just turned back to Jonathan.

Well then. Maybe this was his answer. He didn't come planning to ask her to choose, but it didn't look like he needed to. She seemed to have made her choice. Where was his horse when he needed him? Right. In the stables in Montevaro. It had been way too long since Jonah took his stallion out for a long ride. A hard gallop through an Alpine field would work out some of his frustrations.

"I do not think she loves him." The soft voice didn't startle Jonah, but he did look to see where it came from. The queen stood next to him. She looked like she'd seen better days, and if she didn't get some color in her cheeks soon, she'd be the next one on his patient list.

"Pardon?" He wasn't sure he'd caught her full statement.

"I do not know that Ana loves Jonathan," she repeated. "They are friends, of course, but I am not certain her heart has decided in which direction her future lies."

"I see."

The queen turned her blue eyes his direction. Beautiful eyes, one part of him noticed, but not as alluring as the sometimes brown, sometimes nearly green, eyes of the princess. "I do not think you do. We talked about you. About Jonathan. He understands her in a way you do not. I am nearly certain you would like to understand her that way, but you do not. Not yet. Right now, he is the safe choice. I am not convinced he is the right one. Not for Anastasia."

"I see," he muttered again, turning her words over in his head. What didn't he understand about Ana? And could he fix it?

More importantly, would he be in time?

A sticky substance met Ana's fingers as she brushed Jonathan's hair back off his face. She pulled them out of the thick brown strands and looked before she gasped. "You're bleeding!"

"It's not as bad as it was." Jonathan took hold of her wrist, and she knew he could feel her pulse race. "Go wash your hands." He gave her a smile that made her knees weak. "I'll wait right here."

She hurried toward the bathroom only to find Jonah on her heels. The small room didn't have enough room for two, but she left the door open. He obviously had something on his mind.

"You should be more careful, Ana." His voice wasn't as much concerned as it was... hard?

Surely, he didn't think all of this was her fault! "What are you talking about? I was just standing in the kitchen..."

"No." His interruption annoyed her, even as he nodded toward her hand. "Other people's blood. You should be careful."

Ana rolled her eyes. "Oh, please. You worry too much, Dr. Fontaine." But...Jonathan's words from earlier came back to her. *I used my family name, the money, the cars, to get girls into bed.* He hadn't given her a number, but it was too many. Enough that...

No! She would give him the benefit of the doubt. Surely, if he told her everything else, and wondered if there was a future, he would have mentioned an awful disease like HIV.

Jonah handed her an alcohol wipe when she finished washing her hands. To keep him happy, she wiped her fingers thoroughly before tossing it in the trash. "Why are you even here, Jonah?" That sounded rude. "I'm always glad to see you, but I had no idea you were coming."

"I didn't know I was coming until I had a couple of unexpected days off. That never happens. I talked to Addie. She suggested I come see you." He leaned against the door jamb with his arms crossed over his chest as he stared at the toe of one of his cowboy boots. "She didn't tell me you already had company."

"She likely didn't know. Jonathan was only here about an hour before the incident started."

"What did happen?"

She shrugged. "I have no idea. They have not updated us yet."

"Your Highness?" The voice behind Jonah caught their attention.

"Yes, Tony?"

"We're ready to brief both of you."

"Of course."

Jonah stood to the side allowing her by. He was on her heels when she reached the table, choosing the seat next to Jonathan. Jonah chose the seat on her other side. Great. What a better way to illustrate the turmoil inside her than to sit between them.

Tony started talking again. "Thanks to Princess Ana's sharp eyes, we apprehended five men lurking in the woods near the cottage where Christiana has been staying for the last few days." Ana looked to see Christiana staring at her folded hands. "All of them were armed, though none with guns. We have not yet determined what their goal was. They may have wanted to hurt the queen, kill her, kidnap her, or something else entirely. What we did *not* do, is catch whoever hit Jonathan over the head." He sighed. "From the little we did get from the captives is that the man who escaped is likely the ring leader."

"What now?" Christiana seemed resigned, scared, and a bit like she might be giving up. Alexander moved to stand behind her, just to one side, and rested a hand on her shoulder.

"We keep both of you here for a while longer then secure both of you in the main Bayfield residence. It has more line-of-sight, making it more difficult to sneak up on. We're calling in security forces from Mevendia and Montevaro while we continue sifting through Mr. Eit's records to determine who we might be able to arrest and indict, and who we can trust. They will assist both with that and with security here."

"What about the yacht?" Christiana asked. "It isn't stationary.

Would that be a better place?"

"No, ma'am. We like having you here. If the need arises again, you can get to this location similar to how you arrived today."

Ana noted the wording. Interesting. He didn't want Jonah and Jonathan to know there were secret passages. Just in case one of them was the bad guy? She almost snorted at the thought.

Then, she sobered. Despite his sometimes creepy factor, Uncle Henry had never been suspected of being a bad guy either.

What would it be like? To lose your parents at such a young age and then, years later, find out that your guardian was about to be convicted of treason? Though, Ana reflected, Christiana hadn't spent much of the twelve or so years between her family's deaths and her eighteenth birthday actually in Ravenzario. Was that why? To solidify his power and further marginalize the young girl?

Someone said her name, snapping her out of her thoughts. "Pardon?"

The look on Tony's face told her what he thought about her wool gathering. "The gentlemen will be shown somewhere they can clean up and then meet you at the main residence."

Sure enough both Jonah and Jonathan were standing near the elevator. She nodded at them and they both smiled at her. Before the door shut, she noticed the smiles slid away, and they glared at each other. Great. Just what she needed. Just what Christiana needed.

Alexander took charge. "This way, ladies." He opened another panel in the wall. This one also led to a dank basement-like corridor, and this time, someone gave her a flashlight. It made her feel a bit more in control. But when the door closed behind them, she also wondered just how serious this threat was and if it was over.

Chapter Nine

*J*onah had known all along this would be a fast trip to Ravenzario, and he wouldn't have much time to spend with Ana. He hadn't counted on splitting that time with Jonathan - or with a security crisis. He didn't really need to clean up, not like Jonathan did, but it was clear he would not be allowed to accompany the women to the residence. However they traveled to that location, he wouldn't be privy to it.

The man who had led them to the bunker room stayed behind. It made sense. Jonah now knew he was Alexander Bayfield, whose family owned the property. He likely already knew all the secrets.

"Why are you here, Dr. Fontaine?" Jonathan sat in the seat in front of him. The fifteen passenger van was empty but for the two of them, a driver, and a security guard in the passenger seat.

"Pardon?"

"You heard me. Why are you here?"

"Why aren't you searching for your brother?" Jonah shot back. This man had appeared on the cover of tabloids for decades. They had everything they could ask for. More than anyone could want or use. So why did he decide, out of all the girls in the world, he wanted Ana? It wasn't fair.

But when Jonathan didn't respond, Jonah knew he'd gone too far.

"Sorry, man. Uncalled for."

He could hear the bitterness, anger, and even anguish, in Jonathan's voice. "There are no more leads. We have no idea where he went. Because of who he is, there will likely be a *48 Hours* or *Dateline Mystery* or something done in the next few weeks and once a year or so until we know what happened." Jonathan rubbed the center of his chest with the heel of his hand. "The reality is, he's probably dead somewhere, lying in a gully in the middle of the woods and covered up by brush or a mudslide. Or found unrecognizable in a city after falling into a storm drain. Or in a marsh in Florida. Or who knows where. If he'd been kidnapped, we'd know about it already. Ransom demands would have been made, stings set up, bad guys caught while we prayed Phil was still alive."

Jonah couldn't imagine what it cost the man to admit that his brother had probably died alone, but it could be years before they knew what happened. If they ever found out. "How are your parents doing?"

"My mother refuses to believe it. She thinks he's hiding out somewhere getting high."

"He's a druggie?" That tidbit had escaped Jonah's knowledge.

"It's not common knowledge, but it's not a secret either. Speculation has run rampant for years that he is. I'd appreciate it if you didn't confirm it."

Jonah turned that over in his head. He didn't anticipate contact with the press anytime soon, or ever. But even if he did and he told them what Jonathan said, his imagination conjured up Ana when she found out. The disappointment in her eyes would be too much. Besides, it was the wrong thing to do.

"My cousin was a druggie," Jonah blurted out before he'd

even made the decision to. "He lived with us for a couple years in high school. My uncle was a Vietnam Vet with PTSD and didn't make wise choices. He had a kid with a girl he met on the streets. My cousin was in and out of foster care for years until his mom finally had her rights terminated, and his dad was nowhere to be found. That's when they sent him to us. We were in Texas, and he was in North Dakota at that point. They'd never wanted to ship him out of state before. I never knew much about my uncle. But my cousin was always in a downward spiral. About the time he turned seventeen, he would disappear for weeks at a time. He always came home, though."

"What happened to him?"

"He got clean. Went through a Teen Challenge program in Phoenix. He's married, finishing school to be a therapist who works with kids who are wards of the state in a residential facility. Job's already lined up as soon as he finishes the program next year. His first kid will be here in the next few weeks."

The van slid to a stop in front of a palatial residence but neither of them moved. "I guess we have something in common besides Ana, then." Jonathan finally opened his eyes to look at him. "Thanks for telling me. Maybe he really is just out there, and he'll come back to his senses and come home."

Jonah quirked a smile. "I bet if we really tried, we have more in common than Ana and disappearing druggie relatives."

The other man's laugh turned to a whimper. "Probably. But it hurts to laugh. I need Advil."

Jonah laughed instead. "And I need a long ride on my horse, but only one of us is going to get what we need."

"You ride?" Jonathan started to slide across the seat to the open door.

"I'm a Texas boy, no matter where I was born. Of course, I ride."

A security guard Jonah didn't recognize stood by to help Jonathan if he needed it, but was waved off. "If I didn't have a bump the size of a coconut on my head, I'd talk Alexander into letting us ride. They don't have any for public use, but I know they keep a few horses here for family use."

Jonah turned on his best strict doctor voice, the one usually used on parents not patients. "As your physician of record, I forbid horseback riding for several days at least."

"Don't worry, Doc. I don't think I could get on, much less stay on, right now." Jonah noted his death grip on the railing as they climbed the stairs. He was shakier than he let on. "I won't go galloping around for at least forty-eight hours. Promise."

The doctor in him wouldn't let Jonah go ahead of the man who might turn out to be a friend after all. Good thing too. Because his foot didn't quite clear the top step and when Jonathan tumbled forward, Jonah was there to catch him.

"Thanks, Doc." The slurred words drifted to Jonah, but the slumped, limp body told him Jonathan had passed out.

The scream told him Ana had come outside just in time to see it.

"Jonathan!" Ana knelt next to Jonah and the unconscious man. "Jonah, what happened?"

"We were talking and he insisted on walking up here himself." The doctor shifted to get a better grip, she thought, and used his head to motion to the security guards who were already headed their way. "Let's get him inside."

With help, they moved him to one of the spare bedrooms on the first level of the house. Ana had heard the housekeeper trying to decide where best to put all of them up. This room hadn't been one mentioned, but for now it would do.

Someone brought Jonah his doctor bag and he pulled his stethoscope out, listening to Jonathan's heart for a moment. "I think he's okay, but if that other doctor is around, you might want him to take a look. Head wounds like this aren't my specialty."

"He'll be over in a few minutes." Alexander poked his head in. "Thanks for your help."

"Of course."

Ana sat on the bed across from Jonah and picked up Jonathan's hand, stroking the back of it. "Are you sure?" Tears blurred her vision.

"No, I'm not, Ana." She could still see him shake his head. "I think so, but I wouldn't have expected him to pass out either. I knew he was pushing himself too hard, though. I'll feel better when someone else takes a look at that hard head of his."

They sat in silence until another doctor came in a few minutes later. This one looked very different than Jonah. Severe and strict were two words that came to mind. Mean was the third when he kicked them all out. Even Jonah. They made their way to the balcony, where they both rested their forearms on the railing and looked out over the horizon.

She leaned the side of her head against his shoulder. "I'm glad you're here, Jonah. I know they had another doctor on the way, but I'm glad you were here, too."

"I'm glad I was here." He turned his head to rest it on hers. "How are you? Are you all right?"

"It's not the first time I've been rushed off somewhere because there was a potential danger, and it's probably not the last time either."

"I don't like that." She felt his head move until he brushed a kiss against her hairline. "I understand it's part of your life, but I don't like it."

"We have security for a reason, and they are very good at what they do. Fortunately, they are rarely needed."

"I'm glad." His arm moved and slid around her waist. "I like you way too much to let something happen to you."

Ana turned, her arms finding their way around his waist as he held her close to him. The stress began to bleed off of her just as she had felt it fall away from Jonathan after his arrival earlier in the day. Had it really only been a few hours since he surprised her? Since he'd told her how much he liked her before confessing his deepest sins, biggest regrets?

She relaxed against Jonah, letting him hold up some of her weight. Here, in his arms, she felt safe for the first time since the fireplace opened up behind her at the cottage.

The fiery sunset lit the sky, seeming to set the hay fields around the property on fire.

"Ana..." Jonah's soft voice compelled her to move back enough to turn her head. Before she could say anything, the intensity in his eyes told her what he planned to do half a second before he did it.

He kissed her.

With an urgency, a desperation, a need he hadn't had before.

And she found herself swept away in the emotion of it all. Her fingers slid around his neck, winding into his hair where they held on for dear life.

Minutes may have passed. Or it could have been days. Or years. Or mere seconds, but when they broke apart, both of their chests heaved as they tried to catch their breath.

Jonah rested his forehead against hers. "I can't say I'm sorry, Ana," he whispered. "I know I have no right to kiss you like that." No. He sure didn't, though she couldn't quite remember why at the moment. "But you have to know. I think I love you."

Ana staggered back, her hands clutched to her abdomen. "What?"

Chapter Ten

S tanding at the head of the table in the conference room at the main house, Christiana was not happy. She glared first at Alexander, then Tony, then Alexander again.

Neither of them looked like they'd budge.

"I want answers, gentlemen." Maybe a direct order would get her somewhere.

"Your Majesty, you know everything we can tell you." Tony's use of her more formal title indicated his irritation. "We don't know who was behind it, and we don't know for sure how they found out where you were. We *do* know only one person not on the list was told."

"He had *nothing* to do with this!" She managed to conceal just how mad she was. Maybe.

"Maybe not. But it's possible he let something slip when he left the palace. We told you to tell *no one* for a reason, ma'am."

Alexander stood like a silent sentinel, his arms folded across his chest, and positioned near enough to the door to get to any threat that might barge through. To protect her. Protection was Tony's job. He'd been promoted to head of security the day before the accident. The timing was the only thing that kept him from losing his job. There was no way he could have been aware of the problems with her parents' automobile, and even then maintenance wasn't necessarily his responsibility. He was in charge of making sure the men who maintained the vehicles were trustworthy.

"Ma'am, you need to have a seat." The tension, bordering on anger, in Tony's voice scared her into pulling out the chair. Once seated, he went on. "We've debated telling you this for some time. I spoke with King Antonio, former King Jedediah, and Queen Adeline a few moments ago and decided it's time."

She glanced between the two men. Neither of them gave anything away. "What, Tony?"

He walked to the seat next to her and pulled it out. "There's no easy way to tell you this. If you'd been older you would have known from the start, but you were so young."

Something to do with the accident then. Her belly churned, and she feared she might be sick. She was never sick. Never threw up. But something told her this news just might change that.

"We've long believed the accident wasn't an accident."

Sucker punched, Christiana slumped over the table as it sunk in. "Not an accident?" she whispered.

"We've never found definitive proof, but the gut feeling on my part as well as both kings was that something was done to tamper with the vehicle or to impair your father's judgment."

Her father had been driving that day when the car went over the cliff and into the water many feet below. She shut out the nightmares she had from time to time, mostly around Christmas. They died the morning before Christmas Eve as they finished up a two-month tour of the country, something they did every several years. She hated the holiday for that reason.

As she tried to wrap her mind around the implications, she asked for clarification. "So someone killed my parents, my brother, his nanny? Or caused the accident?"

"It's possible. Once we began to suspect your uncle, we wondered if he might have done something."

"But why?"

Tony shrugged. "Power, I suppose. He's your mother's relative, but she married royalty. Maybe he had some plan to usurp the throne. The next closest kinsman is actually quite removed from your father. You know that."

Wheels spun in her head. "I was supposed to be in the car, too. It would have been the four of us." The bile that already churned kicked up a notch.

"Yes, ma'am. The nanny would have lived as she wouldn't have been with them, but you, most assuredly, would not have survived."

"I can't believe it." An assassination attempt not only of her parents, but her and her brother? "I wasn't even supposed to be queen. We still, even today, have the old rules of primogeniture. My brother was supposed to be king. The Princess Yvette from Mevendia would have married him and been queen. I was the spare." She swallowed the burning liquid that threatened to force its way out as she tried to assimilate the new information.

"Yes, ma'am. But when your brother was declared dead, you became queen."

Something more seemed off. Then it hit her. "Declared dead?"

Tony hesitated and she knew he was about to drop another bombshell.

"What is it?" she demanded, half rising out of her chair.

"Your brother was never found, ma'am. There was no body."

* * *

"But you have to know. I think I love you."

The words drifted through an open window as Jonathan drifted in and out. The poking and prodding stopped.

And everything went blessedly black.

He had no idea how long it had been when his eyes opened again, but the lack of light coming in around the curtains told him it was dark outside.

"How're you feeling?"

Jonathan looked over to see Jonah sitting in one of the chairs next to the bed. He tried to say something, but his mouth felt like he'd swallowed a whole bale of cotton. Jonah reached for a cup on the side table and, much to Jonathan's dismay, helped him drink a few sips.

"That's enough," the doctor told him. "Feeling better?"

"Some, yes. Thanks, Doc." He tried to push himself into a sitting position. The ache in the back of his head turned to shooting pain with the movement.

"Careful." Jonah helped him reposition until he sat with his back against the headboard. Jonathan closed his eyes as the doctor checked his vitals.

"Where's Ana?" He had to know. Did he imagine what he'd heard? What had her response been? Was it over between them? "Is she okay?"

Jonah settled back into his seat and nodded toward the other side of the room. Jonathan didn't have to turn far to see Ana sound asleep on the empty side of the bed. On top of the covers, but with a light blanket tossed over her.

"This can't be appropriate," he muttered.

Jonah's lips twitched. "You were unconscious, my friend. Her virtue was threatened at no time."

"Still." Details of the day came flooding back. "Did they determine if the threat is over?"

"To the best of my knowledge." The other man took a sip of his own drink as he shrugged. "No one tells me anything. I do know both women think you're quite the hero for charging out there on your own and getting wounded for it." Jonathan didn't miss the spark of amusement in his eyes. "Personally, I think it's stupid, but there's no accounting for taste."

Jonathan tried to laugh but it turned to a groan, just like it had in the van, one of his last clear memories of the afternoon. "Don't do that. It hurts."

"Sorry. Occupational hazard. I'm a pediatrician. My job is to make kids forget they're in pain or sick."

He closed his eyes and held out his hand. "You got any meds, Doc?"

After a clicking sound followed by rattling, he felt several pills in his hand. "Do you need any help?"

"I got it." He had to open his eyes to find the water. What he found was an amused doctor holding the cup. "Thanks." Carefully, he tossed back the four extra strength ibuprofen, swallowing all in one gulp. "How long do they take to kick in?"

"Too long when you're in pain. Distraction is the best thing for you until they do."

"Who's going to distract me?" The best distraction for the pounding would come in the form of the slender princess who slept far too close to him. Even though there was a good foot and a half of space between them.

Jonah grinned. "Me, I suppose." He did something to his phone then handed it over. "That's Archer."

The phone had a picture of a horse on the screen. A big one. Through the pain in his head, he couldn't quite tell what color - a bay maybe? Chestnut? It would be easier to tell if there wasn't a white blaze covering his whole face. The horse faced the camera, a western saddle on his back, and a cowboy at his side. The cowboy covered Archer's nose with one hand. The tilt of his head and the angle of the black cowboy hat meant Jonathan couldn't see his face, but it had to be Jonah. The cowboy loved the horse. And the horse loved him back.

"He's the one you were telling me about?"

"Yep. Brought him from Texas to Montevaro with me. Couldn't have left him in Texas. My dad wasn't very happy with me, but he's my horse."

"Dad liked to ride him?"

Jonah chortled. "Nah. The deal was that he got the stud fees as long as they boarded him at home for me."

He handed the phone back. "A stallion." That surprised him. He'd only ever ridden one, and it belonged to his uncle. Geldings were much more common.

"He has quite the lineage. We talked about gelding him but decided to go this route. It's been well worth it."

"I imagine so." He reached out his hand. "Let me look again?" Jonah gave him the phone back. "Do you board him out near the Montago March?"

The doctor took the offered phone and stuck it in his pocket. "Yep."

"I've seen him. I've taken horses from there with both Addie and Ellie. I noticed he was in a paddock by himself and wondered why. They're keeping him away from the lady horses?"

The conversation about horseflesh continued for another half hour until the medicine started to kick in again. "Do you think I could eat something yet, Doc?"

Jonah looked at his watch. "If you feel up to it. Want me to see if I can find something for you?"

"I'd appreciate it."

After he left, Jonathan turned to watch the sleeping beauty lying next to him. He couldn't think straight just yet, but he knew he'd never actually *slept* next to a woman. With one finger, he reached out and brushed a bit of hair off her forehead. When he did it again, she shifted. He stilled but her eyes fluttered open.

"You're awake!" Her sleep-filled voice warmed him. "How're you feeling?"

"Better."

Ana shifted until she could sit up, cross-legged, next to him. Her hair tumbled around her shoulders, clearly the remnants of her earlier partial up do. She'd probably hate how messy it looked.

Jonathan loved it.

"Where's Jonah?" She looked around and twisted to look out the door, but the doc was nowhere to be seen. "He said he was going to stay with you until you woke up."

"He went to get me something to eat. I'm feeling good enough to keep something down." He thought. Maybe. He reached for her hand. "Thank you for staying with me, but you look exhausted. You've had a long day. Why don't you go get some sleep?"

"Are you sure?"

"Absolutely." Jonathan held her hand up until he could kiss her fingers. "Sleep well." He really wanted to kiss her, but he didn't dare.

"You, too." She leaned over and brushed her lips against his cheek. "Good night."

She walked out of the room and he whispered, "Good night." Eyes closed, he dozed off even before Jonah returned. When he woke, there was a tray with a light snack and a note. Jonah told him to eat when he felt up to it but if he didn't, to wait for breakfast.

Alone, he began to eat, but gave up after only a few bites. He doubted the two of them were together, but the fact they'd left him alone didn't bode well for his future with Ana.

Especially not since Jonah loved her.

* * *

After Christiana finished throwing up, Alexander insisted she get some rest. She fell into a restless sleep until voices woke her about midnight. From what she could tell, Ana and Jonah had finally left Jonathan alone after he'd woken up to talk to them.

But she wanted answers. Would she still find Tony in his office? Did Alexander hold the key?

Still dressed, she straightened her clothes and headed to find out. Sure enough, in the office, she found both of them.

"Gentlemen, I want answers."

She'd obviously startled them, but neither jumped.

Tony motioned to one of the chairs on the other side of the desk. "Have a seat, ma'am."

"I *need* answers, Tony."

"I know." He walked around as Alexander sat in the other chair. Tony leaned back against the desk. "Ask away."

"What did you mean when you said there was no body?"

He sighed. "Just that. We never found Nicklaus or his nanny. For years, we wondered if he'd survived somehow and, if so, why didn't he come back? We kept that information very close to the vest though. As far as pretty much anyone knows, Nicklaus was buried the same day as your parents and his nanny two days later."

"Who does know?" Who else had known before her?

"Henry, for one. Alexander found out recently. A few key members of Parliament at the time. No one new there since. The royal families and select members of security in Montevaro and Mevendia. We thought maybe he'd turn up there."

"Did she take advantage of the situation and kidnap him? Was there ever a ransom demand?"

"No, ma'am. As best we could tell, they fell out of the vehicle into the water. It was cold that day. They couldn't have survived long even if they weren't already beat up from the accident."

"I never saw pictures," she whispered. "I thought the car was nose-down. How could they fall out?"

"It was more sideways by the time it stopped. If you really want to see them, I'll show you some, but I wouldn't recommend it."

Christiana shook her head as it all sank in. "No. I trust you." She wiped under her eyes with her fingers. "I just have a hard time thinking about that day at all. Now to find out all four of them didn't die instantly like I always believed..."

Tony and Alexander exchanged a look and she demanded they expound on it.

Her head of security looked defeated. "None of them died instantly, ma'am."

Another sucker punch. "What?"

"Your mother likely died quickly. Your father died as the emergency personnel arrived on the scene. We have no idea about your brother or the nanny."

"Then why..." Christiana had to stop to regain her composure.

"My guess, ma'am? Those who told you they died instantly didn't want you to know they suffered. Not for long, but long enough it wasn't instantaneous."

"Is there anything else I should know?"

Tony hesitated long enough she looked up but then he shook his head. "No, ma'am."

She put her hands on the arms of the chair and pushed up until she stood. "I'm going to bed."

Alexander moved to her side. "Are you sure you don't want someone with you, ma'am?"

She shook her head. "No. I will be fine." Christiana did not want anybody to witness what was sure to be an epic crying jag. "Thank you."

With that she left the office. She managed to keep her composure until she reached the bedroom assigned to her. There she threw herself on the bed and cried herself to sleep.

* * *

Alexander watched the queen as she left the office. "She's

not okay," he told Tony.

"I know." The other man came to stand next to him. "But there's not much we can do about it at this point."

"No. There's not."

They watched the now empty hallway for several minutes, each lost in their own thoughts, before Alexander spoke again. "Are you sure about her boyfriend?"

"As sure as I can be without actual evidence. He's the one who hit Jonathan over the head."

"Do we tell her?"

"Not without incontrovertible proof. She won't believe us."

"He's going to propose. I heard her tell Ana about him this morning. She didn't say so, but that's the impression I got." The idea of Christiana having any kind of relationship with that man made Alexander's skin crawl. The idea she'd agree to marry him? Made him nauseous.

"We'll have to make sure it never gets to a wedding."

"It won't." Alexander would do everything in his power to make sure it didn't. "Are you going to tell her about the rumors about Nicklaus and the nanny?"

"Not until I have to. They've never found any substantiation in the press."

Another minute passed.

"Tony?"

"Yeah?"

"Are you ever going to tell her what her father said before he died?"

Tony didn't answer.

Chapter Eleven

*A*fter a fitful night of sleep, Ana woke to someone knocking on her door.

"Yes?" she called, sitting up and, despite wearing her favorite pajamas, held the sheets to her chest.

Alexander walked in, eyes down. "I'm sorry for bothering you, ma'am, but I've been asked to tell you that you'll be leaving in about two hours."

"What? Why?"

He shook his head. "The queen doesn't want you to be in any danger. Any threat is against her, not you. She's asked that all non-essential personnel be evacuated."

Ana cocked an eyebrow at him. "Evacuated? Isn't that a bit strong?"

With a shrug, he started to back out of the door. "Not my call, ma'am."

"Alexander?" She called him back.

"Yes, ma'am?"

"Is there more to it?"

He didn't answer immediately. "That's all I've been told."

Ana nodded and let him leave. So there was more to it, but he wasn't at liberty to tell her about it. She got ready to leave as quickly as she could. Her suitcase had been packed at the cottage and brought over but not yet unpacked. She wondered if both Jonah and Jonathan would be going with her or if they would both have other arrangements. Could Jonathan even fly yet?

She walked into the hallway and went to the room designated for the queen. "Can I see her?" she asked the guard.

He shook his head. "I'm sorry, ma'am. The queen has asked not to be disturbed."

As much as Ana wanted to press the issue, she decided it would be better not to. Instead, she went down to breakfast. Jonah was already there, as was Jonathan. He'd looked better, but he'd also looked worse. After a quiet meal, they were driven to the airplane as it sat on the tarmac.

Everyone seemed to be in their own worlds, even Marty and Carrie, at least to an extent. The flight didn't last long. As soon as she could, Ana headed for Addie's office. Without calling ahead for an appointment, she walked right past the receptionist and in. She'd checked the schedule. There was nothing on it.

Nothing except a make-out session with the prince consort.

Ana looked away as Addie stepped out of Charlie's embrace. At least it hadn't been anything...more.

"You are back early." Addie moved to sit behind her desk. "I got word, but no one told me why. I thought Christiana would want the company after the incident."

"Something else happened yesterday. I'm not sure what, but it did."

Addie sighed. "I would imagine Tony told her the truth about the accident."

Ana just raised a brow, waiting for an explanation.

"It was not an accident, her parents did not die instantly, her brother and the nanny were never found."

Ana slumped back in her chair, her heart breaking for her friend. "What?" No wonder Christiana didn't want anyone around. "I wish..."

"I know." Addie sat forward in her chair. "She knows we are here for her if she needs us. There is precious little else we can do." She reached for a folder. "In the meantime, I need you to take over this for me."

Ana took it from her. "What is it?"

"Fundraiser. I thought I would have time, but I just do not."

"Rick's the spare." Ana hated planning fundraisers.

"Rick has a wedding to help plan."

Ana's head shot up. "What? When?"

Addie laughed. "I thought you knew."

"No!"

"He asked Ellie on their way back from the States yesterday. I thought he would have told you."

Charlie joined the conversation. "The only reason you knew is because I knew he talked to her father, sweetie."

Not many people could call the monarch sweetie and get away with it. And Ellie's parents had practically raised Charlie. If anyone would know early on her side of the family, it would be him.

"I knew he'd looked at the rings," Ana told them. "I didn't know he'd picked one and actually gone through with it."

"Yes. And they are planning a Christmas Eve wedding, so he has his hands full. You, my dear sister, get the fundraiser."

"Fine." She had no choice. "I do have schoolwork you know."

Addie just smiled politely. "You will do a wonderful job. Jonah is the co-chair this year, so you will get to spend lots of time with him."

Great.

Ana didn't know what to do about that. He'd told her he loved her. She hadn't quite known how to respond. Then they'd been interrupted before she could.

But that kiss...

"Is that a problem?" Addie broke through her thoughts. "I thought things were going well."

"They are." Ana sighed. If Charlie hadn't been there...

Charlie stood. "And that's my cue to leave." He kissed his wife, whispered something that made her blush, and rested his hand on Ana's shoulder as he walked by. "You'll be great, Ana."

"Thanks." She waited for the door to close.

Addie didn't. It hadn't clicked when her sister started the interrogation. "What is it? What is going on with you and Jonah? I thought you liked him."

"I did," Ana insisted. "I do."

"But..."

"But, I've spending a lot of time with Jonathan, too. And I'm just not sure which direction my heart is telling me is the right one."

"Have you prayed about it?" Addie asked gently. "The only reason Charlie is here instead of Jonathan is because God answered my prayers."

That tidbit shocked Ana. "I know you and Jonathan went out a few times, but you were going to marry him?"

Addie lifted one shoulder. "Maybe. We talked about it. He knew I was in love with Charlie. Our parents and Parliament did not approve. They would approve of Jonathan. Jonathan's family, particularly his grandmothers, would approve of me. It would have been good. I like him. He likes me. We could have made it work. But Charlie is the man God intended to be by my side. Prince consort would have been more difficult for Jonathan because of his family connections. God knew what He was doing."

"What about me? Could Jonathan be right for me then? I'm not going to be queen," she pointed out. "I could move to the States at some point."

"You could. And I cannot answer that question for you. Only you can. Do you love him? Do you love Jonah?"

Ana stared at the manila folder. "I don't know, Addie. I just don't know."

Tapping his tablet against his leg, Jonah walked through the halls of the hospital. He used to tap his clipboard like this, but when the hospital upgraded to the tablets, he'd insisted on good covers. Immediately. They hadn't provided the super good ones, so he'd splurged on a fun one for himself.

After a restless second day off, he was back on the children's floor and preparing to visit his favorite kiddo. He washed well at the sink near her room. The transplant would be done soon, and they needed to be extra sure she didn't get sick in the meantime.

The room was dark and quiet when he walked in, pulling a mask up as he did. Sara seemed to be asleep and he didn't need to wake her up just yet.

"How is she?" he asked her mom.

The exhausted woman looked like she could use a nap of her own. "Tired and ready for this to be over."

"I bet both of you are, too."

"Definitely." He could see tears in her eyes. "I'm ready for my baby to be well."

Jonah reached over and took her hand. "I know you are. I'm ready to not see any of you for a very long time. We're almost there." He looked at the clock on the wall. Addie would be there in a little over an hour to start the fundraiser planning. "Why don't you go back to your hotel? Get some rest. We'll go over tomorrow again later."

"I can't leave her alone."

"I'll stay. I have some work to do, but..." He held up his tablet. "I can do it from here. I have someone coming for a meeting, but we can do that here, too. We'll be quiet and if she wakes up, she can listen to boring fundraiser planning talk." And see Addie. He knew that would cheer the girl up.

"Are you sure, Dr. Fontaine?" He could see the hope for a real nap shining from her eyes.

"Absolutely."

"Thank you." She squeezed his hand then gathered her things. He could see her whisper a prayer over her daughter before she left. Jonah made sure the door stayed wide open. He set his tablet up on the extra tray table and began making a list of fundraiser ideas. He looked through the list of past fundraisers. Casino night the year before. Rodeo the year before that. Despite Jonah's thoughts on the matter, it hadn't done very well. He scanned through and didn't see much of anything that intrigued him. He'd have to see what Addie came up with.

He heard his name drift through the door. A nurse replied. "He's in with a patient right now. Can I take a message, ma'am?"

Without waiting to hear the reply, he went to the door, pulling his mask all the way off as he did. "I'm right here, Nancy."

The brunette turned around. Not Addie but Ana.

She smiled at him, though there seemed to be some annoyance. Jonah walked to her side and kissed her cheek. Nothing too unusual right? He would have done the same with Addie. But the giggling nurses told him it must have been a bit out of the ordinary.

"Come into my temporary office." He stopped when they reached the door. "I do need you to wash up very well. Unless...You haven't been sick recently have you? Anything at all? Sniffles you chalked up to allergies from the hay fields? A sneeze you weren't sure came from the lady in the elevator wearing too much perfume? Anything?"

Ana thought about it and shook her head. "I don't think so, but I don't know that I'd risk my life on it." She turned to her ever present body guards. "Can you think of anything?"

They both shook their heads, but still Jonah hesitated. Finally, he walked to the nurses counter and pulled out a mask. "Do you mind? We're being extra careful in here."

She glared his direction. "I just told you I haven't been sick."

"I know. And if you had been, I wouldn't let you in at all. I cannot risk her getting sick."

She pouted and put it on, but he pulled it below her chin. "You can leave it like this until we go in." How he wanted to lean in and kiss those lips! But he couldn't. Not here.

He put his own mask on, hanging under his chin. They washed up next to each other and they found seats in the hospital room. He explained why he was working in there then asked what she was doing here.

"Addie asked me to co-chair the fundraiser."

She didn't seem happy about it. He didn't know how to take that. "Is that a problem?"

"I hate planning these things." Her eyes scrunched as she pouted beneath the mask. "If I have to do it at all, I guess I'm glad it's with you."

He reached out and took her hand, linking their fingers together. "As much as I like Addie, I can't say I'm disappointed to be working with you." And without Jonathan.

Her pout seemed to dissolve into a smile though it was hard to tell with the mask. "I can't say I'm disappointed either."

"Good. We'll work together then. The first thing we need to do is narrow down the dates. The date is currently set for October 31. I wonder if we can push it back." He swiped through the calendar. "The only other option is two days before Christmas."

"That won't work. Rick's getting married." He looked up to see her clap her hands over the mask, her eyes wide as she realized what she'd said. "*No one* knows. I just found out from Addie a couple hours ago."

He made a locking motion in front of his mouth. "No one will hear it from me. So Christmas is out." With one finger, he swiped through the hospital's calendar on his tablet. "October 31 it is. Not my first choice, but there's nothing else before the end of the year."

"We could do a costume ball. It'll fit in with the night, but have guidelines so we don't end up with a bunch of vampires or zombies." She shuddered. "I do not understand the popularity."

Jonah grinned. "Me either." He leaned closer. "Just be sure to tell me what you're wearing so I know it's you."

Ana felt the heat rise in her cheeks and not just from the mask. "You mean you won't be able to tell it's me if I don't tell you ahead of time what I'm wearing?"

"I hope I can, but you never know. You and Addie, for instance, look very similar from the chin down. Really, even from the nose down."

"I'll tell you a secret." She leaned closer. "I'm younger than Addie is. So if the costumed woman looks old, it's not me." Ana struggled to keep the laughter in, but failed. She did her best to keep the volume down. The last thing she wanted to do was wake up the sleeping girl. She'd seen the name on the outside of the room and, unless she was mistaken, this was the girl from Addie's wedding.

Jonah leaned back in his seat. "I know fundraisers are good

and all. We need to raise the money, but I'm more of a get my hands dirty kind of guy. I'd rather be in the trenches treating patients."

"I know." She fiddled with the corner of the folder. "I'd rather be doing publicity, public speaking about the charity in question, press conferences, things like that. But we've been tasked by the queen to plan this fundraiser and we have about seven weeks to make it come together."

"Not much time."

"Which means we need to decide on the theme and get invitations ordered in the next couple of days."

"Costume ball. Further details will come at a later date."

"I'm sure we can get some instructions together in time to send it out. There is likely already some in the information from past years. We can update them a bit. I do not believe zombies were quite the rage last time."

Jonah chuckled. "Can you imagine your mother or Addie at a ball with zombies?"

Ana giggled. "Not a chance." Then she imagined her mother dressed as a zombie and she had to clap a hand over her mouth to keep the sound under control.

"You pictured the former queen as a zombie, didn't you?" The twinkle in his brown eyes was too much. Both of them doubled over.

"Dr. Jonah?" The voice from the bed sobered them both up quickly.

Ana sat quietly, watching as Jonah pulled his stethoscope from around his neck. He sat next to the bed and talked with the patient. After a minute, he turned to her.

"Princess Ana?"

She stood and walked the three steps to his side. "Yes?"

"Princess Anastasia, this is Sara. Sara, this is Princess Ana."

Ana nodded her head. "Hello, Sara. You were in the wedding.

We met then."

Sara nodded. "Queen Adeline asked me to be in it. I almost wasn't well enough." She shifted in the bed. "Dr. Jonah says I'll get better starting tomorrow though."

The man next to her patted the girl's leg. "That's what we're praying for. Miss Sara is tough and the best fighter I know."

With that, Jonah stood. "Sara, I'm going to talk with Princess Ana outside for a minute. Will you be all right?"

"Yeah." Her eyes fluttered closed. "I think I'm gonna go back to sleep."

"Good plan." He patted her leg again and motioned for Ana to walk outside. Once there, he pulled down his mask. "Can we get together tomorrow night?" He looked back at the door. "I don't want to leave her and she needs to rest. I should be done here about six."

Ana tugged her mask all the way off as she nodded. "That would be fine."

Jonah took a step closer. "Then dinner? I'll pick you up at seven." His low, almost gravelly, voice sent shivers up her spine.

"That would be nice."

He leaned over and brushed another kiss against her cheek. "I'll see you then."

Ana felt the color in cheeks as she avoided looking at the nurses' station on the way to the elevator. She knew as soon as the doors slid shut, the giggling would begin. From the way the nurse grinned when Jonah had appeared to talk to her, and the number of nurses who happened to be hanging out there now, news of their relationship had spread. Ana didn't know exactly what their relationship was, but the nurses would speculate anyway.

So would anyone who saw them out for dinner the next night.

Which begged the question...

What would she wear?

Chapter Twelve

Stupid! Jonah tapped his closed tablet case lightly against his forehead. If it had been a yellow pad of paper he would have smacked it a lot harder.

Where was he supposed to pick Ana up? He couldn't just drive up to the palace, park in the driveway, and ring the bell. What was the protocol? Have her meet him at her place? At the restaurant? At the garrison where the boats left for the palace? For their last date, she'd already been out doing a public appearance and so they'd met somewhere. He'd planned to take her on a horseback ride, but that hadn't worked out. Pizza at his apartment had been nice, but maybe he should take her riding this time.

He called the stables to make sure there would be horses available. They wouldn't be able to ride the trails, but he was able to reserve the indoor arena and arrange for some fences to be set up. Ana had mentioned she missed jumping. Jonah had never jumped a fence on purpose, but it might be fun. Little fences. He didn't want to risk hurting himself or his horse.

But he didn't want to look like a wimp either.

Maybe he should come up with a new plan...

Before he could make up his mind, his phone buzzed at him.

CHECKED MY SCHEDULE. I HAVE A MEETING IN TOWN UNTIL 7:15. CAN I MEET YOU AT YOUR PLACE AT 7:30?

Jonah texted back it would be fine. That settled, he went to his office and got back to work.

By the time seven o'clock rolled around the next evening, Jonah was a bundle of nerves. Sara's transplant had gone well, much easier than most other transplants. No open heart surgery or open abdomen, just what amounted to little more than a special kind of blood transfusion. She had a long way to go, but so far, things looked great.

He'd tried to call Ana earlier, but she'd responded with a text. He wore his blue jeans, riding boots instead of his work boots, and a button up shirt. His black cowboy hat hung on its peg near the front door. All that remained was to wait for...

The doorbell.

He took a deep breath and made himself not rush too much. It was still less than half a minute before he opened it and saw Ana standing there. Suddenly, inexplicably, at a loss for words, he managed a, "Hi."

"Hello." He'd told her to wear something comfortable. Something she could move freely in. And she'd done just that. Black leggings hugged her slender legs. A top that could have passed for either a long shirt or short dress flared from the waist to mid-thigh. Black boots came nearly to her knee. How did she make casual look so elegant?

He managed to regain use of his vocal chords. "Would you like to come in?"

Ana tilted her head his direction. "I thought you had reservations somewhere at eight. Do we have time?"

"Um..." How to answer? Without giving away what they were doing? "We have time if we want, but yes, dinner is waiting."

Her smile lit up his world. "Then let's go. Carrie and Marty promised to follow in the car behind if you wanted to drive."

Jonah managed a genuine grin of his own as he closed the door. "I think I like that plan." With a twist of the key in the door, he locked it. Offering his arm, he covered her hand with his as they walked to the elevator. "I hope you like what I've got planned."

She tossed a pout his way. "And you're still not going to tell me?"

"Nope. You'll see."

"Fine."

Despite her pretend pique, they had a great conversation on the way to the stables. She told him a little bit about growing up royal. He shared some about Splendora. And when he turned into the drive of the equestrian center, she gasped. "Horseback riding? At night?"

He glanced over to make sure it was a good gasp. The way her wide eyes lit up, it was. "Sort of. You'll see."

"I'm not dressed to ride, not really."

"Carrie knew where we were going. She was supposed to bring something for you to wear if she needed to." He'd had to clear it with them, after all.

He parked, opened her door, and together they walked into the barn. Many of the horses were out in the assorted paddocks and fields, but he'd asked if Archer could be inside. Jonah stopped next to the stall with Archer's name on it. The big horse nickered as he stuck his head over the half door.

Jonah wrapped one arm around the horse's head and rested his hand along the side of Archer's face. His other hand rubbed along the white blaze. "Hey, boy." Soft tones worked best. Always had. "Did ya miss me?" As though he understood, Archer's head moved up and down. His lips started working against the pocket of Jonah's shirt.

With a laugh, Jonah moved back. "He doesn't really love me." He reached into his pocket and pulled out a few sugar cubes. "He loves these." With his fingers tight together and palm flat, he held one out for Archer to nibble. "Want to give him one?"

Cautiously, Ana approached. She wasn't afraid, he noted. Some girls were. Archer was a big guy. No, she just wanted to give him time to notice her, to make sure he didn't feel threatened. She held up the back of her hand, careful to keep her fingers tucked together. Archer snuffled her fingers, then bumped them with his muzzle, accepting her immediately.

When Ana held out her other hand, Jonah put a sugar cube in it. He could hear her saying something but couldn't make out the words. Archer ate it and bumped against her chest. Ana rested her forehead against him. The snuffling sounds told Jonah all he needed to hear.

His horse had found a new favorite.

"We aren't going to saddle up?" Ana's hand rested snuggly in Jonah's as they walked toward the indoor arena.

"Nope. Not yet." He led her around the side rather than in the door. There, spread out on the grass, was a red-checked cloth with a wicker picnic basket sitting on top.

"A picnic?" When was the last time she had been on a picnic? Ever? Or not since she and Rick had snuck their snack into the garden. Her mother did not believe in eating outside.

Ana sat down, stretching her legs in front of her. The moon and ambient light from the parking lot meant they did not need a light source that would draw more bugs than necessary. She did not wait for Jonah, but opened the basket. Cheese. Crackers. Sliced meats. Fruit and grapes. "This looks wonderful."

He pulled out a bottle and poured bubbly liquid into wine glasses. "Don't worry. No alcohol. Not a good plan for the next part of our evening."

She took a sip of the sparkling white grape juice. "Is this

Mevendian?"

"Good taste buds."

"I grew up on Mevendian sparkling grape juice."

Jonah set a tray of finger foods on the cloth before stretching his own legs out in front of him and leaning up on an elbow facing her. He reached a hand her way. "Shall we pray?"

She slid her fingers into his and did her best to focus on the words of his prayer rather than the warmth of his hand.

Dinner passed with good food and easy conversation. They cleaned up, taking the basket and cloth with them, laughing as they groomed and tacked the horses. Ana loved Archer, but did not want to ride him just yet. Maybe someday. The horse chosen for her was a smaller bay named Miss Dixie. She followed a safe distance behind Jonah and Archer as they walked to the indoor arena. As much as she wanted to go for a long ride through the Montevarian countryside, they could not do so in the dark. The big door to the arena remained open.

Marty was inside and opened the main gate for them. It was not until Jonah moved a bit to the side that Carrie flipped on the overhead lights.

Ana gasped. "Fences? We're going to jump?"

He laughed. "Well, you are. Archer and I haven't jumped a whole lot. At least not on purpose. We jumped a fence once but that was stupid."

"Well, I love it." She led Miss Dixie to a step stool along the side and swung herself up. For the first few minutes, Ana just put the horse through her paces, taking the time to get familiar with each other. She turned her toward one of the small jumps. As they left the ground, Ana could not keep the grin from her face.

For the seconds between take-off and landing, she felt free.

And she loved that feeling.

If only she could always feel that way.

"Careful."

Jonah glared at Marty and Carrie as he helped Ana through the doors into the emergency department. He didn't need to be told to be careful. Not his first choice of venues, and he didn't have his key card with him so couldn't go through the back door. Murmurs from the seating area let him know the bodyguards had been right with their concerns. It would be on social media in minutes.

Complete with pictures of a bloodied princess.

One of the nurses he knew by sight greeted them and they were soon in a room.

"I wish all of you would stop fussing." Ana sat on the exam table while Jonah put on gloves.

"You need stitches." He began looking for the supplies he would need, but hadn't yet found all of them when a nurse walked in with the chief of emergency medicine on her heels.

"Dr. Fontaine, what are you doing?"

Jonah glanced up. The man was too big for his britches, but he held a lot of influence over Jonah's boss. "The princess and I were horseback riding. She got hurt. I'm stitching her up."

Ana's indignant voice took his attention away from Dr. Lovelace. "I did *not* fall off my horse, Dr. Fontaine."

"I never said you did, Your Highness." He didn't look at her, but kept his attention trained on the other doctor.

"You are not authorized to work down here."

Jonah knew that but he also knew he was kind of the golden boy at the hospital at the moment. And Dr. Lovelace was being unreasonable, but..."All right." He snapped off the gloves. "Princess Ana, would you care to go upstairs where I can stitch that up for you? Or would you prefer whatever emergency room doc isn't busy right now?" Bringing the very competent doctors into this wasn't his finest hour, but Dr. Lovelace had been on his last nerve for some time. When Jonah came down to see pediatric ER patients, the man hovered and second-guessed at every turn.

Ana ignored him and turned to the other man, reading his name off his name badge. "Dr. Lovelace, I appreciate the hard work you do to keep this emergency room running smoothly. I have heard nothing but good things when we do our quarterly charitable reviews for the Royal Family Foundation funds. I know the doctors currently staffing the emergency department are wonderfully competent. I noticed a number of patients waiting, and I would hate to be the cause of further delaying their care. Would you be so kind as to allow Dr. Fontaine to take care of this for me?"

And just like that she had the most hard-nosed doctor on staff eating out of her hand, just as Archer had. Dr. Lovelace hesitated then nodded. "Of course, Your Highness." As soon as Ana shifted so she wasn't looking at him, the other man glared at Jonah. He figured he'd get a lecture in the morning, but right now, he didn't care.

In just a few minutes, he had numbed the area and stitched the gash along her hairline. "The good news is your hair isn't much lighter than the stitches," he told her as he clipped the end. "And it normally covers this area right here. You'll want to wash it carefully because you can't get the stitches wet."

"I am certain I can have someone help me."

Right. She probably had several people help her with her hair if she wanted to hang out at the palace in her PJs all day, much less if she actually needed to go out. As gently as he could, he wiped the blood off her forehead and cheek.

"Thank you," she whispered and Jonah found himself doing everything he could not to look down at her delectably kissable lips.

Instead, he took her hand and used the wash cloth to wipe the dried blood off it. The silver ring on the middle finger of her left hand would need to come off. So would her watch. Both would need to be cleaned well.

Of course, she probably had people to do that for her to.

Ana pulled her hand away as he wiped off the last bit. "Thank you for taking care of me."

"It's my fault you were hurt in the first place." He tossed the wash cloth in the appropriate bin. "I shouldn't have turned the light off in the tack room before you were all the way out." He'd been kicking himself over since he heard her cry out.

"It was an accident, Jonah." To his great surprise, she leaned over and brushed a kiss against his lips. Just a light one, but it certainly left him wanting more. Noises outside the room meant it wouldn't happen right now.

"Time to go." Carrie's quiet words broke the moment. "They're going to take us out the back."

Ana squeezed his hand and slid off the table. "No. I want to go out the front. I am certain this is all over local social media, and I would like to make sure everyone knows everything is fine." She went to the sink and washed her hands. "I would also like to visit anyone I can while I am here."

For a minute, Jonah didn't think Carrie was going to let her, but finally the bodyguard nodded. "All right. Let's go."

Jonathan put his feet up on the ottoman in front of him and pulled Facebook up on his tablet. He started to scroll through, but stopped when he saw a picture of Jonah with his arm around a woman with a bloody face. What...?

Before he could complete the thought he'd clicked through and saw another photo.

Ana.

He flipped over to her official Facebook page. Someone had posted a statement.

Princess Anastasia would like to thank all of you for your concern. She had a minor mishap this evening and cut her forehead. As you all know, head wounds bleed much more than their severity would normally indicate. Dr. Jonah Fontaine, a personal friend of the princess, stitched her wound at Montevaro General Hospital. She spent some time visiting with those in the Emergency Department at the hospital and will be returning to the palace momentarily.

Rather than taking the official public word for it, Jonathan texted Ana. Less than two minutes later, she responded that she had a bit of a headache but otherwise felt fine. He fought his urge to head to the hospital and see for himself. Instead, he flipped on the television to whatever show he could find. The most recent Jack Ryan movie popped up, and he decided it would work as a distraction. Thunder rolled in the background as a sudden storm raged outside.

About the time Jack and Kevin Costner's character walked into the Oval Office, he got another text. Pulling a shirt on, he headed out of his designated room whenever he stayed at the Lydia House. When he reached the foyer, the door opened, and the princess herself walked in.

Jonathan frowned as he noticed blood dried on the side of her face. Not much, but at the same time, too much.

She smiled at him. Her eyes looked tired, but overall she seemed fine. "Good evening, Jonathan."

He reached out and brushed her hair back from the injury. "Does it hurt?"

"Not too badly. Jonah gave me some medication." Ana smiled up at him. "The medicine is making me tired, though, so I will say good night."

"Why are you staying here?"

"I am not feeling well, and the idea of the boat trip was just too much for me to handle."

"I'm sorry." Jonathan resisted the urge to kiss her cheek. Just a couple hours earlier, she'd been on a date with another man.

"I'll see you in the morning?"

"Perhaps. I'm clearing my schedule for the first part of the day. I will likely be here for breakfast."

He grinned at her. "I'll see you then."

She turned before she reached the stairs. "How is your head, Jonathan?"

"Pardon?"

"How long has it been since you were knocked out?"

Right. That. "I'm fine." He'd long ago learned to ignore the dull ache that often came with weather changes. This, with Advil, wasn't much different. As long as he didn't touch the bump or let water run over it in the shower, he was fine.

"I am glad. Please let me know if you need further medical attention?"

"Of course." He wouldn't, but if he did...Well, he probably still wouldn't. Jonathan wondered what the protocol was for asking a girl out when she'd just been out with another man. Rather than call after her, he decided to wait for breakfast.

And when he walked downstairs the next morning, he did just that.

"Dinner?" Ana parroted. "Tonight?"

"I would love to take you out."

When she hesitated, he knew she was going to turn him down. "I wish I could, but Jonah and I have a late evening meeting about the fundraiser in October. We have so much we need to get nailed down. We do not have much time."

"Why didn't you pick a date further out then?" Jonathan shoveled a forkful of eggs into his mouth.

"There were only a few dates where the venue was still available and...well, Rick and Ellie are getting married Christmas Eve. They have not made the announcement yet, but they will soon. We did not want to be too close to that. They are planning a very small, intimate ceremony, and will not do a fundraiser ball in celebration, but we decided to schedule the hospital fundraiser further away. The hospital fundraiser, the wedding, the Christmas Eve Ball, and Christmas seemed like too much for one week."

Jonathan nodded. Made sense. And he'd end up watching another ex-girlfriend of sorts get married this year. Would Ana be the third one? Bad things came in threes. Or was third time a charm? The worst part? He could really see himself falling for Ana, much more so than Addie or Ellie.

Ana poked at her breakfast. "You will be invited, of course. I do hope you'll come, but since Jonah and I are co-chairpeople of the planning committee, we will attend together."

"Of course."

"I did hope you would do me a favor though. I think Christiana is planning to come. Would you be her escort?"

And now she was asking him to date another woman. Kind of. "What about Alexander? I thought they were a thing."

"No. She does have a suitor, but they are not ready to make their relationship public just yet. Alexander has escorted her to several events, but will be in the States."

"I see."

She used her napkin to wipe her mouth and set it to the side. "Let me know?"

He nodded but didn't agree. Maybe he'd need to make a trip back to the States over Halloween, instead of seeing her with Jonah.

Ana started to excuse herself, but Jonathan's phone rang - Addie's ring tone. He frowned as Ana looked on. "Hello?"

"Jonathan, we need your help." No preamble. Straight to the chase.

"Sure. What's up?" He'd do just about anything for most of his friends and Addie was a better friend than most.

"Lindsey's birth mother just turned up on television in the States. She's claiming Charlie date-raped her and stole her daughter."

Chapter Thirteen

*A*na did not know what her sister told Jonathan, but it couldn't be good. "What is it?" she mouthed.

He just shook his head and held up a finger. "What do you need me to do?"

Before Ana could ask again, he'd pushed back from the table and started for the stairs. "I'll leave as soon as I can get my things together. If you can get the travel secretary to plan a flight to London, I can get on a company plane there." His voice grew more distant as he started up the stairs.

What was that about?

Something serious. Ana pulled out her own phone to see a missed call from Rick. In seconds, she heard the ludicrous claims from her brother. She didn't know the whole story of Charlie and his ex-girlfriend, but she did know the claims were utterly ridiculous. "What can I do?"

"Just give no comment and if a reporter or someone persists, send them to the palace media office." She could hear the barely concealed fury in her brother's voice. He loved Charlie and Lindsey, but he was also marrying into Charlie's family as well.

"Will this delay your announcement?" She knew he was anxious to get the initial interviews out of the way. She also knew he would elope, if he thought he could get away with it.

"Most likely. The last thing either of us wants, is for our announcement presser to be filled with questions about Charlie. He and Addie wouldn't want that either."

"Lay some ground rules beforehand? Perhaps your news is just what is needed to take the focus off the groundless accusations."

"Maybe. But I don't want to do that to Ellie. She deserves better."

"I know. Talk to her." Ana headed for the front door, knowing her car was waiting for her. "I will be there shortly, and we can decide what we can do, if anything."

"How's your head?"

She trotted down the steps and climbed in to the waiting vehicle. "It hurts some, but I will be fine."

Something took Rick's attention for a moment. "I gotta go, Ana. Just get home."

The car pulled away from the house. "I am on my way."

Even before she reached the garrison, Ana could see reporters milling about. Thank goodness for tinted windows. She had no intention of speaking to anyone and they would not get inside. What did they hope to gain by being outside a guarded fortress? As the vehicle slowed, they shouted questions, but she couldn't be sure they even knew who was behind the windows.

The large doors swung shut behind her and Ana breathed a sigh of relief. She did not have to wait to begin the trip across the lake. The captain had obviously been told to hurry. It was only minutes before they docked on the island.

She found the rest of the family, along with several others, in a conference room. Lindsey, thankfully, was nowhere to be seen. The first thing she did was give Addie a hug, then Charlie. "Does

Lindsey know?" she asked as she turned around.

Charlie shook his head. "Not yet. We didn't want to tell her until we had to." He rubbed the back of his neck. "In fact, her phone might have gone missing overnight. We didn't want to risk a friend texting her. We also kept her home from school today. Didn't say why. Just an unspecified threat and blocked pretty much all Internet and television access."

"We told her something was wrong with the palace's wi-fi." Ana could see the tear tracks on Addie's cheeks. Her tender-hearted sister would want to protect her step-daughter with everything she had. Addie had even talked about adopting Lindsey someday, likely after she and Charlie were done having children. If it weren't for being queen, she already would have.

"So what do we do?"

"Jonathan is heading back to the States." Addie clung to Charlie's hand.

"I heard his side of your conversation."

"He has a lot of resources there. Charlie will give him limited power of attorney to get into the safety deposit box and get copies of paperwork."

Ana glanced at her brother-in-law. He'd left paperwork in the States?

"I thought it would be more convenient if it was there in case Lindsey ever needed any of it while she was back home without me."

Right.

"So what can I do?" Ana wanted to get to work. To do *something*.

Addie shook her head. "Just being here is plenty. I appreciate it. And do not give any comment when you are asked."

"Of course not." She couldn't keep the indignation out of her voice. They still treated her like a youngster. Rick had been born just a few minutes earlier than she was. But he was seen as competent, as a worthy spare and now heir, for the time being. If not for their positioning in the womb, it would have been her. Would they treat Rick as incompetent if their places had been switched?

Of course, she would never know.

Realizing no one would miss her, she told Rick she would be in her office doing some work. He nodded, but she could not be sure he even really heard what she said. Once there, she sat in her desk chair and swiveled until it faced the opposite direction, staring out over Lake Montevero. It wasn't until the phone on her desk trilled that she turned back around and got to work.

"No one who knows Charlie thinks it's true." Jonah tried to draw Ana out of her funk, but knew he had his work cut out for him.

"I know. There has been no indication anyone of any consequence believes it. Lindsey has not come out of her room since Charlie finally told her last night."

Jonah had seen the news when he checked the Montevarian news site the afternoon before. He couldn't figure out why this Tricia girl thought anyone would believe her. He'd never heard anyone say anything cross about Charlie, and when he started searching for more information, the articles from Serenity Landing and the U.S. news sources seemed to say the same thing.

"What does she hope to gain?" Ana stood and paced around his living room. "Lindsey will never be queen. She *will* be marchioness someday, but there's not *that* much money or power associated with it, I don't think so anyway."

"Maybe she's still mad at Charlie and wants to hurt him?" He poured a bit more red wine into both of their glasses. After nearly two hours of fundraiser planning, they'd ordered dinner.

Neither one of them had brought up the topic until they were done.

Ana picked up her glass and took a swallow. "I cannot fathom what she wants. Money? Notoriety? She certainly has that now. Fame? It will not last. Montevaro is not Great Britain. No one is as fascinated with us as they are with the Windsors."

"True. Except those that live here, of course."

Ana snorted. "I would imagine more Montevarians watched William and Kate get married than watched Addie and Charlie."

"Unlikely." He wondered if he could find the stats to prove it.

"Regardless, if she thinks this will force Charlie into something..." Another gulp of her wine. "If, and this if is as big as the Atlantic itself, Charlie had done this awful things, perhaps. But he did not. And she knows it. Jonathan is already in Serenity Landing doing damage control. He has access to Charlie's paperwork and records there. I do not know when or how Charlie plans to present the information to the public, but he will have to."

Jonah watched her walk back and forth, around and around, until he began to get dizzy himself. He stood and blocked her path, resting his hands on her hips when she stopped. "You're just going to worry yourself into an ulcer."

She seemed to relax, just a bit. "Is that your professional, medical opinion, Dr. Fontaine?"

A grin crossed his face and he slid his arms around until his fingers laced at the small of her back. "Absolutely. And my personal opinion as well. I think you need something to distract you."

She put her wine down and rested her hands on his upper arms. "Is that so?" Slim fingers wrapped around his shirt sleeves.

Without answering, he lowered his head until his lips brushed against hers. She responded immediately, leaning into him. Jonah wanted to lose himself in the kiss, but he couldn't. As much as she made him feel, he had to keep a tight rein on the churning inside. Tearing himself away, he kissed her forehead, careful to avoid her stitches. Ana rested the side of her head against him.

"That worked." Her words weren't much more than a sigh. "I forget what we were talking about."

She really hadn't. Jonah knew that, but he'd take what he could get. They stood there, looking out over Lake Montevaro and the palace for several minutes before he broached the subject he'd been wanting to for a while. The more he tried to find the right time, the more he realized there would never be one. "Ana?"

"Yes?" She didn't look up but had that same breathy tone in her voice.

Deep breath in and out. "Would you consider something?"

"Of course."

"Would you be my girlfriend?" He wanted, more than just about anything, to be the only man in her life. But what would she say?

He got an indication when she pulled away and walked closer to the window, her arms wrapped around her waist. He waited, trying to be patient, but it seemed like an eternity before she spoke. "I am not sure how to answer that."

Jonah moved to stand behind her, his arms folding around her until she leaned back against him. Their reflection in the window looked so right. "There are only three possible answers, Ana." He watched himself kiss her head. "Yes. No. Or not yet."

"Not yet?"

"If you're not ready to make a decision, but I hope you are."

She took a few more minutes to think. "I just don't know how to answer. I like you, Jonah. I like you a lot, but..."

He interrupted. "There's someone else."

"I like Jonathan very much, too. You both have so much to offer, and I have much in common with both of you. I am not sure, just yet, which direction my heart is headed." She leaned the back of her head on his chest. "But Jonathan is out of the country for the foreseeable future. I would imagine he will be incredibly busy so we likely will not even talk much, given the time difference."

"So I get your undivided attention by default?" Jonah tried to keep his tone light.

"For now."

Better than nothing.

A discreet knock on the door preempted whatever else either one of them would say. Ana moved to the side, breaking his hold. "It is time for me to leave. I have an early meeting."

He stopped her with a hand on her shoulder, turning her back toward him. Before he could think about it or she could protest, he kissed her. Shorter than before but more intense.

Much more intense.

"I think I'm falling in love with you, Ana. I told you that once already, and it's still true."

She closed her eyes, hiding the dark pools of emotion from him. "Please, Jonah. I am not ready to make a decision. Not yet. Please promise you will not pressure me into one?"

She could have just stabbed him in the chest with his scalpel.

Did he even have a scalpel? He wasn't a surgeon. Even as he thought it, Jonah knew he was avoiding the real issue.

"Fine." He moved away, letting her go.

"I will talk to you tomorrow." She reached up and brushed her thumb across his lips. "Thank you for being here for me tonight." Before he could respond, she walked to the door and out of the apartment.

"My pleasure," he whispered after her. "Anytime."

Jonathan stood in front of another bank of microphones and a different set of cameras. This time, he was the public voice and face of the Montevarian royal family, at least in the States. Ana had done an excellent job of being their official spokesperson in Montevaro. There hadn't been much to say.

Until today.

"Ladies and gentlemen, thank you for your time." He shifted his papers just a bit. "I will be making a short statement on behalf of Queen Adeline and Prince Charlemagne of Montevaro." Charlie had to hate that. He'd gone his whole life with very few people knowing his given name. "Prince Charlemagne has provided the authorities investigating the allegations of Ms. Tricia Goodson with all of the documentation they need to prove none of the stories are true. This includes statements contradicting those made by Ms. Goodson."

He looked back down at his speech. "On behalf of Prince Charlemagne, I have provided the investigators with copies of documents proving Ms. Goodson is the one who abandoned their daughter, leaving her with the prince when Ms. Lindsey Brewer was just a few weeks old and never returning. There are also documents and statements from Ms. Goodson informing the prince that she was giving up not only custody but all parental rights. Those rights were terminated by a judge nearly a decade ago."

Jonathan took a breath and looked straight at the cameras. "Ms. Goodson, if you will come forward publicly and admit the truth of the matter, Prince Charlemagne will let the whole matter drop. If you do not, be prepared for lawsuits for both libel and slander. Despite Prince Charlemagne's position in the public spotlight, you will not win." He picked up the sheets of paper. "Please, think of your daughter and let this go."

With that, he turned and walked away, ignoring the questions shouted from behind him. Hopefully, Tricia would take him up on the offer and drop all of it, telling everyone she'd lied. If need be, Charlie would sue. He didn't want to, and Jonathan didn't blame him. Maybe Tricia was hoping to sell "sordid" details about her relationship with Charlie. When they were teenagers and got carried away one time in the back of an SUV. There was no sordid to be found.

His phone buzzed as he climbed into the back seat of a car driven by an employee of his father's security company. A smile slid into place when he saw who it was from.

WATCHED ONLINE. YOU WERE GREAT. THINK SHE'LL COOPERATE?

He had to tell Ana he had no idea. Though he'd asked for a meeting with Tricia, and her lawyer if she wanted, there had been no response to the request. He also wondered what he'd been missing out on back in Montevaro. Had Jonah been spending as much time with Ana as Jonathan feared? Would he get back to Montevaro to find they were serious? Or worse - nearly engaged?

At least he'd avoided questions from the press about his brother. They knew nothing more than they had two days after the disappearance, except more about where he *wasn't*. Everyone, even lawyers and investigators, had asked. He didn't look at his phone before swiping to answer the call.

"Still doing their dirty work?" His father's voice grated on every nerve he'd ever had.

"I'm helping out a friend." Why did it bother his father that he was helping Addie and Charlie?

"More than you help your family?"

There it was. And it didn't deserve a response. "What do you need, Dad?"

"Are you coming home?"

"I don't plan on it. I'm here in Serenity Landing for the time being, and I'll probably go straight back to Montevaro. Why?"

"Just wondering when you're going to give up this globe-trotting and elbow rubbing to take your place in the family business."

Jonathan closed his eyes and prayed for patience. "I don't know what I'm going to do." Someday soon he was going to have to tell his dad he had no desire to work for the family's multinational corporation. He wasn't sure what he wanted to do with his life long term, but it didn't involve being CEO of Cranston International.

His father droned on and on about something or other, but Jonathan tuned him out. The car pulled into the drive to Jonathan's way-too-big house, and he cut his father off. "Dad, I've got to go. I'll talk to you later."

He hung up over his father's angry sputters and immediately changed his father's ring tone and vibration pattern. No need to be caught off-guard again. His next call was to Addie's office. As he waited for her to come on the line, he wondered how long until he'd be back in Montevaro.

And have Ana back in his arms.

Chapter Fourteen

*H*ow long had it been since Jonah told her he was falling in love with her? A month? Longer? Ana was no closer to making up her mind about the men in her life. She and Jonah had been working together on the fundraiser, but both of their schedules were too busy to spend much other time together. Jonathan hadn't come back from Serenity Landing yet, though he was supposed to be back before the fundraiser in just a couple of days. Tricia hadn't said anything except through her lawyers and even then not much.

Jonah had kissed her several more times, but none like that night at his apartment when he told her he thought he was falling in love with her.

She did not have time to worry about all of that just yet, though. This fundraiser was in less than forty-eight hours and she still had so much to do. Ana stood in the venue and turned slowly around. Tables were already set up. Place settings would not be put out until the next day. Neither would the table cloths and centerpieces. They were being assembled over on one of the tables to the side though. She went over to look more closely.

"Is this right, ma'am?" The director of the facility looked worried. The woman had been nothing but kind and accommodating. Ana could not think of anything she might have done to give the woman the impression she was displeased, but she seemed to constantly worry about Ana being upset.

Ana leaned over to smell one of the lilies. "Lovely." The vase was really a clear funky shaped thing. Not technically a vase. Black and white marbles filled the bottom inch. In the water above swam two small fish. All of the vases had different kinds, some with only one slightly larger fish, and some with several smaller ones.

"This is what you wanted?"

"Yes." She'd spent a late night or two when she could not sleep scouring Pinterest for fun ideas that might irritate her mother a little bit but not too much. Her mother would never quite approve of live centerpieces. Staff members were tying bows around the base of each one.

A door opened on the other side of the room and she turned to see Dr. Jonah walking in, complete with scrubs and white jacket. She could see the smile light up his face as he caught sight of her. Her heart did the same.

"Good morning," he told her when he was close enough. He reached for her hand and gave it a light squeeze as he kissed her cheek. "How's it going?"

"Fine. I didn't expect you so early, though."

He grinned down at her. "I got someone to cover for me for an hour so I could run over. It didn't seem right to let you do all of this yourself."

They moved away from the others. "You hate this sort of thing," she pointed out. "You would much rather get your hands dirty building something or actually taking care of the children, not setting up for a banquet." He'd made it very clear he only did these sorts of things because he had to.

"It still didn't seem right for you to have to do it yourself."

They walked over to another part of the room where the seating chart lay stretched out on a table. "Did we get this all done right?"

"I think so." Her parents were seated at the head table along with top donors and winners of the raffle drawing. She and Jonah were at the next table over. Jonathan had agreed to escort Christiana after all. They were at the table on the other side of the head table. Two rows of tables ringed the dance floor.

"Do you have your costume ready for tomorrow night?"

Ana shook her head. "I am not wearing one. I have a dress for the occasion but I will have too much else to deal with. I do not want to try to do it all in a costume."

Jonah chuckled. "It's a good thing I planned just to wear a tux then. No costume for this guy either."

"The invitation said black tie, costume optional. I would imagine we will have a number of people who wear costumes and a number who do not." Ana studied the seating chart and realized someone had moved the head of the minority party in Parliament to a table much too far away from the head table. She rearranged the names again. "Done. As long as no one ruins it again."

"No one should." Jonah took out his phone and snapped several pictures. "Just in case." He texted the photos to Ana, so she would have them.

"The place cards are being finished this afternoon. Once the table assignments are written on them, it will not matter if someone moves them again." Her stomach churned. This was so big. Nothing had gone wrong. Not really. Not yet. She still waited for something to happen, to prove that she could not do this.

Jonah slipped his arm around her waist and led her through a side door, into an empty hallway. "How are you, Ana? Really?"

She tilted her head, puzzled. "Fine. Why do you ask?"

"Everything with Charlie and his ex-girlfriend has to be taking a toll on your whole family."

"It has somewhat, but she has disappeared back under the rock she crawled from. That's how Jonathan put it anyway."

"You talked with him?" Did his voice sound overly possessive?

"For a few minutes last night." She moved back towards the ballroom. "I have some more things I need to get done and have a meeting with Adeline in about an hour and a half."

He followed her into the room, talking with the director of the facility while Ana scrolled through her to do list on her tablet. The calligrapher chose that moment to arrive and Ana spent half an hour going over exactly what needed doing. The name cards had been printed by the printer the palace often used, but this woman would need to write the actual seat locations on the back of each one so they could be placed properly.

Jonah's laugh reverberated through the room.

The calligrapher looked away from what Ana was showing her. "Is that Jonah Fontaine?" she interrupted.

Ana felt her eyebrows go up. "Pardon?" No one interrupted her. Ever. Except her family. And maybe Jonah. Or Jonathan. And another close friend or two. But never people working for her.

The calligrapher ignored her - something else very few people did - and started walking toward him. "Jonah!"

Ana crossed her arms and stared after her. What was that about? She did not know. But she did not like it.

Jonah looked up when he heard his name called from the other side of the ball room. His eyes widened a bit, then his heart fell.

Rachel.

Probably not the *last* person he wanted to see, but not too far off. He still caught the woman as she threw herself at him.

"I thought that was you," she gushed.

"Yes. It's me." And across the room he could see a very displeased Princess Ana. Why was she displeased? Because he was hugging another woman? Or because this other woman was supposed to be doing something else? "What are you doing here?"

"I'm doing calligraphy for tomorrow night's event." Rachel stepped back, but didn't let go of his arms. "Putting the seating on the back of the name cards."

There it was. "So you're working with the princess?"

Rachel winced. "Uh oh. I sort of interrupted her and walked off. That's not good, is it?"

No reason to be mean. "Let's go talk to her." When they started walking, he could distance himself from her. He did, too, until she grabbed his arm.

"She looks mad," Rachel whispered.

"We have a lot to do to get ready for tomorrow night. Someone running off while she's talking probably isn't going to put her in the best mood."

"Right."

"Have you actually been introduced?"

"Not really."

They neared Ana and Jonah took care of it. "Princess Anastasia, this is an old friend of mine, Rachel Gray. Rachel, Her Royal Highness, Anastasia, princess of Montevaro."

Rachel gave a small curtsy. "I'm sorry for running off, Your Highness. I haven't seen Jonah in a long time. We used to date and then get together sometimes, but it's been over a year?" She looked up at him to confirm.

Jonah was sure Ana was about to explode. He nodded,

anyway. "Something like that." He glanced at his watch. "I need to get back to the hospital." He took a step back. "Rachel, it was good to see you again. Ana, I'll call you later?"

Ana nodded. "I do need to speak with you before three-thirty this afternoon. There are a few things to finalize."

"I have a meeting at two, but it should be done before then. I'll call as soon as I'm done." Jonah moved close enough to give her a kiss on the cheek. That would give Rachel something to think about.

"That will be fine." Ana turned back to the tablet in front of her. "Ms. Gray, we have quite a bit to go over and not much time to do it in. Shall we get started?" Jonah could hear the undertones of snark, but doubted Rachel would pick up on it.

He was too far to hear by the time Rachel replied. The hospital was a short distance away, and it didn't take long to reach the pediatric floor. One of the nurses seemed to be containing a smile when she told him someone was waiting for him in Room 725.

Curious, he went in, stopping to sanitize his hands first. "Hello?" he called as he walked in.

"Hi, Dr. Jonah!"

He could hardly believe his eyes when he looked at the bed. "Sara! You look wonderful."

The little girl stood up on the bed so she could give him a hug. "I feel good!"

He held on far longer than he likely should, but he did anyway. Sara had wormed her way into his heart. When she finally let go, he turned to her parents. "What are y'all doing here? I didn't expect to see you for another month."

Sara's mom smiled. "We were in the hospital to get some blood work done, and we thought we'd stop in. They told us you were out, but Sara insisted on waiting."

"I'm so glad you did." He sat on the rolling stool. "Tell me all about what you've been up to."

Sara told him about how much she loved being home and how good she was feeling, about her friends coming to visit, and how much she hated doing school at home. She wanted to go back and play with her friends.

"Soon," he promised her. "You're still recovering from the transplant, but..." After a few taps on his tablet, he brought her chart up. "Just as I thought. You're doing very well. Better than we could have hoped for."

"Thank you, Dr. Jonah." He looked over to see tears in her mother's eyes.

"Hey. I just helped coordinate." His best grin went to Sara. "This young lady did all the hard work."

"God did it," Sara told him, as serious as she could be. "I prayed to Jesus that I'd get better because I didn't want my mom and dad to be sad. The next day we met Princess Addie, and she sent us here and paid for everything."

"God works through all sorts of people," he told her. "The queen is very glad you're doing well. The donor is very glad, too, I'm sure. Or is praying hard that you are, anyway. God uses everyone in different ways. Sometimes to pay the bills. Sometimes to donate the bone marrow. Sometimes to dig in the dirt and build something." He tried to forget the trip he'd had to back out of. "Sometimes to be the doctor." Jonah reached out and tweaked her nose. "And sometimes to be an inspiration to others."

He knew there was a plan in the works for Sara to be the honorary grand marshal of Montevaro's Christmas parade. She'd be perfect. If she was still well enough.

"I would love to talk to you all afternoon, Miss Sara, but I have some paperwork to do before a meeting." He stood and put his arm around her shoulders. "Thanks for coming to see me."

"I'm glad we got to."

"Anytime you're in the hospital, you better stop by." He gave her a mock-glare. "Or I'll never speak to you again."

Sara giggled. "Yes, you would."

Jonah clutched his heart and staggered backwards a step or two toward the door. "You're right. You know me too well." He winked at her. "Stay well, Miss Sara." After shaking her mother's hand, he headed to his office. Time to get some work done.

Ana looked in the mirror and tugged at the top of her dress. One strap went over her right shoulder, but her left shoulder remained bare. The green dress with darker green accents suited her well. With her long bangs brushed just right, the scar from the tack room incident was not visible.

A discreet knock on the door told her it was time to go. Jonah would meet her at the facility. Jonathan would arrive with Christiana who was getting ready at the Lydia House. Her family was supposed to arrive about twenty minutes before it started. Rick and Ellie would be early. Addie and Charlie would be right on time. Her mother and father, would show up last. If Ana was lucky, they'd be there early enough the program wouldn't have to be delayed. She rode inside the boat taking her across the lake. No need to mess her hair up. The deceptively simple ponytail had taken nearly an hour to get just right.

The impossibly high heels would likely be her downfall. Her stylist insisted they were the right ones, though. Ana had argued, but the woman was insistent.

A car took her from the dock to the venue. Paparazzi were already lined up as her door opened. She took the hand extended to help her out of the car with one hand, while the other clutched her handbag and her skirt to keep it out of her way.

"You look beautiful, Princess Ana." The quiet words caused her to look up and realize the man helping her was none other than her date for the night.

"And you are quite dashing yourself this evening, Dr. Fontaine." She slid her hand into his offered elbow. "We must now run the gauntlet."

As much as she wanted to bypass the reporters stalking the red carpet, Ana knew she needed to speak with them. She greeted them, thanking all for covering the hospital fundraiser. The first few questions were relevant. Jonah answered some, she answered others. But then...

"What about the allegations against Prince Charlemagne?"

Ana managed to stop herself from glaring at the reporter. "The accusations are groundless. The investigation in the States has come to nothing. Mr. Jonathan Langley-Cranston has acted on the family's behalf in Serenity Landing, and he assures us they are doing everything they can to bring this woman to justice. My sister and brother-in-law would prefer to come to an amicable agreement with her, and arrange for her to spend some time with my new niece, if that is what they both want. Beyond that, we have no comment."

A different reporter shouted the next question. "Are you dating Jonathan Langley-Cranston?"

"Mr. Langley-Cranston is a dear friend of my family's, and I enjoy spending time with him."

The same person called out again. "So you're dating Dr. Fontaine?"

Ana felt Jonah's arm tense under her hand. "Dr. Fontaine is also a dear friend of my family's. He and I have worked hard to put together tonight's fundraiser. I could not have done it without him. If there are any other questions about this evening and not about my personal life or the personal lives of my family, I would be happy to answer them."

"Is Prince Richard really engaged to Ellie Brewer?"

Rather than answer, she smiled at those assembled. "Thank

you all for your time." Together, she and Jonah walked into the building.

"You handled that well." His hand covered hers as they walked to the offices set aside for them.

"It is not the first time, and I doubt it will be the last."

He dropped his arm and slid her hand into his, fingers interlacing. "Am I just a dear family friend?"

She sighed and turned away, taking her hand back. "We have been over this, Jonah. You and Jonathan are both dear friends. I enjoy spending time with both of you."

"You're going to have to make a choice sooner or later." He stood behind her and rested his hands on her shoulders. "I know you know what I think you should do."

"And Jonathan could say the same thing and mean the exact opposite." If she was being honest with herself, Ana knew which direction her heart was leaning. In fact, it was leaning further than the Tower of Pisa.

Toward Jonah.

Though they had not been on many dates and had only spent their time working on the fundraiser, she had learned a great deal about him, about his childhood, his family. And he had brought out a side of her she had not shared with many people. A more vulnerable side. She'd opened up about what she wanted out of life more than she had with anyone else. Though she did not think he agreed with what she wanted, he certainly seemed to support it.

She twisted her head to look up at him. "I promise. I'll let you know soon."

Her eyes fluttered closed as his lips pressed against the spot where her neck met her bare shoulder. "I'll be waiting." Another kiss further up her neck, and she found herself tilting her head to the side for another even closer to her ear.

"We have too much to do." Ana's protest sounded weak even to her own ears.

"I know." One final kiss just below and behind her ear. "Later."

"Later," she promised. The butterflies had taken up permanent residence in her stomach and picked up the pace of their flutters at the thought of a proper kiss before she went home.

"Then let's get to work."

The next two hours passed in a blur. Final questions from the director of the facility, more from the chef as half the strawberries delivered were bad. Last minute RSVPs had to be accommodated. Fortunately, none were of the "important enough to warrant rearranging the seating" variety.

Addie and Charlie arrived moments before Rick and Ellie did, with Prince Malachi and a date in tow. All four of them made it into the ante room about the same time. None had chosen to wear costumes. Addie didn't think it befitting her position. Charlie agreed and refused himself. Rick flat didn't want to and Ellie went along with it. Ana was half surprised they didn't come as mountaineers or something.

"Your answers were perfect." Addie gave her a hug as she walked in. "Thank you."

"I have said the same thing before. So have you and Charlie. And the press office. Do they really think we will change our answer?"

"Who knows?"

Rick jumped in. "We changed one answer."

"You confirmed the engagement?"

He held up his hand, linked with Ellie's to show off the engagement ring. "Decided we were tired of hiding it. Told them the official announcement would be next week."

"The wedding is in less than two months," Ana pointed out. "You had to tell them sometime."

The turmoil inside began to calm down as she chatted with

her siblings and their significant others. And Jonah. His hand on her back had a calming effect on her.

Tonight, she would talk to Jonathan. And tell both of them her decision.

Chapter Fifteen

J onathan didn't understand his father's attitude. He'd always emphasized that Jonathan was to marry someone of equal or greater social status. But escorting royalty to a function put on by other royalty didn't cut it. Maybe because he was clearly just friends, if that, with the queen of Ravenzario. Maybe because if he were to marry Ana, his father believed the odds of him working for Cranston Enterprises would fall dramatically.

More than anything, Jonathan wanted to be out from under the yoke of expectations, but that didn't seem to be happening. He escorted Queen Christiana into the ante room where Ana, her siblings, and their dates all waited on her parents. All six greeted both him and Christiana, but they went back to their conversation about Rick and Ellie's wedding plans. Jonathan didn't think they meant to cut him and his date out, but they did.

Or maybe Christiana was doing it herself. She'd been quiet in the car. He leaned toward her and spoke quietly. "Can I get you a glass of water? Or something else to drink?"

She shook a head full of blonde curls. "No. Thank you,

Jonathan. I am fine."

"Let me know if you change your mind?"

"Of course."

Two minutes before the program was to begin, the door opened again, allowing the former king and queen to enter. The former queen looked a bit vexed when Ana asked Addie if they were ready to begin. If he had to guess, he'd bet money she didn't like someone else being the center of attention.

He and Christiana were the first to be introduced, followed by Prince Malachi and Lizbeth Bence, then Rick and Ellie, the former king and queen, Addie and Charlie, and finally Anastasia and Jonah.

The possessive way the other man's hand had rested on Ana's back stuck in Jonathan's mind. Had she made a decision without telling him? Surely not.

Dinner was delicious and passed quickly. So did the speeches, complete with a slide show of the good things the hospital had done. Dr. Jonah had a place of prominence in many of them, but he was the main pediatrician on staff and much of the funds raised would go to his department. Pictures of Jonah with a bald little girl on his back, or signing a bright purple leg cast, or playing video games with a boy in a wheelchair.

How could she help but choose him?

Jonathan liked kids as much as the next guy and volunteered at different places pretty regularly, but he couldn't hold a candle to Dr. Jonah Fontaine, pediatrician extraordinaire and all around good guy.

The first dance, as always, was reserved for Montevarian royalty. He watched as Ana gave Jonah a shy smile. The kind he wished she'd give him. She was smitten. No doubt about it.

"I am sorry."

His date's quiet words cut through his fog. "Pardon?"

"I know you believe you love Ana."

Love? He'd never used that word, not even to himself.

"Maybe," he finally conceded.

"I do not know what is happening between her and Dr. Fontaine, but you need to tell her."

Right. Lay his heart on the line and get it trampled. Sounded like his idea of a great time. The second dance started, but when he turned to ask Christiana if she would like to, he realized she'd excused herself seconds earlier. Ana had already been handed off to another dance partner.

For the first time in quite a while, Jonathan wished he still drank.

A shot of Jack would really hit the spot.

He slid his hand into his pocket and rubbed his thumb over his token of sobriety. He'd made it too far to fall off the wagon over a girl.

His family had made a large donation. He had made one. Maybe he'd see if Christiana wanted to blow this Popsicle stand and they could sneak out the back. She didn't seem to want to be here anymore than he did.

Right now, he just wanted to leave. Before he gave in to the open bar calling his name.

Christiana stared into the mirror. Bright blue eyes stared back. A face wet from the water she had splashed on it. So tired. All she wanted to do was sleep for about a week.

It had not been easy, but she had been taking back the reins to her kingdom. Her uncle had pled guilty and was in prison for the rest of his life. More secure than the famed Rock in San Francisco, there was only one way off Pirate's Island.

In a body bag.

Despite his betrayal, she did not wish that on her uncle, but he would never see freedom again. One of the first things she had done was undo as much of the recent damage she could.

Tourism had taken a big hit, but the laws were back to the way they used to be and the Ministry of Tourism was hopeful it would rebound quickly. As soon as she'd heard about Rick's plan to cross-promote tourism within the Commonwealth, she directed the Minister of Tourism to make sure it got done. It would help all three of their countries.

A thousand and one other issues had been coming at her left and right. This person wanting funding restored to that project. Another person wanting her patronage for the other charity.

It was overwhelming.

She felt like she was drowning.

In over her head.

Another little girl playing dress-up, pretending to be a queen.

Even her boyfriend, who had been hinting at a proposal before the end of the year, wanted more than she had to give. More attention from her for his organization's interests. A change to import taxes she did not quite understand - and had no idea what relevance it would have to him.

Tony limited the number of people allowed to see her. A few members of Parliament had been cleared. Her boyfriend. Alexander. A few leaders of significant cities or businesses, but otherwise everything funneled through Alexander for the time being. She knew that would not last. He had his own family business to run. His parents had been incredibly patient as he helped her get a handle on so many different things.

With an expert touch, she fixed her make-up and went back toward the ballroom. The hallway reserved for the VIP guests remained blessedly vacant, until Dr. Fontaine walked out of the kitchen.

He bowed slightly at the waist. "Your Majesty, it is good to see you again. Did you enjoy dinner?"

"Yes. I did." She did not want to stand here and talk to him, but she could not be rude.

"I hoped to get a chance to talk with you this evening." His hands went behind his back and he clasped them there, a serious look on his face.

"What can I help you with?" She did not mean it. Not really. She was tired of so many people wanting so much. Until everything her uncle had done was undone, she would get little rest.

"The orphanage in Ravenz-by-the-Sea is run by a friend and colleague of mine. For nearly a century, their funding has been a combination of government monies and donations. Their largest donor for most of that time was the Ravenzarian Royal Foundation's Children's division."

Christiana's heart sank. Even this man wanted something from her. Something she did not know if she could give. "Yes?" she asked when he did not go on. "Many things are funded by the government and the Foundation. As much as I would like to know every detail of every one, I fear that is impossible. I am not certain of the details without seeing them."

"The government funding was cut without explanation four years ago. They've been able to make up for it, barely, with private donations, but the Foundation cut their donations to barely one-hundredth what they had been, also with no explanation, despite repeated requests. It is the only orphanage for a dozen or more towns in that part of the country. Could you at least look into the why of it? Is there something he's done that he doesn't realize to warrant it? If not, he's going to have to close down. Already, he's behind in repairs and upkeep to the grounds. Not just prettifying things, but needed repairs." The man was passionate about his cause, Christiana would give him that.

"Have him contact Alexander Bayfield. I will tell him to expect the correspondence, and hopefully he will have an answer soon."

The door opened and Jonathan exited. Likely, her escort had been worried about her. Dr. Fontaine bowed his head to her and held the door open as Jonathan let go of it. "Thank you, Your

Majesty."

A forced, tight smile crossed her face. "My pleasure, Dr. Fontaine." But it was not. Not really.

"Why don't we get out of here, Christiana?" Jonathan held out his elbow. "Let's grab some ice cream and go to Lydia House until it's time for you to go to the airport."

She smiled and slid her hand into his arm. "That sounds lovely."

In just a few minutes, they had snuck out a side entrance and were on their way. The further away they got, the more her stress bled off.

Ice cream and maybe a late night nap.

Just what the doctor ordered.

As she sank into the couch, Ana watched Jonah undo his bow tie and the top button on his shirt. Her shoes clunked, one at a time, to the floor. "I cannot be sad this is over," she told him, her eyes closing. As much as she loved speaking to people about good causes, she did not love the long spans of time where she had to be "on." A few minutes here and there while she gave statements or one on one? She could do that. But nearly five hours of dinner, dancing and speeches, mixed with auctions for items worth far less than their stated values? All for a good cause, but not her favorite thing.

Not even close.

Jonah settled next to her and stretched his arm along the back of the couch. It did not take much for him to urge her to scoot next to him, to rest her head on his sturdy shoulder. To let him take some of the burden, some of the stress.

"This is why I would rather get in there and work," he told her. She could feel the rise and fall of his chest as he spoke. "Not even hard work, putting in a full day's labor, wears me out like things like this event does."

"I cannot say I disagree with you."

His thumb rubbed up and down her arm. "I could see us doing that together one day. Spending weeks at a time helping build orphanages in Africa or teaching you enough to help me at a clinic for kids in Central America."

Her heart constricted in her chest. "I still think I would rather be a spokesperson." Would he accept that? "I am not good at the kinds of things you are talking about, but I can do more by bringing awareness to situations."

Jonah's head leaned against hers. "You just haven't had a chance to do those sorts of things. I bet you'd be even better than I am at mudding bricks or getting a child to open his mouth so I can take a look."

Ana didn't answer, but listened to Jonah go on and on...and on...and on about how well they would work together in the slums of a town in India she had never heard of or in neighborhoods made of cardboard near Rio. Her heart constricted further, for multiple reasons. She wanted to do more, give more, to all the causes he talked about, and she would see what she could do to raise those funds from her family and elsewhere. She also felt more than a bit of guilt at her comfortable surroundings and her not-quite-light-hearted complaining about shoes that likely cost more than many people in those places made in a year.

But her heart also squeezed as Jonah continued to downplay her desired role.

Finally, Ana sat up and slid her shoes back on. "Jonah," she interrupted. "Did Rachel do those sorts of things with you?"

She did not have to look at him to know he wore a puzzled look. "Yeah. We met on a trip to Ravenzario to work there."

Ana stood, ignoring the screaming pain in her feet. "Then perhaps you should consider doing those things with her." Without waiting for a response, she left the room, motioning to

Carrie and Marty that she was ready to leave.

Alone.

Her heart had fallen for Dr. Jonah Fontaine, but he had not proven worthy, not at this point. He did not make any move to see her side, where her strengths and talents lay. She could hear him calling after her, but she did not turn around. She would have to tell Jonathan in the next few days that not only were she and Jonah over, but that she did not love Jonathan and likely never would.

Too tired and worn out to even let tears fall, she collapsed against the seat in the car. She pressed a button. "Has Christiana left for home yet?"

"Just a moment," came Marty's voice and a second later, "Yes, ma'am. Her flight took off twenty minutes ago."

"Can you take me to Lydia House, please?"

Marty hesitated then answered. "Of course, ma'am."

Ana texted Jonathan that she would be there to see him in a few moments. A return message said he would be glad to see her. About ten minutes later, the car pulled up in front of Lydia House. Jonathan waited outside, still in his tuxedo. His tie hung loose. Three buttons were undone. His jacked had been dispensed with and his suspenders rested over a crisp white shirt with the sleeves rolled to the elbows.

He opened the door and helped her out. His arm went around her waist, allowing her to lean on him. They came to a halt in the more comfortable living area. A fire roared in the stone hearth.

"Sit here." She followed his instructions, too numb to do much else. "Turn this way." Ana did and found herself sitting with her feet up on the couch. Jonathan lifted them and sat down, holding her feet in his hands.

"What are you doing?" she murmured.

"Giving you a foot rub."

His thumbs expertly kneaded the arch of her right foot. She

felt the stress bleeding away.

"Want to talk about it?"

He didn't really want to hear how her night had gone with Jonah, but she looked like she needed a friend.

"It was a long night."

"You did an excellent job."

"Thank you." Her eyes were closed as her head hung back against the arm of the couch. "I do need to talk to you, though, Jonathan."

He didn't stop working his thumbs against her delicate arch. "You choose Jonah." He'd known it was coming and seeing them together confirmed it.

She didn't confirm immediately, and he changed feet. "Not exactly."

"I'm not sure what that means."

"It means I had planned to tell you I chose Jonah. It means I think I have fallen for him. But it also means he said some things tonight that made me realize there is no future for us, at least not at this point in time."

Jonathan's hands stilled. "I'm sorry, Ana."

Her eyes opened, and he could see her fighting sleep. "Why are you sorry? I am the one telling you I planned to choose another man."

"Because I want you to be happy. Anyone watching you two tonight could tell he makes you happy."

"In general, perhaps, but the reality is we do not see eye-to-eye on things of utmost importance. Without agreement there, it can never work."

"I'm sorry to hear that."

"Are you really?"

"Yes." He was. Sort of. He did want her to be happy. His

first choice would have been with him, but if not, he wished for someone who would treat her well. Jonah would do that.

"Why did I not fall for you, Jonathan? The areas where Jonah and I disagree are not a problem for you and me. In fact, I believe we would be quite compatible in all the ways that matter." Her voice started to trail off. "Why couldn't I fall in love with you?"

A question that would haunt Jonathan's dreams for days to come most likely. Her head fell to the side. Jonathan set her feet on the couch and stood up. Lifting her easily into his arms, he carried her up the stairs and to the room Christiana had used earlier in the day. Gently, he laid her on the bed and covered her with a blanket he found in the closet. Back downstairs, he told Marty and Carrie where he had left her. The two guards exchanged a look Jonathan didn't know how to read. He went upstairs to his own room and pondered his next move.

Could he put himself through what happened with Addie again? If Ana was even interested, would he date her knowing she was in love with another man at the start? He couldn't answer that question. Not yet. Not until she told him it was something she might want to do. Then he'd have to consider it.

Because whatever he'd felt for Addie paled in comparison to his feelings for Ana. Did he love her? He couldn't honestly say he did, but he couldn't be far off. With the slightest of pushes, he could find himself lost in those chocolate eyes for eternity.

He changed into a pair of pajama pants and flopped onto the couch. For a while, he stared at the ceiling, but his jumbled thoughts gave him no rest. He grabbed his phone and opened it to his favorite Bible app. Not quite the same as picking up the good book itself, but he chose Psalms and picked one at random. Twenty-three. Not intentional, but just what he needed. Reassurance that the Good Shepherd was standing next to him, taking care that he didn't wander into danger.

Several chapters later, he put the phone down, his eyelids

finally growing heavy. Deciding to sleep on the comfortable couch in front of a blazing fire, Jonathan started to doze. He didn't know how long he'd been asleep when a knock at his door startled him. It couldn't have been long, because the fire still burned brightly.

Running a hand through his hair and stifling a yawn, he crossed the room to open it. Ana stood there, her hair out of its ponytail and flowing over her shoulders. She still wore her dress, though her feet remained bare.

Concern flooded him. "Is everything okay?"

She nodded, though she didn't seem quite all together. "There are no clothes in the room I'm in. Do you have something I can borrow to sleep in?"

He backed away from the door but didn't invite her in. "I'm sure I do. I think a pair of my sister's shorts got mixed in with my stuff when I got back from the search for Philip." He dug through one of the drawers and pulled them out, finding a soft Avengers t-shirt at the same time. "Here you go." He started to head back for the door when he realized she'd followed him in.

He might be a gentleman, willing to step aside for another man who captured her heart and loved her the way she deserved. But woken from a deep sleep to an adorably tousled princess, he couldn't help but want to slide his fingers into the tousled, sexy hair that hung over her bare shoulders and kiss her senseless.

Jonathan swallowed. He needed to keep his libido under control. She had told him she was in love with Jonah, even if things didn't seem to be working out just yet.

She took the clothes from him. "Thank you." But instead of leaving, she wandered into the large walk-in closet.

A minute later, "Jonathan?"

He had to swallow twice. "Yes?"

"Can you help me?"

Jonathan blinked twice. Then again. "What?"

"I can't get the zipper started."

If she was using so many contractions, he knew she had to be tired. "Um, sure." He should call Carrie, but surely the security guard had gone to bed herself by now. Taking a deep breath, he walked to the closet. She stood with her back to him, hair swept to one side and her head hanging forward. His fingers fumbled with the tiny zipper as he tried not to touch the skin of her back. He didn't watch as he lowered it about six inches. Surely she could get it from there. He couldn't trust himself to say anything but turned and quickly returned to the other room.

She called her thanks. Jonathan braced his hands against the mantle, his own head hanging down. *God, are you trying to torture me?*

Soft hands touched the skin on his back and slid around to the front. His eyes opened to see hands clasped against his stomach. Her forehead rested against his backbone between his shoulder blades.

"Why can't I fall in love with you, Jonathan? We're perfect for each other."

"I don't know, Ana."

"Do you love me?" Her voice tore at his very being. The small, scared little girl who hid deep inside the poised, polished princess.

Jonathan pushed off the mantle and turned in her arms, wrapping his around her and holding her close. He could feel hot tears on his bare chest and he wished he'd thought to toss on a shirt.

She looked up and he could see tears swimming in her eyes. "Do you?"

The last bit of control broke and he kissed her. His fingers tangled in her hair, her hands holding his back. Everything he thought he'd felt for Addie, the bit he'd felt for Ellie, anything he'd ever felt for another woman - paled in comparison to what he felt for the woman in his arms. In that kiss, he told her what he couldn't with words. That he would spend his days loving her.

If only she would let him.

Chapter Sixteen

*T*he intensity of Jonathan's kiss caught her off-guard, but Ana found herself sinking into it. Sinking against his warm skin.

Wanting more.

His lips left hers and found their way across her cheek toward her ear then down her neck.

Behind him, a loud *pop* sounded as the fire reached a wet spot in the wood. Breathing heavily, Jonathan rested his forehead on her shoulder as he held her even closer. Ana clung to him as an anchor in her emotional storm.

"I'm sorry, Ana," he whispered. "I shouldn't have kissed you like that. No one should. Not yet."

Ana tried to make sense of his statement in her kiss-addled mind. "What?" she finally whispered.

He moved away from her and back to face the fireplace, bracing himself against it like he had moments earlier. "The night of the Renaissance Ball, Lindsey and I got Addie and Charlie alone on the balcony. We knew they belonged together. She told me later he kissed her like she'd never been kissed before. Incredibly intense. And when it ended he told her only one man should ever have the privilege of kissing her like that. Her husband. Then he left, and he and Lindsey were going to go back to the States."

She wrapped her arms around her stomach and tried to make sense of what he was saying.

"Only one man should ever kiss you like I just did, Ana. The man you marry. After you marry him."

Her sleep-filled, kiss-addled mind could not make sense of it. "And that won't be you?"

Flames danced on the other side of him, illuminating the skin of his back. "I don't know. You told me you loved Jonah. Could something change and the two of us end up together? It's possible. But unless, and until, there are rings and a preacher..."

"I understand." But she did not. Not really.

Ana did not move as Jonathan did. He went somewhere she could not see and came back with a t-shirt on. He came to stand in front of her, unclenching her hands and holding them in his. "I think, princess, that it would be best if we put kissing on the 'do not do' list for now. If, at some point in the future, we decide there's a future for us that includes holy matrimony, we'll talk." He lifted one set of their joined hands and used his knuckle to tilt her chin up. "You, love, are much too great a temptation, and one I have a hard time convincing myself I want to resist." He let go of one hand and led her to the door. "I think it's best we say good night."

Ana finally found her voice. "Can we talk tomorrow?"

"Of course." He kissed her forehead gently. "Good night."

With more emotions than she knew she had churning inside, Ana went back to the room she'd come from. No one had ever kissed her like that. And no one had ever told her she was too great a temptation.

She curled under the covers and relived every fire lit moment in Jonathan's room until she fell asleep.

Sunlight streaming in the windows woke her the next

morning.

With arms stretched toward the headboard, Ana reached her toes toward the end of the bed, enjoying the feeling. She rolled to the side to see her dress from the night before lying draped over a chair. Leaning against it was a card-sized envelope with her name on it. She sat up, visions of that kiss fresh in her mind. The back of the envelope wasn't sealed and she pulled out a sheet of Lydia House stationery.

> Beautiful Ana,
> I can't tell you how much I regret leaving like this, but matters in Serenity Landing demand my attention. Addie or Charlie can tell you all about it.
> It's probably for the best, though. After last night, I am not sure I can trust myself to remain a gentleman. You asked if I love you. I didn't give you a verbal answer, though I'm sure you can figure out what it would be. I won't say it, not here and now, but I know you know.
> I don't know what the future holds for us, my wonderful princess, but I do know the God who placed the stars in the sky holds both of us in the palms of His hands. He knows even if we don't just yet.
> You are always in my heart, my thoughts, and no matter what, forever in my prayers.
> Always,
> Jonathan

No. He didn't say the words, but the implications were certainly there. Jonathan loved her. He wouldn't have kissed her like that if he didn't. He wouldn't have said those things if he cared for her the same way he cared for Addie or Ellie or his sister.

She read the note again and caught the second line. Dropping it on the bed, she reached for her phone to find a missed call from her sister.

"What is going on?" Ana asked as soon as Addie answered.

"Tricia finally made her move."

Ana groaned. "What is she doing?"

"Selling the story in a made-for-TV movie."

"You have to be joking."

"I wish I were."

"Is anyone buying it?"

Addie's voice grew grim. "One of the seedy premium channels. Which means it will be a sordid distortion of reality, complete with profanity and..." Ana heard her take a deep breath. "Well, you can imagine."

Ana cringed. "Can you stop it?"

"Jonathan is on his way back to the States."

"I know. I stayed at Lydia House last night and he left me a note. Can he stop it?"

"There is no way to know. Charlie is furious. He had hoped Tricia would cooperate and Lindsey could at least get to know her mother a bit, but he told Jonathan to hire the best lawyer in the U.S and sue the daylights out of her. He is done having Lindsey put through this."

"I am surprised he had this much patience."

"You and me both. He had to talk me out of doing this weeks ago."

"I am on my way back to the palace. We will figure this out."

"Thank you, sister." Something changed in Addie's voice. "Now, what were you doing at Lydia House last night? You went to the fundraiser with Jonah, but saw Jonathan afterward?"

"The last thing you need to worry about right now is my love life or lack thereof. I will be there soon and we can talk then." Or not, she added silently. The last thing she needed was Charlie and Rick finding out how things ended with Jonah or how Jonathan kissed her. Both of them would go what Charlie called "all big brother on their hides."

She hung up before Addie could ask her anything else. Ana did not know what all of it meant. So how could she possibly explain it to her sister?

Jonah went to work, did his job, did it well, went home, ate, went for a run, and wondered where it had all gone wrong. Over and over. And not necessarily in that order.

But, even a week later, always hovering in the back of his mind was Ana's parting words.

"Jonah, did Rachel do those sorts of things with you?"

"Yeah. We met on a trip to Ravenzario to work there."

"Then perhaps you should consider doing those things with her."

Where had he gone wrong? Talking with Rachel the day before the fundraiser? Talking about his upcoming trip to Ravenzario?

Telling Ana she should do more of the physical work?

That couldn't be it, could it? That's where the reward was. In seeing a building take shape. In knowing children were vaccinated against malaria and tuberculosis. To see the smiles when he gave them a lollipop or a first teddy bear or other toy. Those were the truly rewarding things in life. To know you'd done something to make a difference. Could Ana not see that? Had his suggestion offended her in some way?

But she was too well-grounded to let an imagined slight get in the way of their relationship. Were her parting words and ignoring him when he called after her a way of breaking up with him?

Had there been anything to break up?

Shaking it off, Jonah went back to his laptop. Planning was nearly done for the Ravenzario trip. He left in four days. Would he see Ana before he left? Should he call her? It had been a week and he would be gone for nearly two. Just over a week in

Ravenzario working at the orphanage, then back to Texas for American Thanksgiving with his family. Turkey. Dressing. Party potatoes. His stomach nearly growled at the thought of the goodness.

Finally, he made up his mind and pulled out his phone.

I WOULD LOVE TO SEE YOU. I'M NOT SURE WHAT HAPPENED, BUT I WANT TO MAKE THINGS RIGHT BEFORE I GO OUT OF TOWN.

And send.

Rather than sit by his phone waiting for a response, he took a shower, washing the hospital and three-mile-run grime off. With a towel still wrapped around his waist, he picked his phone up from where he'd tossed it on his bed. No reply.

He dressed, made a quick dinner, and went back to his packing. Work boots instead of cowboy boots. Tool belt. Worn but tough jeans. Flannel shirts. One nice pair of slacks and a button-down shirt just in case. Nothing he'd need in the next couple of days.

His phone buzzed.

HAVE A GOOD TRIP.

Nothing more.

CAN I SEE YOU? he sent back.

He had to wait ten agonizing minutes before she agreed. They made arrangements to meet at the stables. He couldn't imagine why, but he didn't wait. She wanted to meet now. As fast as traffic would let him, Jonah made his way to the outskirts of town. The sedan with the dark tinted windows was already there. He made his way inside to find Ana standing in front of Archer's stall. His big ol' horse just knocked against her torso until she laughed and held out her palm.

"You want another one, boy?" Whatever she held, Archer used his lips to pick it up.

"You're bribing my horse?"

"No. Archer likes me, bribes or not."

"What are you giving him?" The white on her palm looked to be the wrong shape for a sugar cube.

"Peppermints. One of the horses I had while growing up loved them." She abruptly walked away from Archer's stall and headed for the tack room. "I want to go for a ride."

Jonah looked around to see Miss Dixie already in her stall, cross-tied and waiting for someone to saddle her. He snagged a halter and slid it on Archer before cross-tying him. By the time he finished grooming - Archer hadn't needed much - and saddling - something he did well - Ana was waiting impatiently.

Rather than waiting for a leg up, she led Miss Dixie outside and used the fence to hop on. She started down the trail while Jonah mounted Archer and trotted to catch up. He pulled to a walk when he reached Ana's side.

"Care to tell me what's going on?"

"We are going for a trail ride. Not a long one, but I have not ridden in far too long. I was not far from here anyway so it seemed ideal." She kicked the sides of her horse until Miss Dixie took off at a canter.

Archer didn't have to be asked twice to catch up. In fact, he wanted to blow right past, to take control and gallop to blow off a bit of energy but Jonah didn't let him. Instead, they cantered side by side along the path until it reached the tree line. Ana pulled up first slowing Miss Dixie to a trot and then a walk.

"Are we going to talk?" He couldn't tell what was going on inside her head, covered as it was by a helmet, something he'd very irresponsibly forgotten.

Too late now.

They walked their horses for several minutes before she answered. "You want me to be someone I am not."

He turned to look at her face. It remained impassive. "I do? That's news to me."

Now she shook her head, her expression a bit sad. "That you do not understand tells me all I need to know."

"Explain it, please. Because I don't get it. Really."

"You want me to be like you, Jonah. I am not." Her voice held almost eerie calm.

He snorted. "I don't think so. You're not anything like me in most ways. In the important ones we are, but that's all that matters."

"You are right," she conceded. "We are alike in the important matters. You have compassion for those less fortunate. You want to do all you can to help them. I like to think I am the same way. Where we differ is what constitutes help. From what you have told me, the only way I can help is to build an orphanage or give tetanus shots. I disagree, but you refuse to see my perspective as valid."

Because it wasn't, but he didn't say that. "I never said your perspective wasn't valid," he argued.

"Very well. You did not. But you strongly implied that what I wish to do to help is not of any value, or very little." She clicked and her horse moved into a fast trot as the path opened into a field.

"I never said that!" He didn't need to kick Archer into a canter to catch up. "But anyone can stand up and ask for money or whatever. It takes more than that to get in there and do the actual work. Most people won't."

"You are correct. And incorrect at the same time. That is why we will never come to an agreement on this. If we cannot agree, there is no future for us as an us."

"Is this because of Jonathan?" Had the other man managed to convince Ana the two of them belonged together?

She shook her head. "It has nothing to do with Jonathan." With a click, she directed her horse off the path and through the waist high grasses. When she reached an area where the city of Montero and Lake Montevaro spread below them, Ana stopped Miss Dixie.

He pulled a restless Archer to a stop as well. "Then what is it?"

An exasperated sigh was her only response.

"Come with me," he pleaded on an impulse. "Come to Ravenzario with me and see for yourself."

She turned her horse back around and headed for the trail, this time going back toward the barn. So not a long ride. The trip was silent but for the sounds of the forest around them and the occasional snort from one of the horses. When they neared the barn, she pulled Miss Dixie to a halt again.

"Very well. I will accompany you to Ravenzario. And I will have a challenge of my own for you."

"What's that?"

"Which one of us can raise more support. Both in dollars and in terms of people who show up to help. No money either of us donates will count, and I will not talk to Christiana. There will be separate addresses or phone numbers that we each give out and a slightly different location for volunteers."

Jonah barely managed not to roll his eyes. "Fine. Whatever works to get you there so you can see I'm right."

She shook her head again, with that sad look he hated. "You may be. Or you may end up admitting there is validity to my view."

Miss Dixie started for the barn as he answered. "And if I don't, there's not a future for us?"

Her words drifted back to him. "You said it. Not me."

"I can't believe you're going with him." Jonathan's voice spilled from Ana's speaker phone.

"I cannot know if there might be a future for us, Jonathan, until I know for certain there is not one with Jonah."

"I'm not sure how I feel knowing I'm second choice," he muttered.

She did not know how she felt either. Despite everything he stirred in her on a physical level, she was not convinced Jonathan was the right man for her. "I do not want you to be second choice. I have to know, or you and I will both always wonder."

Though he did not say anything, she could practically hear him admit she was right. Finally, he went with, "You know he's already started fundraising and looking for more volunteers."

"I know."

"That doesn't concern you?"

"Do you think it should?" She knew Jonathan understood.

"Probably not. You have star power."

"That might not be quite right, but I have name recognition Jonah does not outside of Montevaro."

Jonathan sighed. "I miss you."

Ana did not know how to respond to that. She knew what Jonathan wanted to hear. That she missed him the same way, but she was not sure it was the truth. "I miss you, too," she finally said, hurrying to move on. "I know Charlie and Addie appreciate everything you are doing on their behalf."

"I know you don't miss me quite the same way, Ana." His voice took on a new gravitas. "Is there a chance? If this thing with Jonah doesn't work out, do you really see a chance for a future for us?"

Ana closed her eyes and prayed for the words to say. "I do not want to discuss this on the phone, Jonathan. I have told you that."

"I know." He seemed to muffle a scream. "I promised I wouldn't push you. I'm sorry."

A small smile played on her lips. "I know." She glanced at the clock. "But it is time for me to go. I likely will not have much time to talk until I get back in about a week."

"I'll be praying for you. Praying you find the answers you need."

She knew what it cost him to say that. "Thank you, Jonathan.

I appreciate you more than you can ever know." How many other men would not only step aside but pray for the woman they loved to find answers, even if those answers included another man?

With an admonition to be careful, he ended the call.

Ana left the Ravenzarian palace where she had been staying with Christiana. A car took her to the church where they were meeting with the group of local volunteers. Carrie would be with her at all times, and Marty would never be far away.

Jonah seemed to be the leader of the expedition, something she had not realized before.

"Good morning!" he called to everyone. "Thanks for coming. We'll be heading for Ravenz-by-the-Sea in just a few minutes. I'll be handing out dorm assignments on the road. Work group details are in your information packets that Ana will give you as you board the bus. Thank you again!" He hopped down off the chair he'd been standing on and handed her a stack of papers. "One to everyone, please."

Right. She went to stand by the bus and smiled at each person as they boarded, handing every one of them a packet of about ten papers. There were four left when everyone had filed in. One for her and she supposed the others were for Carrie, Marty, and Jonah. Marty took one as he climbed the steps into the former city bus. Carrie motioned with her head for Ana to go ahead of her. When she did, Ana found the smell to be overwhelming. The people likely smelled fine, but the bus itself was another matter. Breathing in through her mouth, Ana took one of the last seats on the left side of the bus and near an open window. Carrie sat next to her.

"I'm proud of you," her bodyguard told her. "But Marty and I have final say over everything."

"I know." They had gone over this several times. In great detail.

"Then everything will be just fine."

A sense of foreboding came over Ana, and she prayed Carrie was right.

Chapter Seventeen

*J*onah flipped through the papers on his clipboard, satisfied everything was in order and ready to go. He'd seen Ana hesitate as she boarded the bus. He didn't take pleasure in her discomfort, but she needed to get the full experience. This trip wouldn't be nearly as challenging as many trips were. They'd be sleeping in college dorms. Fairly old ones, to be sure, but in good shape and well maintained. The building they'd be working on wasn't falling down or made from cardboard and corrugated metal, but it wasn't up to royal standards either. Not even close.

He got to the page with the dorm assignments and shook his head. Marty had insisted Ana be with someone who had already been cleared by them or stay by herself. The only person who met those requirements was Rachel because of her association with the fundraiser. So his ex-girlfriend and the woman he was falling in love with would be staying in the same room for the next eight days.

It couldn't be good.

Unless Rachel could change the way Ana looked at things.

The next page included his recent fundraising efforts. He was happy with the amount of pledges he'd gotten from his colleagues at work. The rules Ana had laid out said he couldn't tell them he was in a competition with her, but it was the reason Rachel came on the trip. She'd stopped by to see him, and he'd been talking about it with another doctor.

As far as he knew, Ana hadn't done anything just yet and had tried to keep her arrival in Ravenzario quiet.

"Have you seen the weather forecast?" Marty leaned over the seat behind Jonah.

"Not today. Why?" There hadn't been anything concerning the day before.

"They're talking about major storms heading this way. A Medicane."

Jonah nearly snorted. "A what now?" Medicane? That didn't even sound real.

"Mediterranean hurricane. They're rare but they do happen. They're also not as bad as the ones you may have experienced in Texas, but they bring plenty of wind and rain."

"And it's headed for us?"

"The track isn't set yet, obviously, but Ravenz-by-the-Sea is dead center of the potential path."

"Are you going to let her stay?" If they wouldn't, the whole thing was for nothing.

"For now."

"We'll be watching it, I'm sure."

"So will I." The unspoken implication that Jonah wouldn't do everything he could to protect the princess hung in the air.

Marty moved back and pulled out a well-worn paperback. Jonah tilted his head, but still couldn't read the title. Something by Louis L'Amour. Not what he would have picked for Marty. Shifting so his back rested against the window, Jonah made a few more notations on his to do list for the week. Not just for him but for the entire crew.

The drive lasted a bit over ninety minutes with no stops. For the most part they followed the coastline, the awe-inspiring sunrise views getting comments from just about everyone. As they neared their destination, the bus turned inland, winding up into the mountains a bit. The town of Ravenz-by-the-Sea sat a couple hundred feet above sea level, nestled into the mountainside. The population was only a few thousand, but the orphanage served the surrounding area.

The bus crossed the bridge over the river and into a bit of a valley where the orphanage sat nestled against a wooded backdrop. So picturesque and yet such sad stories. Jonah closed his eyes and breathed a prayer. They needed far more funding not only for repairs but to keep going at all.

They arrived about seven-thirty. Jonah couldn't help but smile as he saw the kids, ages newborn to about fifteen, waiting in front of the main entrance. They were holding signs welcoming the workers. He didn't think any of them knew a genuine princess was coming. The only person he'd told was the director, Louis.

Everyone piled out of the bus and onto the grass in front of the building.

Louis counted to three and the kids all shouted. "Welcome to Ravenz-by-the-Sea!"

All of the volunteers broke out into applause as the kids started to sing the national anthem.

Louis turned to the twenty or so people Jonah had brought with him. "Thank you, all of you, for coming. We can't tell you how much we appreciate it. I'm Louis and I'll let everyone else tell you their names. We don't expect you to remember all of us, if you don't expect us to remember all of you - at least not right off the bat!" Everyone laughed. Each of the orphanage employees spoke followed by each of the kids, who mentioned how old they were. The oldest, Matty, was fifteen and held the youngest, his little sister, Ramona. She was all of eight months.

The last to go was a little girl who said she was five. Jonah would have guessed younger based on her size. She seemed very serious and he knew he would try to draw her out. Maybe the little girl would be a good project for Ana. And then he caught her words.

"My name is Anastasia." Pronounced like the Russian princess, not like Ana said her name - Ah-na-stah-shia. "My mama grew up in Montevaro," she told them. "She named me after Princess Ana but everyone calls me Stacy."

Jonah glanced over at Ana to see her hiding a smile before Stacy caught his attention again.

"And I have diabetes."

Louis caught Jonah's eye and nodded. They'd talked about this girl, though Jonah hadn't remembered her name. She'd been diagnosed just a few weeks earlier and didn't much like it. No one could blame her for that, of course. It would be Jonah's job to help her figure it out. Louis had been doing his best, with the help of the nurse on staff, but she didn't have much experience with diabetes. Louis caught his attention and brought Jonah back to the present.

"All right, so that's all of you. We'll do our best! I promise!" he told them. "I'm Dr. Fontaine, but everyone calls me Dr. Jonah. And I'm a pediatrician, so I'll be talking with each of you, making sure you're growing like you should. I was born in Montevaro but grew up in Texas. Who knows where Texas is?" Several hands went up. "It's the best place on the whole earth, at least I think so and so does just about everyone I know."

"Are you a cowboy?" Stacy asked.

Jonah grinned and held out a foot. "I've got the boots and the horse. Archer's back in Montevaro, but he's a Texas horse through and through." Even if he had never punched cows. Ever. He turned to his crew and pointed to the closest person. "Why don't you start, Marty?"

Marty only gave his first name and said he worked in security. They went around the group. Ana didn't give her full name, just

Ana, and said she worked for a non-profit organization. True in some ways. She did a lot of charity work, but few of the people with them knew who she was. Would word leak out? It surely would when she started her fund raising and volunteer efforts in a few days.

And with that, it was time to get to work.

"Hi, Ana." The little girl plopped down next to her. "I like you. We have kind of the same name."

Ana smiled. "Your name is Stacy, correct?"

"That's what ever'one calls me, but my real name starts like yours does."

"Yes, it does." She leaned closer to the small brunette. "You want to know a secret?"

Stacy nodded enthusiastically. "Yes!"

"My name is really Anastasia. They're not pronounced the same, but they are spelled alike."

"Like the princess?"

Oh! How she didn't want to lie! But she also didn't want more people than necessary knowing. "Yes," she finally said. "Just like the princess. You know there was another Princess Anastasia from Russia."

Stacy nodded again, this time much more serious. "I know. Everyone thought she escaped the bad guys, but really she died."

"Well, for a long time no one *really* knew for sure what happened to her, but yes, a few years ago, they found out for sure she did die with the rest of her family." Ana leaned closer. "It's kind of fun to wonder what might have happened to her if she had escaped."

"Just like Prince Nicky." Stacy picked up one of the paintbrushes Ana had been cleaning and fanned the bristles.

"Prince Nicky?" This was a story Ana was not familiar with.

"Queen Christ'ana's brother. Mama said they never found him either."

Ana blinked several times in rapid succession. "You mean after the car accident?"

Stacy gave another serious nod. "Mama said they found the queen's mommy and daddy but not her brother." She shrugged. "Maybe he's still 'live, too."

Her mind whirled with the possibilities. Did Christiana know the public suspected? Ana did not know much about the accident except the king had been driving and slid off a dangerous mountain road. Until her conversation with Addie, she had always been told the four of them - king, queen, prince, and nanny - had been killed instantly, and the only reason why Christiana still lived was the stomach flu.

She had to change the subject. "So, young lady, have you seen Dr. Jonah yet?"

"Yep! I was the first one. 'Cause of my diabetes. He's gonna help me figure it out."

"Dr. Jonah is an excellent doctor." She wiped her hand on a towel and held back her bangs where they had fallen out of her French braid. "See this scar?"

Stacy wrinkled her nose. "Ow."

"Yep. I boinked my head while I was with Dr. Jonah and he took me to the hospital and sewed it back up." She leaned closer and whispered. "It did not even hurt."

"I hope he can make it not hurt when they poke my finger and give me shots."

"Do you have to have shots often?"

"Every day."

"I'm so sorry to hear that, sweet thing."

Stacy looked up at her, a very serious look on her face. "I like you, Miss Ana."

Ana felt tears fill her eyes, and she put an arm around the little girl's shoulders. "I am so glad, Stacy. I like you, too. Very much."

Stacy leaned closer and whispered, "You look like Princess Ana."

Ana used a hand to shield the side of her face as she whispered in Stacy's ear. "Wanna know another secret?" Stacy nodded. "I am Princess Ana. But shh. Don't tell anyone, okay?"

Stacy turned to look at her again, her eyes wide. "Really?"

"Yep. Dr. Jonah asked me to come."

The little girl flung her arms around Ana's neck. "I'm so glad you're here." Ana hugged her back, holding on as long as Stacy wanted her to. She knew this was some of what Jonah was talking about when he said there was nothing like a thank you from a child. She had never disputed that, and she was glad to help from time to time. It conflicted her even more. She *knew* she had a valid point. Her time, often, would be better spent doing publicity. She wondered if Jonah would come to see that by the end of the week.

A clanging sound caught her attention, and Stacy moved back. "I won't tell anyone, Princess Ana." Her eyes went wide again, but this time she appeared to be scared. "I shouldn't call you that, then, huh?" Ana shook her head as tears pooled in the big blue eyes. "And I shouldn't hug ya, should I? You're a princess and all. You probably aren't supposed to let little girls hug you without permission."

Ana took Stacy's face in her hands. "You, sweet girl, can hug me *anytime* you want." She kissed her forehead. "But you're right. Just call me Miss Ana while we're here, okay?"

Stacy nodded and pushed up. "It's lunch time. I gotta get my finger poked by Dr. Jonah."

With the little hand snug in hers, Ana headed for the office Jonah had set up in one of the spare bedrooms. She looked around while Jonah finished putting a Teenage Mutant Ninja Turtles Band-Aid on the knee of one of the boys. Water stains colored the ceiling, the brown circles telling her the roof was in need of repair. Some of the stains extended down the walls. The carpet had obviously seen much better days, though it was not a health hazard. Yet.

"Well, hello there." Jonah grinned at them as the boy ran off. "My two favorite Anastasias." He leaned toward Stacy. "Did she tell you that's her name, too?"

Stacy nodded and looked up at Ana. "Does he know?"

Ana laughed. "Yes, he knows."

Jonah pulled a pouch out of a drawer and unzipped it. "Does he know what?"

After looking around for eavesdroppers, Stacy whispered, "She's really Princess Ana."

He took something about the size of a pen out of the pouch. "Yep. She sure is. Do you know who first introduced me to her?"

"Who?"

"Queen Adeline. I met her last spring when Duchess Lindsey needed a doctor. I met Prince Charlie, because he's Lindsey's dad, you know. And I met Princess Ana, too." He patted Stacy's shoulder. "All done. Let's see what the reading is."

Stacy and Ana looked down to see a red spot on one of the small fingers. "You already sticked me?" Stacy sounded as incredulous as Ana felt.

"Yep." Jonah winked at both of them. "I'm just that good." He looked at the readout. "I think you're okay for now, young lady. But you better go get some lunch."

Stacy tugged on Ana's hand. "Are you comin'?"

Jonah answered. "I need to talk to Miss Ana for a minute, but we'll be in. Can you save us seats?"

With a serious nod, Stacy turned and ran off.

Jonah made a notation in a little book and put all of it back in the black pouch. "She's a cutie."

"She is," Ana confirmed.

"I'm surprised you told her." The pouch went back in the

bottom drawer.

"We have the same name. She's named after me, and she's a sweet thing. It seemed like the right thing to do."

Jonah held up his hands at her tone. "Don't get all defensive with me. I didn't say it was wrong, just that I was surprised." He stood and took her hands in his. "Now, care to have lunch with me?"

Jonah wanted to kiss her. More than he'd ever wanted just about anything in his life.

"What's her story?" Ana asked, oblivious to the war in his head. "She talks about her mom like she talked to her the other day."

He dropped one of her hands and sat back down, his heart heavy. "She did. Stacy's not technically an orphan. Her mother is in the hospital, very ill. Cancer of some sort. There's no one else, so she's here. Because she's not orphaned yet, there's no money coming in from the government to support her or her medical needs. Her mother hasn't worked in over a year and..." He shook his head. This was why he needed to get through to Queen Christiana. Kids like this had no one else. Even if the government funding never came through, the royal family's foundation always had until about five years earlier.

Ana had noticed the water stains. He'd seen her looking at them. They were just the tip of the iceberg, but the roof needed to be patched. And soon. He'd looked at the information on the Medicane forming further east. Even if they didn't get hit directly, there was likely rain coming in the very near future. He'd heard steps up there earlier. As soon as he finished with the last kids this afternoon, he'd be up there helping.

"Can she get a sponsor or patron of some kind to help?"

Jonah looked up at the princess. Unless he was very much

mistaken, Ana would be that person in the very near future. Just like Addie had taken care of Sara, Ana would make sure Stacy was taken care of until she was adopted after the death of her mother, something he feared would happen any day. Louis had made some comments to that effect anyway. "I'm sure Louis would love it if he could find a sponsor for her," he finally said. "Right now, he's struggling to make ends meet as it is. The employees aren't much more than volunteers at this point. Even Louis isn't taking a salary, just room and board. The vehicles are a decade too old and held together more by duct tape than anything else."

He could see the emotions playing over her face. "I want to sponsor her. Separate from our agreement."

"Of course." He couldn't resist, though he knew he should. "You know, if you hadn't come..."

Sure enough the brown eyes flashed at him. "Do not start with me, Dr. Fontaine. I am well aware of that. I never protested spending time like this. I always said it was not the *best* use of my time on a regular basis. Wait until the week ends. You will see."

He didn't answer her. She didn't give him a chance, but spun on her heel and walked out. With a sigh, he locked the door and followed her to the lunchroom. Once there, he found himself sitting on the other side of Stacy from Ana. The princess had barely acknowledged him and certainly hadn't spoken to him. Fortunately, Matty sat across from him. That kid liked to talk. He kept Jonah and the others at the table in stitches the whole time.

Louis came in as the meal wound down. He motioned to Jonah. When they were alone in the hallway, he gave Jonah the news he'd been dreading for two days. "It's time. We need to get Stacy to the hospital."

"I'll take her." And Ana. No way would Ana let her go without going along.

Ten minutes later, he steered one of the orphanage's twenty-year-old SUVs along the road toward the bridge and across it to the hospital.

"Is my mama gonna die today, Dr. Jonah?" The little voice from the back seat tore at his heart, and he could see Ana wiping a tear from her cheek.

"I wish I could tell you I knew she was going to be all right, Stacy." He blew out a breath. "But only God knows how long someone is going to live. He knew before your mama was born just how long she would be needed on Earth."

"And her time is up?"

"I don't know, sugar. Not for sure. But tell you what? As soon as we get there, I'll talk to her doctors, okay?"

In the rear view mirror, he saw her nod. It only took about ten minutes to reach the hospital and a few minutes longer to get to her mother's bedside. Jonah didn't need to talk to the doctors or look at her chart to know she didn't have long left. She reached an almost skeletal hand out to Stacy. He noted the care the little girl took, gently holding the nearly translucent skin. Given his choice, Jonah didn't know if he'd want Stacy to see her mother like this.

"I am so glad to see you, Anastasia." Her other hand brushed the little girl's hair back. "I have missed you."

"I've missed you, too, Mama," Stacy whispered.

"Are they nice to you at the orphanage?"

She nodded. "Mr. Louis is super nice."

"And they're helping with your diabetes?"

Jonah couldn't imagine. Struggling to survive a losing battle with cancer only to find out your only child had diabetes.

"Dr. Jonah stuck my finger, and I didn't even feel it."

"Who is Dr. Jonah?"

Stacy pointed at him. "He and Princess Ana came to help us at the orphanage."

Her mother's head turned until she could see them. "Thank you, Dr. Jonah." Her daughter's words seemed to sink in and she looked a bit past him. "Princess Ana?"

Stacy suddenly looked scared. "I'm sorry Miss Ana. I know you said it was a secret."

"It's okay, sweet girl." Ana didn't even try to stop the tears. "I am glad your mother knows. I want to tell her what an honor it is to have you named after me."

"I met your mother once," the woman whispered. "She was pregnant with you and your brother, though no one knew it yet. It was obvious she didn't feel well, but she was so kind and gracious. When you were born and had the same name as the character from my favorite story, I knew I would name my oldest daughter after both of you."

"Thank you."

The tired eyes closed. "Will you make sure the orphanage takes care of her? We have no one left but each other."

Chapter Eighteen

*T*ears fell unheeded as Ana heard the unspoken words. The two of them had no one else and very soon, Stacy wouldn't have anyone. "I will make sure she is taken care of," she whispered. If she had to take the little girl home with her herself, she would make sure of it. "I swear it."

"Thank you." Somehow, she managed to give Stacy a hug. Ana marveled at the little girl's gentleness. "Can I talk to you alone, Dr. Jonah?" The look she gave Ana told her everything she needed to know.

Her strength was about to give out, and she did not want her daughter to see it.

Ana held out a hand to Stacy. "Come with me. We will find a snack that will make Dr. Jonah jealous." She knew they needed to be careful because of her diabetes, but surely they could find something.

A glance at Jonah confirmed her fears. But rather than find a snack, they found a seat. Stacy crawled onto her lap and just sat there as Ana held her. Less than twenty minutes later, a drained Jonah walked out of the room and nodded at the nurses manning the nearby station.

He came to sit next to them resting his large hand on Stacy's smaller one. "I'm sorry, sweet thing."

"Mama's with Jesus." Stacy spoke so matter-of-fact it tore at Ana's heart. "Jesus told me last night He was going to come get her soon, but that it was okay to be sad."

Ana exchanged a look with Jonah over Stacy's head.

"Jesus told you?" Jonah asked.

Stacy nodded against Ana. "Sometimes, when I'm sleeping I see angels. They sit on our roofs. They have big swords to protect us from bad things."

It was not the first time Ana had heard of such things, though she had never known anyone who had had it happen.

"Jesus came to see me twice. He was sad both times. The first time he said my mommy was sick, and He knew it would make me sad, but He would make sure someone took care of me. I went to the orphanage the next day. Last night, He told me soon it would be Mama's time to come home with Him."

Ana tightened her arms around the little frame. "Then I am sure Jesus has her now."

Stacy seemed quite certain. "Jesus said she wouldn't hurt anymore, and she would look even better than her old self instead of looking so sick."

The only thing Ana knew to do was hold the little girl tighter and pray for comfort.

Louis appeared a few minutes later and Jonah left to talk with him. Ana heard them whispering about funeral arrangements. She also heard Jonah telling Louis he would take care of it. Ana had already decided she would help.

"Can we go back?" Stacy whispered.

"Back where?"

"To the orphanage. I don't like it here, and Mama's not here anymore, not really."

"Of course." The two of them rode back with Louis while

Jonah took care of things at the hospital. Stacy insisted on staying close to Ana while she went back to work on the painting task she'd been assigned. She tried to get the little girl to do something else, but Stacy refused.

"Miss Ana! Miss Ana!" One of the other girls ran in holding a mess of something. "Look what we found!"

Ana could not help wrinkling her nose. "What is it?"

"A dog!"

That ball of mud was a dog?

"Can you help us wash her?"

Ana looked down at Stacy who seemed to have brightened. "Of course. How about outside?"

They stood on the driveway while Matty hooked up the hose. "Who wants to hold him?"

"Hang on!" One of the girls darted around the side of the building and came back with a plastic swimming pool. "Fill this up and we'll put him in here."

They did just that, letting the water fill up around the matted mess of a dog. Though, the more Ana considered him, he did not seem to be too impoverished. Perhaps he had run away just a couple of days earlier instead of being dumped. However long it had been, he had found a mud puddle to play in. One of the other girls brought some shampoo out and together about seven of them worked to get the little dog clean. When they finally rinsed the last of the grime away, a quite adorable black and white dog appeared. She had seen one not too long before. A Havanese perhaps? At least partially. The girl - Ana had checked - couldn't weigh much more than ten pounds, maybe fifteen soaking wet, but that was stretching it.

"Can we keep her, Miss Ana?" The question had been asked over and over.

"That is not my decision, children. But she looks like she has been taken care of, so I would imagine someone is missing her."

They all protested, but Ana stuck by her statement. Just as

she realized what a mess she was, Jonah drove up. The grin on his face almost made the mud spattered all over both arms and her face worth it.

"Who is this little girl?" he asked, kneeling down to pet the still dripping wet dog.

All of children talked over each other, telling how they had found her in the woods. Jonah laughed at the different versions of the tale, but finally seemed to get the general idea.

"Why don't we find a box and a blanket for her? I bet she would like a chance to rest."

The kids ran ahead to do just that, but Stacy hung back not minding that she got even more wet when the dog crawled right into her lap as she sat on the ground. It was almost as if the dog knew she needed a friend.

"They're sweet together." Jonah's arm brushed against hers. "It's going to break her heart when we find the owner."

"I know." Ana would try to buy the dog if she had to, if that's what it took to comfort the little girl.

Jonah wrapped the dog in his old sweatshirt and helped Stacy stand up. He sent them inside but stayed behind to talk with Ana.

"The funeral will likely be in a few days. It seems like there are a few friends, but none terribly close either geographically or relationally. Her mother left a few instructions. Given her choice, she would prefer to be buried near Montevaro where she grew up, but realized she would likely end up elsewhere. I read some of the notes she'd written. She wanted to move back to Montevaro and had planned to before the cancer struck. She wanted to raise Stacy there."

"We can arrange it. I do not know how just yet, but Christiana and I will come to an agreement if we need to. Somehow, we will grant her mother's wishes."

"I thought you'd say that. I'll talk to Louis and see what we need to do to get Stacy transferred to an orphanage in

Montevaro until a permanent home can be found for her. I hope the queen's uncle didn't screw those laws up when he was in a bad mood."

"We will sort it out." Her hand rested on his arm.

Jonah's nose wrinkled and he picked up her pinky finger with his thumb and forefinger. "You are a mess. Don't touch me."

She could see the twinkle in his eye and knew what she had to do. Ana launched herself at him, trusting that he would not let her fall.

"You're a mess!" Jonah hollered, easily deflecting her while not letting her stumble. Personally, he thought she looked utterly adorable with her hair streaked with mud and her clothes dripping wet.

"You will be too in a moment!"

He needed to teach her to trash talk a bit better. Her formal phrasing didn't translate well.

She tried again to get him, but he dodged, laughing, until he slipped. Fell. Landed right in the plastic pool full of we-had-to-clean-a-muddy-dog water.

He used a wet hand to push dripping hair off his forehead and saw Ana laughing so hard she could barely breathe. Bending over with her hands on her knees, she gasped between chuckles.

"Help me up?" One hand out, Jonah contemplated pulling her in with him, but when she hesitated, he promised not to.

Once back on solid ground, he noticed Ana had turned more serious. "It seems wrong." She wrapped her arms around herself, something he'd noticed she did a lot.

"What?"

"Laughing and playing around. Stacy's mother died just a couple of hours ago."

"You heard Stacy though. Jesus promised her He would take

care of her. I'm sure He has someone here on earth to be His hands and feet, but she's trusting the Savior to take care of her. I'm sure most of us could learn from her example."

"You are correct, of course." She looked up at the darkening sky. "It still seems wrong though."

"It's nearly time for dinner. Why don't you get Carrie to take you back to the dorms and take a quick shower?"

"I think that is a good idea." She walked toward the house just as Carrie came out the front door. The two of them left on foot to walk the quarter mile to the campus.

Jonah borrowed Louis's bathroom to clean up and change into a fresh pair of jeans and flannel shirt. He didn't figure he'd ever get his sweatshirt back and he was fine with that. When he made it to the dining room, the dog had won over the hearts of everyone present. Someone had found dog food and a bowl for water.

"Does she have a name yet?" he asked.

Matty shook his head. "No. We decided to let Stacy pick." The word must have gotten around. No one would say anything to the girl about her mother, but they would do what they could to keep her mind off her loss. He just hoped it didn't backfire when the owners came forward.

Jonah turned to her. "Have you picked a name yet, Stacy?"

"Lexi."

"You want to name the dog Lexi?" he clarified.

She nodded. "My mama's name was Lexi."

"Lexi it is."

"Can Lexi sleep with me tonight, Dr. Jonah?"

How could a guy say no to that? "We'll have to ask Mr. Louis, but I bet she can."

"Thanks, Dr. Jonah."

Dinner was both subdued and lively. A strange dichotomy as the realization of Stacy's loss spread among the kids, but also influenced by the presence of the new Lexi-dog. Ana slipped in a bit after everyone else started and sat off to one side with Carrie and Marty. The three of them seemed to be whispering urgently about something, though Jonah couldn't figure out what. Probably something to do with Stacy and possibly the burial of Stacy's mother.

With her dinner half-completed, Ana took a call and walked outside to take it. Jonah excused himself to follow her.

"You should see her, Jonathan. She is stronger than anyone I know."

He didn't mean to eavesdrop, not really, but he also hadn't expected her to be talking to Jonathan. Jonah stopped, allowing her to walk farther away so he couldn't hear any longer. Marty joined him a minute later.

"We may need to move her out tomorrow."

"Why?"

"The storm looks to be heading this way. Likely just a bunch of rain, but the office in Montevaro is concerned about potential flooding. It's still shaping up and we'll know more in the morning."

Jonah continued to watch Ana's back as she stood in the distance. "Keep me posted? We may need to move everyone out if it's bad enough."

"Agreed."

"We'll talk about taking her to the hospital without one of us later."

Jonah didn't answer.

Ana hung up and turned around to see them. She looked like the weight of the world had lifted from her despite everything with Stacy. "That was Jonathan," she told both men as she neared. Neither replied but waited for her to go on. "He said they've reached an agreement with Tricia. She will stop everything in exchange for no charges being brought against her. Jonathan and an investigator realized the circumstances were such they could threaten to have her brought up with child abandonment charges. Charlie promised not to pursue any of those or defamation of character charges if she would crawl back into the woodwork, he said."

"Good." That had to be the weight that lifted. Jonah knew it had bothered her. But something bothered him. "Was she really guilty of child abandonment? She left Lindsey with her biological father, not on the side of the road?"

Ana shrugged. "I have no idea, but the threat was enough. Perhaps she thought she would be given money by Addie and Charlie. When she realized none was forthcoming, she decided to..."

"Get while the gettin's good?"

She smiled. "I believe that is how Jonathan put it. I had not heard the phrase before."

"I'm glad." Jonah realized Marty had disappeared. "How are you doing, Ana? It's been a tough day."

"It is not my mother who passed," she pointed out, turning to walk back out to the yard. "I wish there was more I could do."

"You're going to get her to Montevaro, right? Both of them, I would imagine. Make sure her mother is buried where she wanted to be and get Stacy well-taken care of. I would expect nothing less from you."

"I still wish I could do something more."

He turned her words over in his head. "You wish you could adopt her, don't you?"

Ana raised a single shoulder. "I know there are others who would be a much better choice for a permanent home, but perhaps I could be her foster parent."

Jonah stood behind her and wrapped her in his arms. "Do you know how hard it would be to give her over to another family if you spent time as her foster mother? It would be better for both of you if we could find a good family right off the bat."

"I know. I just wish..."

He kissed the side of her head and noticed the still damp hair. "I know. You're too wonderful to not want to take care of her. I know some good places back in Montevaro. She'll be well taken care of."

"If I were married, I could take care of her forever."

Chapter Nineteen

*A*na would never know what possessed her to say such a thing. She did know that if Jonah did not respond "correctly" and if this week went as she anticipated, she would talk to Jonathan about that very thing. As far back as the coronation, he had insinuated he would be open to such a relationship. Essentially an arranged marriage they both prayed would turn into something more. Unless she missed her guess, it already had turned into "more" on his side.

Before Jonah could answer, they were called back inside for the evening Bible reading and prayer session. Stacy sat on Ana's lap and the now-dry Lexi-dog curled up in the chair beside them, something Ana was sure Louis would not allow under normal circumstances. The children each took a turn reading if they were old enough. Stacy did not, though Ana noticed the version of the Bible was one the girl would be able to read. Louis did not press her. Ana noted the applicability of the passage being read.

Louis talked about the verses as they finished. "I Corinthians 12. Who has any idea what all of that means?"

One of the girls Ana had met, but could not name, answered.

"It means we all have different jobs." She took the Bible from the girl next to her. "Verse 17. Basically, it points out that if we were one giant eye, we wouldn't be able to hear. And if we were a giant ear, we couldn't smell. Or walk. Or talk."

The little girl on Ana's lap giggled.

Louis looked at her and smiled. "Yes, Stacy?"

"That's funny." She clapped her hands over her mouth.

"The idea of a giant ear talking and walking around?"

Stacy nodded.

"I agree. But in order for a giant ear to do that, it would still need a mouth and feet." He looked at the Bible in his hands. "This section talks about how some people are teachers and some perform miracles and some do other things. We each have a job to do and each job is important. Is it possible to live without a foot? Sure. But it makes life more difficult. Same if you can't hear. Or smell. I knew a girl in high school who had to have surgery on her brain. When it was over and she healed, she couldn't smell anything. The foods she used to love, she didn't anymore. And the foods she liked afterward, some of them she couldn't stand before. So we're all important."

Ana glanced at Jonah out of the corner of her eye. Had it sunk in for him? Would he recognize the meaning?

"Why don't we pray?" Louis started and gave each of the children and staff members a chance to pray if they wanted. Most of them prayed for Stacy. Stacy prayed for Lexi-dog and thanked Jesus that her mother no longer felt any pain.

After supervising the brushing of teeth for the girls, Ana tucked each of them into bed in the rooms shared by two or three of them. She saved Stacy for last. Lexi-dog curled up next to the little girl. "Did you take her outside so she could go to the bathroom?" Ana asked. The last thing they needed was a mess to clean up.

Stacy nodded. "After I brushed my teeth."

"Good job." She kissed the little girl's forehead. "I will see you in the morning, sweet one."

"Goo'ni', Miss Ana." A big yawn muffled her words. "Thank you for sittin' with me while Mama went to see Jesus."

Ana squeezed her hand, amazed again at the strength found in one so young. "It was my privilege."

She struggled against the tears again as she left the room, pulling the door most of the way shut behind her. Walking downstairs, she found most of the staff and volunteers back in the living area. Leaning against the door frame, she listened to the conversation.

"We need to get a plan together," Louis was saying. "I'm hearing rumbles that this could be a huge storm."

"Storm?" she asked walking all the way in.

He nodded. "It's one of those things where they're not really sure. It could be nothing. It could be a medicane."

"Medicane?" she asked.

"Mediterranean hurricane. They're not technically hurricanes," Louis went on with a roll of his eyes. "The water temperature around here isn't quite warm enough, but otherwise, essentially. Lots of wind. Lots of rain. All in a short period of time. We don't want to be here if it gets bad."

"Why not?" Rachel asked.

"The orphanage is in a valley of sorts. We're above sea level, so even in a worst case, we shouldn't see anything like they did after Hurricane Katrina in New Orleans." He nodded toward Jonah. "Dr. Fontaine and I both helped after that one. But it's very possible the first floor will be partially flooded. I don't think it would get to the second floor, but the roads will likely be covered and..." He glanced at Ana.

"What?" she asked.

"Forgive me," he muttered. "For those of you who haven't put it together yet, this is Princess Anastasia from Montevaro. She will likely leave before the rest of us for that reason, but I also know she and her family are quite close to our own Queen

Christiana. We all know what's gone on with her uncle trying to run the country into the ground. We've all been concerned about the bridge for several years. Request after request has been put in for it to be repaired, or even replaced, but they've fallen on deaf ears. We're all hopeful now that the queen is in control, things will start getting the funding they need, but for now, we don't want to be on this side of the bridge if things go bad."

"What do we need to do?" Ana asked. "I will be here until the last people are evacuated." She did not look at Marty or Carrie. She already knew they would be furious.

Louis turned back to the group. "First thing in the morning, we need to get as much as we can onto the second floor. We need to pack clothes and special things for all of the kids. By dinner, we need to be packed up and heading out."

"We'll have all hands on deck," Jonah promised. "A few people working on the roof still, but the rest of us are at your disposal."

Louis thanked him and everyone talked logistics, though none would actually ask her opinion or for her help. This was why she did not want people knowing who she was.

Rather than wait around for them to not ask for her help, she went to the office and called the palace in Montevaro. She told the public relations office what they needed and they promised to get on the arrangements. Then she texted Carrie and together they went back to the dorms to get ready for morning.

He should have known. Ana disappeared even before the planning for the work was done. Cuddle a little girl and clean a few paint brushes? Sure, she could do that. Even "supervise" a bunch of kids washing a dog, but work? Real, hard work? Not gonna happen.

Jonah tried not to think the worst, but couldn't help it. There had to be another reason. What it could be? No clue, but they were giving out assignments and she was gone, along with both Marty and Carrie. For a minute, he wondered if they'd made her evacuate already, but Marty had said it would be morning at the earliest before they left.

Instead, Jonah helped Louis make the assignments and then went to the office serving as his dorm room. Still in his "fresh" clothes, he fell asleep in the recliner. It had seen better days, but still retained that sort of comfortableness that couldn't be replaced by something new. He woke early, even before his alarm went off and started packing up everything he wouldn't need in the next few hours. The bus would arrive shortly and they'd fill the back half of it to the gills with everything they could. The passengers would cram three or four to a seat in the front half if needed. The drive was only about eight miles. They hoped to make several trips in the SUVs, but couldn't know for sure.

Every twenty minutes, he'd stop and check the news. Sure enough, the forecast grew more grim with every passing hour. Heavy rains. Strong winds. No one knew for sure where the worst would be, but Ravenz-by-the-Sea would get hit unless something drastic occurred.

"Dr. Jonah!" Was that Matty? "Come here!"

He went out to the living area. All of the seating had already been moved upstairs, but the television had been left so they could keep up to date on the weather.

"And now, we're joined from Ravenz-by-the-Sea, by Princess Anastasia of Montevaro. Your Highness, thank you for joining us."

That's where she was. Jonah fumed silently. They needed her here. Helping get ready.

Variations of "It's Miss Ana!" sounded from around the room as she spoke.

"Thank you for having me. I am in the town of Ravenz-by-the-Sea, volunteering at the local orphanage. I am sure many of you have heard that

there is a storm headed this way. By morning, we are expecting the orphanage to be at least partially cut off from the world. We plan to have everyone and everything out long before then, but we could use help. Not just here in Ravenz-Sea." When had she picked up the local shorthand? "*Many areas in this part of Ravenzario are scrambling to sandbag, to get the elderly and infirm to safer locations. To make sure family members and friends are to safety. If you are in the area, or close enough to get here, we would greatly appreciate the help.*"

The news anchor went on to get a phone number people could call for more information. Jonah turned away in disgust and went back to the office, packing everything he could move into boxes.

"What's your problem?"

Jonah jumped. Then tried to calm his pounding heart as he turned back to his work. "I don't have a problem."

"Liar. What's your problem with Ana?" Jonah should have known Louis had been his friend too long.

"There's a lot of other things she could be doing with her time. Lots of kids here who need help getting ready to move for who knows how long."

"Oh please! There are at least thirty adults here to help pack things up. We'll be ready to go by lunchtime at the rate we're going. Having her, or even Marty and Carrie, here wouldn't make an appreciable difference. What's she's doing on television? That could."

Jonah couldn't keep in his snort. "I don't see it."

"How many people just outside this region have no idea there's a major storm headed our way? People who will now drop everything and drive an hour or two and help sandbag along rivers or evacuate nursing homes?"

Jonah just shook his head. Nothing would convince him Louis was right. Because Louis was wrong. No two ways about it.

Louis didn't say anything else but left him to finish his work.

They worked solidly for several more hours. At the lunch break, one of the kids found Ana on another channel. This time, Stacy sat next to her.

"This is Stacy. She is one of the children being displaced by this storm." A number flashed on the screen. *"If there is anything you can do to help the people of this area get ready for this storm, children like Stacy would be most grateful."*

And pulling a child into it. Jonah couldn't stay and watch the rest.

An hour later, Marty pulled back in the driveway, alone. He helped finish loading everything into the van and SUVs. Shortly before three, they pulled out, just as the first sprinkles started to fall. As all of the vehicles crossed the bridge and climbed into the mountains far enough to be out of danger, Jonah breathed a huge sigh of relief. They didn't unload the vehicles, except the one with the medical supplies and records. They left everything boxed up, in case they needed to evacuate rapidly again, but easily accessible if needed.

Ana walked in a few minutes later, her expensive shoes clicking on the linoleum. He didn't say anything but watched as the children scrambled around her. Her carefully constructed hairdo had already been ravaged by wind and rain and the storm wasn't even there yet.

He went back to work, organizing what he had with him. Twenty minutes had passed before she walked in.

"Where's Stacy?" she asked.

He looked up and noticed she'd changed into jeans and hiking boots. "Last time I saw her, she was with you on television."

The fear crossed her features in a millisecond. "She went back with Marty."

Jonah's heart stopped. "What? Are you sure?"

"Yes. She said she wanted to check on Lexi-dog and ran after him. I saw her talk to him as they walked outside."

He grabbed his phone and called Marty. Easier than trying to find him in the maze of an unfamiliar middle school. "Marty, did Stacy come back with you?"

His heart sunk as he heard the answer. "Thanks." He hung up and stared at Ana's stricken face. "He told her to stay with you and thought she did."

Ana looked like she'd seen a ghost. "Then where is she?"

Chapter Twenty

*T*his is Stacy. She is one of the children being displaced by this storm."

Jonathan watched with pride as Ana did what she did best. Bring light to a situation that was rapidly turning desperate.

"Thank you for coming." He turned to see Christiana walk in.

"My pleasure. What can I help you with? Addie wasn't very clear."

"There is a lot going on." He could see the stress on her features. "Alexander and Tony are a huge help to me, but I need someone the people know as more than a press secretary. Someone familiar to the people of both Ravenzario and Montevaro. That is where you come in. Can you please be the public face of this for right now? With Ana in the area about to get hit, someone needs to be in front of the cameras."

"Of course. Whatever you need from me. You got it."

"We are expecting a call from Jonah momentarily that everyone is safely at the local middle school."

As though the good doctor heard her, Christiana's phone

rang. She hit the speaker button. "Yes?"

"Ma'am, this is Marty from Princess Ana's security detail."

She exchanged a glance with Jonathan. "Yes, Marty?"

"I hate to say it, but the princess is missing. She and Dr. Fontaine have disappeared."

Jonathan pushed down the snarky thoughts as they rose up. Surely, they wouldn't take this chance to go make out. The uneasy feeling in his stomach grew worse. Almost without realizing it, he began to pray.

"Jonah called me to see where the little girl, Stacy, is. I told them she didn't come back with me. But she wasn't with Ana and Carrie either. One of the two SUVs is gone. The other one won't start. The only vehicle we have right now is the bus and I don't dare drive it in this wind. It's too high profile. Even if we knew for sure where they had gone but we don't."

Jonathan spoke up. "Marty, this is Jonathan. Where do you think they are?"

"I think they went back to the orphanage to look for her."

The prayers intensified. "Do you have any way to get there?"

"Not right now. We're looking for a vehicle we can use, but the rain is really coming down hard. Everyone else here has smaller vehicles. We need a full size truck or SUV."

Christiana took a turn. "Have you talked to city officials yet?"

"Carrie is working on that as we speak. We believe they're not much better off than we are." Jonathan could hear the hesitation in his voice. "The budget cuts have hit this part of the country hard, ma'am. The consensus around here is that it isn't really your fault because much of it started before your age of majority, but national government officials aren't terribly popular around here at the moment, including you. Ana is because she's here and doing something, but..."

He could see the pain on Christiana's face. She had grown up with Ana. In many ways, Ana was her sister. "Anything the national government can do to help, we will. I have already given orders for troops to get there as quickly as possible. They should have started arriving this afternoon."

"Yes, ma'am. Carrie hopes the city officials can get in touch with them because they should have better equipment."

"Do whatever you have to, Marty," Christiana said. Jonathan admired her ability to keep the panic out of her voice. He doubted he'd be able to if he tried to talk. "She is not answering her phone?"

"No, ma'am. We tried both phones."

"I thought you would have, but I had to ask."

"I understand." A scuffling sound muffled Marty's discussion with someone else. "Carrie found the mayor. I'm going to confer with them. We'll keep you in the loop."

"Thank..." Before the queen could finish her statement, the line disconnected. She looked up at Jonathan, tears in her eyes. "How will I ever face Jedidiah and Alexandra? Or Addie? Rick? If something happens to her..." Jonathan moved to her side and gave her the biggest hug he could.

"You have to get yourself together, ma'am." It was odd - giving a woman so much younger than him a hug and calling her ma'am at the same time. "We're all praying for their safety. Jonah isn't stupid. He won't let her get into a situation where she'll get hurt." He knew that wasn't entirely true. Hurt? Maybe. But Jonah would give his life to save Ana's. Jonathan knew that.

Because it's what he would do for the woman he loved.

There was something helpless about being the one in charge.

Sure she was queen. Christiana could order men and women to the area to help prepare and help in the aftermath, but she could actually do very little.

Christiana stared out the window of her apartment. She had moved in just weeks earlier, after her uncle's things had been moved out. All of the furniture, save the family heirlooms, were removed and replaced. The monarch had lived in these rooms for centuries. It was time she took her country back.

In the distance, the waves crashed against the shore. The sky, dark and foreboding, hung low. Only a few splatters had landed on her window. She couldn't see the southern island of Ravenzario from here, but she knew they were getting battered. At least the phone lines still worked.

The door opened behind her, and she watched the reflection in the window as Jonathan came in. How she wished Alexander were here! But he had gone to his family's property nearby to help protect everything there. She depended on him far too much, Christiana knew that.

She could not help it.

Her life, in recent months, had been too much like the sea out there. No rhyme or reason to the waves. Coming at her from all sides. She needed a calm port. Her boyfriend's business had been hit hard by the changes in the wake of her uncle's arrest, and he struggled to keep it afloat. Alexander had somehow been promoted to trusted aide.

"Is there any word?" she finally asked.

"No, ma'am. Not yet."

"Did you talk to Marty or Carrie?"

"I spoke with Marty a few minutes ago. They have not yet secured a vehicle to take them to the orphanage. Based on the footage coming from a local television station, it would not be safe for them even if they could."

Lightning flashed in the distance. Too far away to hear the thunder, but too close to Ana and Jonah and that little girl.

"They still have power?"

"Everyone does as far as they know."

"Electrical teams are ready?"

"They are assembling on this island. We are praying the docks on the other island will be operational so we can get the ferries to them and the trucks off. Others are on their way to a location about fifty miles away. They're getting rain and wind, but not nearly as bad as the shoreline is."

"What else can we do?"

"Nothing, ma'am. Just pray."

"I have not stopped."

"Neither have I. The entire country and all of Montevaro are praying, too."

"It does not feel like enough."

"It has to be."

But it was not. And it never would be.

Perhaps her uncle was correct. Perhaps she was not cut out to be queen.

Perhaps she should have died in the car accident instead of her brother.

Ana had never been so cold. Soaked to the skin. Rain pelting her with the precision of a million tiny hammers. Wind had blown her hair out of its tidy braid, but water now plastered the strands to her skin.

"Can you fix it?" she yelled, flashlight in her hand.

Jonah slammed the hood down. "No. Not here. We have to walk to the orphanage."

Eight miles. The distance from the school to the orphanage. They had made it six and a half. Jonah managed to fix the SUV the first time, but after another quarter mile, it stopped again. He hoisted a rope out of the back and tied it around his waist.

"We'll walk. I think there's an extra car battery there. This one died. If that's all it is, we can fix it. If not, we'll walk over the bridge."

"Why not stay at the orphanage?" She held her arms up as he wrapped the rope around her waist.

He did not answer, and she feared she knew why. Jonah was not convinced the orphanage would survive this storm.

The water had not yet passed the one inch mark in most places. It was like walking through a giant puddle. The yards on the one side of the road were filling faster than she would have liked. With her poncho hood pulled tight and a ball cap on, she managed to keep most of it out of her face. A backpack with medical supplies and a poncho for Stacy was barely visible under Jonah's slicker.

They passed the dorms. She had suggested staying there, but Jonah told her they were locked up tight and he did not have a key. They were solid, World War II construction, designed to keep an enemy out, though they were never used for that.

Almost there.

Ana feared her legs would give out as they turned down the drive for the orphanage. Jonah's flashlight showed the water nearly at the porch. As they got closer, it rose until it reached her knees. Once on the still-dry porch, Jonah tried the door.

Locked.

After taking half a step back, he kicked it in.

How did he have the energy?

"Stacy!" he hollered.

Ana followed suit. They searched the bottom floor, still tied together.

Then it hit her.

"Lexi-dog!"

Jonah turned, flashing the light in her eyes. "What?"

"Lexi-dog. Did you take her with you?"

She could see the realization cross his face. "No. None of us thought about it. I don't think anyone even saw her this morning. Where was she last night?"

"With Stacy, in her room."

Water began to seep in the open front door as they darted toward the stairs. "Stacy!" Ana shouted with all her strength.

There! A tiny voice. Yelling for help?

"I hear her!" Jonah took the steps two at a time, dragging Ana with him.

By the time they crossed into Stacy's room, Ana had caught up. Stacy sat there, completely dry but for the tears on her cheeks.

Ana pushed past Jonah. "Are you all right, sweetheart?"

Stacy shook her head. "I'm hungry and I don't feel right."

Jonah was at her side, taking his backpack off. "When was the last time you ate?" He stuck the flashlight between his cheek and shoulder.

"Lunch with Miss Ana before the TV show."

"Too long," he muttered as he reached for her finger. He thrust the flashlight toward Ana. "Hold this."

She could hear the "make yourself useful, finally" undertones to his words. Without saying a thing, she took it from him while he pricked Stacy's finger. He squeezed until a good drop of blood soaked into the strip and put it into the meter.

"All right, Miss Stacy. You've been doing pretty good keeping it under control, but your numbers are a lot lower than I'd like." He handed her a smushed candy bar. "Try to eat some of that as you can."

Ana set the light down to help Stacy, but Jonah rebuked her. "I need that light, Ana."

Right. Because he was digging out a syringe and a bottle of life saving medicine. He filled the body of the syringe with the liquid. "All right. Let's do this, Miss Stacy."

Unable to watch, Ana closed her eyes. Stacy whimpered before Jonah pronounced them all done.

"Now, let's get going." She saw him pack up the supplies.

"We can't." Stacy's tear-filled voice broke Ana's heart.

She moved closer and rested a hand on the girl's head. "Why not, sweetie?"

"Lexi-dog had puppies. We can't leave them."

Ana looked at Jonah who looked back, eyes wide. "Where are they?"

That's when the other noise Ana had been hearing registered. Whimpering. On the other side of the bed. She crawled over, annoyed by the rope that still attached her to Jonah. There they were. The little black and white dog and three tiny pups. She could probably fit all three of them in both hands. With room to spare.

She looked over to see Jonah's grim face as he tried to decide what to do.

"We have to take them," Ana whispered.

"I know," he replied.

"How?"

"I haven't figured that out yet."

"I did." The voice behind them told Ana they had not been quiet enough.

"How?" Jonah asked her.

Stacy climbed down off the bed and went to her closet. She pulled out an over-the-shoulder satchel like a high schooler might use. "Lexi-dog can fit in here and you can carry her, Dr. Jonah."

Ana could sense his reluctance but knew he would do anything in his power to get the dogs to safety - as long as it didn't endanger their own.

"What about the puppies, Stacy?" he asked her. "We wouldn't want to put them in there, too."

She opened it and pulled out a little girl purse. "They'll fit in here, right?" Jonah nodded as Stacy opened that bag and pulled out a baggie of dog food and a covered cup with milk. "See? This can go in my backpack."

Ana had to hand it to her. She had thought of everything.

Except how to get across a water-covered street without a car.

She could see the wheels turning in Jonah's head. "All right.

Here's how we're going to do this."

Ten minutes later, the original rope, with water-swollen knots, had been cut off. Another rope had been tied to Jonah, then Stacy, then Ana. Jonah still carried the full backpack, but would also have a battery for the SUV. They all prayed it was the problem. Ana now carried Lexi-dog in the satchel across her chest. The strap had been shortened so it was almost like a baby carrier she had seen advertised.

Stacy insisted she would carry the puppies. Ana and Jonah had exchanged glances, deciding to let her. For now. If need be, they could attach the small purse to Ana's satchel and keep the puppies close to their mother.

Jonah gathered both of them close and prayed aloud for their safety. With the flashlight in his hand, they started down the stairs, scared of what they'd find.

Chapter
Twenty-One

*J*onah prayed harder than he had ever prayed in his life. The flashlight didn't illuminate much, but enough. As he feared, by the time they reached the bottom step, they were already in the water. He turned around.

Handing the flashlight to Ana, he scooped up Stacy. "I'm going to carry you the first little bit, okay? The water's pretty high."

She nodded and Ana held the light where he could see. He picked up the battery he'd left sitting on a built-in shelving unit near the front door and stepped out onto the porch. By the time they reached the ground, the water came nearly to his hips.

He glanced back to see it coming to Ana's waist, but it wouldn't last long. She'd been a trooper. He'd give her that. Now, if the battery would just work.

It was grueling, but eventually they made it to the SUV. He'd tied the rope so it would be easier to get off and he set Stacy inside the SUV with the dogs while Ana helped him. He thanked God and all the designers of this particular vehicle that the battery was easy to get to and didn't really require tools. It would be nice to tighten the nuts a bit more but as long it had enough spark to get started, that's all he cared about. In ten minutes, he had the batteries changed out.

"Go try to start it," he yelled to Ana. She nodded and handed him the flashlight. There was a small one in her pocket. It would be enough. They had decided to save it for later. He could hear it trying to turn over and at one point it almost caught and then...

Nothing.

Plan B.

If he only knew what that was.

"What now?" Ana yelled at him.

"I don't know!" he yelled back.

"Go back to the orphanage?"

He didn't want to do that. She had to have picked up on his fear that it wouldn't be there come morning. If hard pressed, he didn't *really* think it would float away, but he didn't trust it to stay put either.

"So we walk to the bridge?"

"The bridge is closed by now. I'm surprised we got across."

Ana's hood slipped off her head. "But if we get to the bridge there will be someone on the other side we can signal, right?" Even with her hair plastered to her scalp and rain pouring down, she managed to look beautiful.

But he couldn't worry about that now.

And she was right.

"Okay. So we walk. It's about a mile and a half to the bridge."

"Can Stacy make it that far?"

Jonah doubted he would make it much farther than the bridge himself. Ana was questionable. Not with the dips the road took, now sure to be full of water. "I'll go. You two wait here." The SUV had stopped high enough it shouldn't be in danger of washing away for quite some time.

"No!" The force of Ana's voice nearly blew him over in the way the wind never could. "We stay together. Rick always taught me that. In an emergency, unless there is *absolutely* no other way, you stay with your party. Always."

She had a point, and Jonah conceded it with a nod. "Fine. I'll carry her if I have to. Put the puppies with you this time, though. We don't want to have to switch it later."

Ana nodded and they worked their way back to the door. While she explained the plan to the little girl, Jonah dug around in the back and came up with another ball cap. Ana had given hers to Stacy to keep the rain out of her eyes. Now all three of them would have one again.

He retied the ropes and made sure Lexi-dog and the puppies were secure. "Let's go."

They trudged up and down a few of the smaller hills. Water ran toward them on the uphill side and with them as they went down. At the base of these hills, the water was still only to mid-calf on Jonah. He carried Lexi through them. As they reached the crest of the last hill before the descent to the bridge a crashing sound reached them.

On instinct, he rushed to Ana and Stacy, just two steps behind, covering them with his body as they ducked. After a few seconds with nothing hitting them, he started to relax. A smidge.

"What was that?" Stacy yelled.

He shook his head. "I don't know." This time, they both held Stacy's hands as they walked up the last bit. As they breached the top, the wind caught them full force. Lightning flashed. As the thunder cracked overhead, Jonah stopped all three of them, waiting for another one.

It didn't take long for another one, and he saw what he'd feared with the last flash. He turned to Ana and yelled, "We have to go back!"

Jonathan had never felt so helpless. Not even in those early days of searching for his brother. Then, police and countless searchers were out doing the hunting, but now, no one could do anything but pray.

The door opened and he turned to see Tony walk in. "Anything yet?"

Tony shook his head. "Not yet. They're supposed to call in about ten minutes with another update unless they know something sooner."

"How's Christiana holding up?" He hadn't seen the queen since he'd left her apartment several hours earlier.

"She's trying to take charge. Doing her best. She has a few people around her who are helping her. Alexander is on his way back."

Jonathan looked out the window. "He has a boat he can use in this weather?"

"Apparently. And one of the harbors on the island is sheltered enough to launch it. He won't be able to dock here, but there's another spot a few miles up the coast where he can. A car will meet him there. I know he's worried about the queen and wants to help her."

The phone rang, cutting off any follow-up questions Jonathan might have asked.

The other man jabbed the speaker button. "Tony."

"It's Marty. We got a vehicle."

Jonathan nearly sank to the chair in relief but kept himself upright.

"About a minute before we reached the bridge, it collapsed. I don't know why, I just know we were sixty seconds from being swept away with it."

Anxiety and relief warred within Jonathan, and he felt sure the others felt the same.

"We're glad you're okay," Tony confirmed. "Do they have any idea what happened to it?"

"I think they suspect it's the lack of funding over the years.

There was a rush of water, but not *that* much and the river certainly hadn't topped the bridge. There didn't *seem* to be anything in the water big enough to do that sort of damage. At least that's what I've been told."

"So now what?" Jonathan paced the room.

"Nothing for now. We can't launch a boat across that river and there's no possible air rescue at the moment."

"There's no other bridge into that area?" How was that even possible?

"Not really. That section of the city isn't very big. Under a hundred buildings total. There are other roads in, but all of them have low-water crossings that would have been filled hours ago."

Of course.

"So what do we do?"

"Pray."

"We've been doing that."

"Then pray har..." The line went dead.

Jonathan looked up to see Tony looking as grim as he'd ever seen anyone. "Now what?"

Tony shook his head. "There's only one thing we can do right now."

"Pray?"

"You got it."

Ana thought she had been cold on the way to the orphanage the first time, but that didn't compare to how she felt now. She had seen the same thing Jonah had. The bridge had been swept away and with it, their route to safety.

He had ushered them to the side of the road and a somewhat sheltered spot under a few trees. "Now what?" She had to yell to be heard.

"I don't know!" She knew he had to yell back, but she still did not appreciate the tone.

"The orphanage?"

"No!"

"Another house?"

"I don't know the area well enough."

"The dorms?" Wind whipped her words away.

Jonah moved closer, Stacy in his arms, and yelled in her ear. "I told you. They're locked tight."

"I know, but there's a fire escape. Can we climb it to the second or third floor and get in that way?"

Through the light of the dimming flashlight, she could see him thinking about it. "They use doors on the fire escape, not windows," he finally answered. "But I think that's our best bet. The windows are supposed to be shatter proof, but it's all we've got."

For the next two miles, it took everything she had - and some that had to come from elsewhere - just to put one foot in front of the other. Her feet ached. Pain shot through her knee where she'd wrenched it at one point. She hadn't mentioned it to Jonah. Lexi-dog had behaved better once her puppies were nearby, but the weight still took its toll. Ana was beginning to worry that even curled together and relatively dry under her poncho they would be too cold to survive. Stacy's heart wouldn't be the only one that would break.

Ahead of her, she could make out the outline of Jonah. He carried a full backpack and a little girl. She should not complain about what she had to carry.

The driveway to the dorms was uphill, something she was grateful for when it came to flooding, but not when it came to actually climbing it. They reached the dorm that had been her home for the last several days and realized the stairs were on the far side of the building. The good thing, she realized when they got to them, the building would block the worst of the wind.

"Can we rest a minute?" she asked Jonah.

"Let's get to the first landing."

Good plan. Even on this side, the water was starting to puddle around their feet. Ana took half a second to thank God the stairs went all the way to the ground level. There was no ladder to climb, something Ana did not think would be possible with the rain and the wind, even with the lesser force where they were.

But even those few steps were a struggle.

Stacy snuggled close as Ana collapsed to the metal floor. "We won't stop long," Jonah told her. "We need to keep going."

"How high?"

He looked up, squinting toward the top of the building. "Let me check it out and see what I can find." He looked at the knot in the rope and apparently decided he couldn't undo it. Instead, he pulled a pocket knife out and sliced through the rope.

She watched him go and prayed as she had never prayed before. For the rain to stop. For the wind to cease. For shelter. Dry clothes. A blanket.

Mostly, though, she asked God to keep all three of them safe.

The wind did not calm. The rain still came in sheets. But a sense of peace filled Ana's spirit. Somehow, God would make a way for them.

Come daybreak, they would be rescued.

The phrase *pray without ceasing* took on new meaning for Jonah. He prayed for the kids at the school, for the residents of Ravenz-Sea, for Stacy, Ana, and even the dogs. He prayed for himself. For an inner reserve of strength to get him where he needed to go and back to get Ana and Stacy somewhere safer.

He struggled up the metal stairs, praying for an open door. Six floors. Ground floor and second floor had been locked. Third, fourth, and fifth were too. Jonah flattened himself next to the door and rested a moment.

The back of his head leaned against the metal door. With his eyes closed, he struggled to take a deep breath or two before heading up to the last floor. He gripped the handle and prayed it was open. He twisted the knob.

Locked.

His eyes landed on the stairs that continued up to the roof. He hadn't wanted to go that far. The wind would whip every direction, full force, and he'd be lucky to stay upright. Ana and Stacy wouldn't have a chance. Jonah took another deep breath and started for the roof, thanking God and his lucky stars the stairs went all the way to the top.

Bracing himself, he went up the last few steps. As his head breached the top of the building, the wind hit him full in the face, whipping rain into his eyes.

The waning beam of the flashlight cut through the droplets enough to make sure he didn't trip over debris littering the roof. Was there access to the interior of building from up here? Surely there was.

Stumbling from a particularly strong gust of wind, Jonah went forward. He made it around about half the roof line when he saw it. A door. Leading to stairs. He hoped.

He prayed.

But would it be unlocked?

Reaching for the knob, he prayed even harder. Twisted. And nearly wept in relief when it pulled open.

Jonah only took the time to make sure there was room for them in there. Emergency lighting still worked and there were the stairs. At the bottom would be dry sheets. Towels. Food. Maybe even a working land line.

He swung his backpack off and left it inside. After finding a piece of debris to prop the door open - just in case - he took a deep breath and went back into the driving wind and rain. Finding the opening in the roof and climbing back down the stairs took less time than going the other direction.

Ana and Stacy huddled together against the door.

"Come on!" he yelled, not more than two feet from them. "There's access on the roof!"

Ana nodded, struggling to her feet before reaching for Stacy.

He wanted to take some of her burden. Maybe her backpack or the dogs, but it would be more difficult to trade now than to just get up to shelter. Instead, he reached for Stacy. But the little girl stuck close to Ana. The walk back up the stairs took more time but he had to give them credit. They put one foot in front of the other. Over and over.

When they neared the roof, Jonah took the lead. He had Stacy thread her fingers through the belt loops on the back of his pants. Ana did the same, sandwiching the girl between them. He could help break the wind, protecting them just a bit from the worst of it.

That had been his theory, his desire, but the wind came from all different directions. A swirling vortex. Stinging pelts of water had to be hurting both of them. Finally, they reached the door, still propped open by that debris. With a crash bar on the inside, Jonah let it close behind them as they all made it out of the storm.

"How are the puppies?" Stacy's first question popped out as she reached for Ana's poncho.

Jonah stopped her. "First, let's get downstairs to a dorm room where we'll be more comfortable."

Stacy waited for him to cut the rope holding her to Ana then started for the stairs. The dim lighting was enough, though barely. The little girl gripped the railing as she took the steps. While he'd left it propped open, water had begun streaming in, wetting the linoleum. Rivulets ran down the staircase, but soon it wouldn't be a worry.

Jonah turned to look at Ana. She leaned over with her hands braced against her knees and her side pressed against the wall.

With her head covered by the hood from the poncho and ball cap, he could barely see her face. Her eyes were closed, and he was sure those were tears running down her cheeks, not just water.

He might have to reassess his opinion of her. Beautiful? Without a doubt. Smart? Yes. Charming? Vivacious? Capable of looking good on television? Yes to all of those things.

Spoiled rich girl who refused to get her hands dirty?

Maybe not.

Jonah opened his mouth to ask if she was all right when a cry sounded down the stairs.

Ana bolted before he could move, taking the stairs with the agility of a mountain goat. He was only a step behind, but came to a screeching halt when she did, seeing what she saw. What had made Stacy cry out.

A gate barred their exit from the stairwell into the hall way.

They were stuck.

Chapter
Twenty-Two

*I*f Ana could have cried harder, she would have.

As it was, tears had been streaming down her cheeks since the moment they stepped in out of the wind. She wanted to sob but could not find the energy. One look at Stacy's stricken face told her it would be the wrong move anyway.

Every ounce of positivity she had ever possessed went into her next words. "Look on the bright side. We are out of the rain. The wind cannot get to us here. Just by being inside, we can get relatively dry even without towels. The power is out, but we have emergency lighting. We will be all right until the storm blows over."

If they had enough medicine for Stacy.

And the rescue crews could find them.

And the building did not blow away.

And...

She knew she had to put a stop to the million runaway thoughts.

Stacy's words penetrated her fog. The dogs. Ana pulled her poncho off, praying with all her might that the three little ones had not already succumbed. First, she pulled Lexi-dog out of the satchel, handing her to Jonah. Jonah took the now wiggly bundle of wet fur and tucked her close, bending so Stacy could pet her head. The little girl had been remarkably still as they walked, as though she somehow understood what was needed of her.

But now, her shrill barks echoed through the cinder block hall.

Reaching for the smaller bag, Ana breathed a sigh of relief as she noted movement. She pulled out one tiny puppy then another followed by the third. All still alive. In just a moment, Lexi-dog was settled on the floor, allowing her puppies to nurse.

All three of the human occupants of the stairwell pulled off their outerwear. Ana found herself wishing she could take her jeans off. Was there anything worse to wear than wet denim? Stiff, now-dry denim would come a close second.

"Do you have that other flashlight?" Jonah's voice caught her attention and she handed over the small key chain LCD light. He used it to examine the lock on the gate and look around for any way to get through.

Ana sank to the stairs, three up, and stretched her legs out in front of her. Her head leaned against the wall, her eyes closed, and she felt her whole body go limp. What she would not give to get through that gate and into one of the beds on the other side.

The crashes of thunder could still be heard, but no longer carried the bone-rattling intensity they had outside.

"I think we're stuck in here," Jonah told them, handing her the little flashlight back. "The gate's locked and I don't think we could break it down. I know I don't really have the energy to try right now."

"We are inside," she told him, her eyes closing again. "We are safe. That is the important part."

"I know."

She could not see with her eyes closed, but knew Stacy sat on the floor next to Lexi-dog and the still-nursing puppies. Soon, they would have to find something dry for the dog to curl up on with her babies.

"What time is it?" Stacy asked.

Ana did not even look at her watch. It was not water proof and likely had expired some time earlier.

"I don't have my watch."

One of Ana's eyes opened to look at Jonah. "You do not have a watch? You always have one."

How did she know that? Had she been paying that much attention to him and his accessories?

"The battery died the other day, and I haven't had a chance to replace it. I tossed it in my suitcase before we left. My phone is at the office in the school. I left it there."

"Mine is in my purse." Also left behind. When they realized where Stacy was, the two of them had left without stopping to grab anything.

"It doesn't really matter, I guess." She could hear Jonah digging through his backpack. "Let's get this mama settled." The quiet conversation between Jonah and Stacy told Ana he had found something dry for her to lay on.

Ana wanted to help, but her muscles were quivering masses of gelatin. She thanked God she had gotten as far as she had before collapsing.

"Can you tell if the puppies are okay, Dr. Jonah?" The fear in Stacy's voice echoed Ana's fear for all of them.

"I'm a kid doctor, Miss Stacy, not a puppy doctor." Ana could hear him moving around. "But they're alive. They just ate. I can't promise they'll be okay if we don't get out of here soon. For now, though, I think they're fine." More movement. "I'm more worried about you, though, kiddo. Let's check that blood sugar."

Ana tried to open her eyes, to make sure Stacy was all right. It was a losing battle. She drifted, their voices coming from a great distance as she succumbed to the Sandman's call.

"What do you mean?" Christiana wanted to close her eyes as the military commander gave her the update. She wanted to scream. To do *something*. To order someone else to do something.

To *find* Ana and Jonah and little Stacy.

"We still can't get across the river, ma'am."

She expected they would not be able to. The rain still came down in sheets at the palace. Christiana could not imagine what it was like in Ravenz-Sea.

"What does the radar look like?" She had looked at it herself, but she had never paid much attention to what the colors meant.

"There is a bit of break coming soon, but not enough for us to get a helicopter over there. Not yet. It is *possible* we will be able to get across the river then if it lets up long enough, but I doubt it."

"So what is the plan?"

"Ma'am, the only thing we can do is wait and pray."

The answer she expected but not the one she hoped for. "Keep me posted."

"Of course, ma'am." A click told her the line had disconnected.

Christiana tugged the rubber band out of her hair before pulling it back into another ponytail. Rarely was she so casual, but after being awake for nearly a full day worrying about Ana, Jonah, the little girl, and the rest of her people caught in the path of this storm, she did not much care. If she went on television, she would have to, but for now she had Jonathan to do that for her. She rested her hands against the table in front of her, leaning against them as her head hung down.

"You need to get some rest, ma'am." Alexander's voice cut

through her thoughts, dragging her out of them.

"My people are out there. How can I rest when they are struggling for their lives? When it is my fault they are trapped?"

"You can't know that, Your Majesty. The neglect started when you were young. You couldn't have stopped your uncle when you were twelve. I checked. That's when the funding for that particular bridge was cut."

She turned, folding her arms around her. Staring at the window only turned it into a mirror. The darkness of night combined with the clouds from the storm and the light behind her meant she could only see herself. Bedraggled. No make-up. Stress showing in every pore. If she was closer, she would likely see blood shot, red rimmed eyes. Her cheeks held the pink stain of recent tears.

Behind her, Alexander stood looking at her, not the window. The compassion on his face warmed her desperate heart. He was a good man in a storm. Literally. How had he come to be in her inner circle? Less than a year ago, she had known him casually. They had met a number of years earlier at the house of mutual friends, but he had not known who she was then. Not until the day she left. There had been a few lovely moments of possible connection, though he was several years older. At sixteen, she had been too young for him at the time. Nothing would have happened between them, regardless. But when he found out who she was, a wall had gone up. He had treated her with the same deference and distance so many others did.

But something had changed. Suddenly, he was around regularly. She knew Tony trusted him.

Maybe that had something to do with it. Tony knew he could trust the outsider as he investigated her uncle.

Her phone buzzed and she pulled it out of her pocket. A text from the main man in her life made her smile. He was thinking about her. He wished he could have whisked her away from everything going on so she would not have to deal with the stresses.

As sweet as the sentiment was, she needed to be here, to be doing whatever she could to help those living through the worst of this storm.

"Ma'am, you need to rest." Alexander opened the door behind him. "I know you are anxious for information. Your apartment isn't far. We will get you at the slightest change or bit of news."

She shook her head. "No. I need to be here."

"Then at least lay down on the couch in your office."

Christiana hesitated, then nodded. Just a few more minutes and she likely would not be able to keep her eyes open anyway. As she passed Alexander, she noted a hint of a smile on his face and realized this had likely been his goal all along. He would have known she would refuse to go to bed but might agree to the couch. Before long, she had kicked off her shoes and stretched out.

"Give me your phone." Alexander stood over her with his hand outstretched.

"Why?"

"If anything happens that you need to know about, Tony, Jonathan, or I will make sure you know about it."

Too tired to argue, she handed the phone over, closing her eyes again. Breathing deeply, she let herself sink into the beckoning darkness of sleep. Yes, she was the queen. Yes, she was ultimately responsible. But it was nice to know there were people she could lean on when she needed to.

Letting the nothingness overtake her, she slept.

"What are you doing?" Jonathan walked into the outer office to find Alexander with an open laptop, plugging a phone into it.

"Backing up the queen's phone."

It seemed like an odd time to do such a thing, but Jonathan supposed they needed something to fill the hours.

"I missed the press briefing. How did it go?" Alexander didn't look up as he clicked the mouse.

"Fine. There's not much to tell. Few reports are coming in except for heavy rain and flooding. We have few specifics except for the bridge. We have no word from Ana and those with her. I answered a few questions about what the plans are as soon as the weather lets up. The next briefing won't be until after dawn."

"When is the storm supposed to break?"

Alexander didn't know? He'd been following it like the rest of them, hadn't he? "Not until noon or a bit after."

"The helicopters will be ready to go as soon as the weather allows for flight?"

"You were there when Christiana talked to the military commanders." He crossed his arms in front of him.

"I was." Alexander glanced up. "I was working on something else at the same time."

Jonathan sensed a secret in the words, but knew the other man wouldn't share. "Yes. They'll be ready. They already are, just in case the weather breaks earlier than expected. Pilots are rotating readiness status. They just need a window in the weather."

A frown crossed Alexander's face as he stared at the screen before he glanced back up. "Good. Have you talked to Queen Adeline?"

Who did this guy think he was? But Jonathan knew he was one of the few people Tony trusted implicitly with the queen's safety. "Not in a few hours. Charlie insisted she needed some rest. They'll call when she wakes up, or I'll call when we know something."

Jonathan did his best to keep his mind off what Ana could be going through. Likely cold and wet, she would be scared. He prayed she wasn't also hurt. Or worse.

He knew the possibility existed that she was already dead, but he refused to believe that - or to even give time to those thoughts.

Alexander looked up again. "Could you go get Tony? I need him to see this."

Jonathan tossed an annoyed glance Alexander's way, but the other man was completely absorbed in what he was doing. Muttering something unseemly, he headed out the door and for the security office.

Ana felt something warm on her hand. She struggled to open her eyes to see what it could be. When she managed to crack them, just a bit, Lexi-dog was licking her fingers where they dangled over the step.

She could not have slept long and every portion of her body ached in ways she did not know were possible. Turning to look for the rest of her little group, she found Jonah seated much the same as she was, but he had a little girl on his lap. With his arms wrapped tight around her, Stacy rested her head on his shoulder.

Tears filled Ana's eyes. Again. But this time it was for a different reason. He would make an excellent father someday. His care for children was evident to anyone, anywhere. Not just because of his profession, but because he genuinely cared for them. Deep inside, a longing to be the mother of those children rose inside her, though she knew it could never be. She could admit to herself that she had fallen in love with him, but she could not spend her life with a man who undermined and belittled what she wanted to do.

After a few minutes, Lexi-dog let out a little yip and Ana rescued one of the pups as he inched too close to the edge of the step.

"Why are you precious things up here?" she whispered. "The floor would be safer."

"She's partial to you." Ana looked up to see Jonah watching her. "She wouldn't stay down there once the puppies were done eating. You did such a good job protecting her, she wanted to be near you."

"How long did I sleep?"

"Not very long. Maybe an hour." He glanced down at the still-sleeping little girl. "I have to go back out."

Ana blinked as she tried to assimilate that. "What? Why?"

"She needs food, not just the little bit we brought for her."

"She can have mine." The offer was instantaneous. She could do without for a day or two if she had to. Stacy came first.

"She could have mine, too. But it's not enough. We only have a couple more protein bars left. We didn't expect to get stuck."

"And there was nothing at the orphanage that would have helped," she finished for him. "What are you going to do?"

"Try to find a car I can break into."

"What? You cannot break..." Ana stopped the thought. This was life or death. Whatever damage was done she would help pay for. "Why?"

"If I can get a tire iron or a crowbar, I might be able to get the gate open. The SUV didn't have either." He shifted until he had both arms under Stacy. "But I need to go."

"Wait until morning? Even with the clouds, there will be sunlight."

"I can't wait that long. She needs to eat, and I'm afraid the water may rise too high for me to get where I need to."

Before he could hand her over, Ana stood. "Let me sit on the floor. It will be safer for all of us."

Once situated, Ana held out her arms and took Stacy from him as he laid her on Ana's lap. He gently moved Lexi-dog and the puppies, too.

"Take the little flashlight. We will not need it."

Jonah hesitated. "And if the emergency lights go out?"

"We are in a confined space. We will make do much more easily in the dark than you will outside."

He looked at it, then nodded. "Thanks." Two steps up, he stopped and turned. "Pray for me?"

Ana smiled at him. "I have not stopped."

Jonah came back down the steps and knelt next to her. "I know." He leaned over and before she knew what he planned, he kissed her.

Short and full of longing for...something more she could not put her finger on. A relationship?

In the dim lighting, she could see his dark eyes had turned even more serious. "I love you, Ana. I'm not sure what the problems are between us, but if we make it out of this alive, I want to find a way to work them out." Another kiss and he left.

Ana closed her eyes and her muddled mind tried to make sense of it. When she realized she could not, she instead succumbed to sleep once more.

Chapter
Twenty-Three

*S*tupid!

Just what a girl, a princess no less, wanted to hear while trapped in a life or death situation. *I love you*, his inner self mocked. She hadn't said anything back. Not that he'd given her much chance. Something he'd done had put a wall between them, but he still had no idea what it could be. After wracking his brain for hours on end over the last few days, he had come to no conclusions.

Bracing himself, he opened the door to the outside. Was it his imagination or had the wind died down some? Another gust countered his first thought. Once onto the fire escape, he stopped for a short breather.

On their walk to the dorms, he knew he'd seen cars parked in driveways or on the street, but would they have been swept away? Could he find one now? Would he have to break into a house? Jonah knew he would do what he needed to. His nearly empty backpack would be full. Even if he found a crowbar, he would still try to find some food. Wasn't there a bait and tackle type shop nearby? Or a convenience store? Petrol station? He'd feet less...icky? Not a very manly word, but he'd feel less icky than breaking into someone's home.

Hugging the tree line held several advantages, a bit more protection from the wind being the main one. But it was harder walking. At least on the paved drive, he had firmer footing. Finally, he chose that route. As the water began to lap over the top of his sturdy work boots, he needed all the help he could get to stay upright.

By the time he reached the main road, the water was to his mid-thigh and he thanked the Lord again for Ana and Stacy's relative safety. The little flashlight worked better than the one he'd abandoned but still fought a losing battle against the nighttime storm. He would be on top of a vehicle before he saw it.

But then he saw one. Just a glimpse through the trees with a flash of lightning.

Encouraged, he slogged on but when he saw it, his heart fell again. Upside down. It would be too difficult to get to anything. He knelt down to make sure no one was in the vehicle, breathing a sigh of relief when he saw it was empty. Using the car as a bit of a wind break for the moment, he tried to reconstruct the layout of this part of town in his head. Where was he?

If only life came with a "You are here" sticker.

Orienting himself as best he could, he headed away from the river and toward the residential area. He was more likely to find a car there, wasn't he? Deliberating with himself for a few moments, he decided to take a paved pathway up a small hill and through a partially wooded park. He had explored it just two days earlier with Matty. Praying he wouldn't get lost, Jonah headed that way.

Forcing one foot in front of the other grew easier as he went uphill. Water still ran down the trail, but it no longer reached even his ankle at the worst points. The trees whipped around him, but the break from the wind itself was much needed. He reached the clearing with playground equipment. Eerily still and freakishly frenetic with every crack of lightning. Swings moved in directions they were never designed for. The tall metal slide rocked with each new blast of wind. When he reached the other side and started back downhill, Jonah thanked God everyone else had gotten out.

With little to fill his mind outside of the wind and rain, he found himself thinking back over his relationship with Ana. When had it all gone wrong? She responded to his kisses, seemed to enjoy their dates, charmed the head of the ER for him. And been honest with him all along. She had feelings for Jonathan, too. Jonah believed her to be falling for him moreso than the other man, but he still couldn't figure out when that changed.

Ahead he could see the end of the path. The rising water testified to his downhill movement. Matty had told him where it came out, but they hadn't come this far earlier in the week. Another flash of lightning made him want to sink to his knees and cry for joy. A little store. Not much. Just a few necessities, most likely but it would be enough.

But when he reached the building, the door was locked. The windows wouldn't break. No rocks, no anything he could use to help shatter them enough to get in.

Discouraged, but not defeated, he trudged back to higher ground and found a sturdy stick. A sense of urgency rose inside. He needed to get back. He'd been gone at least an hour already, probably a lot longer. All along, he'd prayed Ana and Stacy would sleep through most of his trek.

Jonah stumbled back into the small parking lot, landing on his hands and knees in the water, still managing to scrape his hands. He could feel the bits of rock and asphalt rubbing in the wounds as he struggled to his feet. It took several minutes of feeling around, but he found the stick again. Praying for forgiveness, he held it up like a baseball bat. He'd hit a few home runs in his day, even a walk-off one or two, but this could well be his most important swing. The noise behind him stopped his forward motion and lightning flashed as he turned.

To see a double barreled shotgun just a few feet away.

"Don't move."

Jonah dropped the stick, one part of his mind registering the splash as the water splattered his already soaked legs. His hands in the air, he turned slowly to face whoever stood behind the barrels.

"I said don't move. When I shoot, I don't miss."

Jonathan gripped the podium and wanted to "reach out and touch someone." But he wanted to deck them. He didn't think that counted. And he knew he needed to keep it under control.

"The queen is sleeping?" the reporter asked again. "How can she sleep at a time like this?"

Praying for patience, Jonathan kept his voice even. "Everyone knows you cannot make your best decisions when you are exhausted. The queen was up until just a couple of hours ago, going over contingency plans and conferring with military and civilian leaders. Some of those communications were lost due to the storm and all of the decisions that could be made had been made. She protested, but it was decided it would be best for her to get some rest before it was time to actually begin deploying assets. There is nothing she can do at the moment except watch and worry with the rest of us. As difficult as it is to do, I would recommend the same for everyone who is able. Get some rest. When the storm breaks, it will be better to be well-rested."

The reporter still looked furious.

Jonathan didn't care.

Hopefully, the people would understand.

He pointed to a different reporter. "Yes, sir?"

"What about Princess Anastasia, Dr. Fontaine, and the girl with them?" The man held his pen over his notebook.

"We have had no word since the princess and Dr. Fontaine left to search for the little girl." He pointed to another reporter. "Yes, ma'am."

"Do you have any idea just how many people are trapped on the other side of that bridge?"

Jonathan shook his head. "No, ma'am. To the best of my knowledge, the only people we are aware of are Princess Anastasia, Dr. Fontaine, and the girl, but a thorough search will be made when we can get troops and other personnel into the area."

After another few questions, he wrapped it up. There was no information to give really, not at this point. In a few hours, when the sun came up, there might be more, but not until then.

He headed back to the queen's office, just a few feet away. Alexander was still in the outer office, doing something on his laptop. The queen's phone was still plugged in. Tony had been and gone several times. They wouldn't tell him what they were doing or what they were concerned about.

"I set your laptop up on the conference table in the queen's office. There's a land line in there as well."

Jonathan felt like he was being sent to the kids' table. Like he wasn't supposed to notice he was being shifted to the side. But he went into the office and to his computer. A text came in on his phone and he picked it up, dialing the familiar number.

"Hello, Jonathan."

He closed his eyes and prayed for peace. "Hi, Mom."

"Why aren't you home, Jonny?"

Had she been drinking? "You know why I'm here. I was home to do some work for the Montevarian crown. Now, I'm in Ravenzario doing work for Queen Christiana and Queen Adeline."

"I need you here, Jonny." No, she didn't. She needed someone to pander to her, something Jonathan refused to do even when he was nearby.

"I don't know when I'll be home. If there's news on Philip or if I have business there, I'll be there." For now, his course work was being done via long distance. Adeline's asking the university president to cooperate sure helped.

"Your brother is dead." Her words slurred, but lacked conviction.

"What are you talking about, Mother?" If there had been news, he would have heard.

"He has to be dead. He wouldn't do this to his mother if he wasn't."

Jonathan pinched the bridge of his nose. "We don't know that, Mom. He could be anywhere. Maybe he fell and got hit on the head and has amnesia. No one knows."

She rambled on for a few more minutes before Jonathan noticed another text come in. One he needed to deal with. "Mom, I have to go. I'll call you soon. Promise." And maybe she'd be sober.

They hung up but he didn't even replace the receiver before dialing another number. "Can I speak with Prince Charlemagne, please? I had a text from him."

"Yes, sir." The operator clicked off and Montevarian music took over.

"Jonathan?" Charlie's voice came on the line.

"What's up?"

"Any news?"

"You know I'd call you."

"I know, but I had to check. Addie won't sleep much longer. I wanted to tell her I'd talked to you."

"Sorry, man. No news." Jonathan ran a hand through his hair. "I wish we did. You'll be my first call. Or someone's anyway."

"Thanks." They talked for a few more minutes as well, before Charlie asked the question Jonathan knew it had all been leading up to.

"Are they still alive, Jon?"

Jonathan blew out a breath. "We have to believe they are. We'll keep praying until we find them."

"Before she went to bed, Addie told me she had a gut feeling something was very wrong. Her gut is usually right."

"I know." After good-byes, they hung up and Jonathan turned to stare out the window.

His gut was telling him something was very wrong, too.

And there was nothing anyone could do about it.

"Ana?"

The sleep-filled voice woke Ana from her light sleep. She looked down at the little girl. "Hello, princess."

As she hoped, smile crossed Stacy's face. "I'm not a princess. You are."

"You are right. I am. But you are, too, you know."

"I am?"

"You are a child of God, correct?" She knew from talking to Stacy's mother that the woman had been a believer. Stacy's conversations about Jesus let her know the girl was, too.

"Yes, ma'am."

"Well, if you are a child of God, you are a child of the King. And little girls who are children of the King are princesses."

Stacy snuggled in a bit closer. "I guess I am a princess, then."

Ana kissed the side of the little girl's head. "Yes, you are."

"Where's Dr. Jonah?"

Ana hesitated. She didn't want to tell her, but Ana knew she had to. "He went to find some food."

The little girl looked at the gate. "Where?"

"He had to go outside."

Tears filled her eyes, and the little lip trembled. "Is he gonna be okay?"

"God will take care of him. Even though we could hardly see outside, God can see us. He knows and He's got us in the palm of His hand." She hugged Stacy closer.

"Promise?"

"Of course." Ana knew that could mean all sorts of things. He could take all three of them Home or He could see all three of them to safety in just a few hours.

"I'm hungry, Miss Ana."

She helped Stacy move to the side and reached into the backpack. "Jonah has a few more bars for you."

Stacy tore off the wrapper and ate it quickly. "Aren't you going to eat, Miss Ana?"

Though her stomach gave a different answer, Ana shook her head. "I will not eat right now. Perhaps in a little while." If Jonah came back with enough for all of them.

Stacy finished her bar and sat down next to Lexi-dog. The dog licked her hand. "Did you feed her?"

Ana mentally chastised herself. "The food you brought is in the bag. Why don't you feed her?"

The girl did just that. Lexi-dog did not eat much, but she was not a very big dog either. "What about water?"

For all the rain outside, they did not have much water to drink. "What if we took her up and let her drink near the top of the stairs?" Not a first choice, but she did not know how else to handle it.

Stacy seemed to be thinking about it for a moment. "I think that's a good idea. Can you carry her?"

"Of course." Ana picked up the little dog and carried her to the top, Stacy on her heels. Lexi-dog lapped up the water standing there on the floor. After a few minutes, she looked up and wagged her tail, then started for the stairs before she stopped.

Turning to look at the door, Lexi-dog's ears perked up and the only way to describe her posture was rigid and at attention.

"What is it?" Ana asked her, knowing she could not answer.

A thump. From outside.

Ana found herself at attention too, reaching for Stacy and stepping in front of her. "Go down the stairs," she whispered. "Take Lexi-dog."

Stacy reached for the dog but she wouldn't go. "She won't come."

"Then you go. Get down in the corner."

Without another word, Stacy followed instructions. Lexi-dog stood at Ana's side, a low growl coming from her throat. Ana wished she had something to use as a weapon, but there was nothing.

A few more thumps and indistinct shouts.

Fear gripped Ana's heart. It was not Jonah. It could not be. Who would he be shouting at? There was too much noise for just one man. The feeling intensified as she heard scraping against the door and more yelling. She still could not make out the words, but they came from just on the other side of the door.

A second later, the handle began to turn. Light blinded Ana, causing her to cry out and duck, shielding her face.

Another shout. One she still could not understand. And then...

"Are you Ana?"

She managed to look over. A mountain of a man stood in the doorway. She could not see his face. The flashlight kept him obscured. Behind him, she could see a sky still filled with black clouds but lighter than it had been.

It must be morning.

She blinked rapidly, trying to take it all in. "Pardon?" she finally asked.

He took a step closer and Ana had to look up to see him. A long, scraggly beard covered his face and he wore an army green slicker.

"I said, are you Ana?"

Darkness tried to envelop her, but she thought of Stacy, of the dog now yipping at her side. She drew herself to her full height. "I am Ana."

He turned and yelled something outside. He moved farther in and she could see two more men coming through the door, another man hanging between them.

The first man through spoke. "We found your doc."

Ana gasped as she recognized the unconscious man. Blood ran down his face, mixing with the rain water. She ran two steps forward until she could reach for him.

"Jonah!"

Chapter Twenty-Four

Christiana opened her eyes to see a sliver of dawn out the window. Just a tiny bit less black and a little more gray. How long had she slept?

The clock on the wall was little help since she had no idea what time she laid down.

"You're awake."

She sat and turned to see Jonathan at the conference table to the side. He had a laptop open and papers spread all around.

"Any word?" she asked, even knowing there would be no news. They would have woken her.

"No, ma'am. There's still at least three or four hours before the storm lets up most likely. Even then, they're not sure how long before the winds die down enough to get the helicopters up, but if the sea calms down enough they *might* be able to get a boat close enough to get on shore even if the dock isn't standing. Forces are waiting to go at the first chance."

"Thank you."

Jonathan smiled at her. "Why don't you go take a quick shower, ma'am? You'll feel better."

She gave him a small grin. "And look better?"

"You said it, not me." He grinned back. "I know better than to tell the queen she's not looking her best."

Christiana laughed. Something she needed very badly. "You did not have to tell me." She stood and stretched, facing the windows, watching the angry waves visible in the increasing light. Turning, she started for the door. "Thank you for your help, Jonathan."

"My pleasure, ma'am."

Rather than going back to the apartment she still hated, Christiana wished she could go to the cottage that was her home for so long. She had spent more than one storm there, cut off from the outside world unless she was willing to dash for the palace without cover. She rarely did. Her uncle had taken care of all the emergency planning and rebuilding.

She came to a complete stop. Had he really helped rebuild when necessary? Or had the national government shirked their duties there, too? Would Parliament have let him?

"Can I help you, ma'am?"

Christiana turned to see a nervous looking maid. She forced herself to relax and smile. "No. Thank you. I was lost in thought." A closer look showed strain around the woman's eyes. "Are you all right?"

Something akin to a smile crossed her face. "Yes, ma'am."

Christiana did not believe her. "Please. If there is something I should know, please tell me."

"Oh, no, ma'am. It's nothing for you to worry about."

"Which means it is something to you. Please?"

The woman looked right and left, as though looking for someone listening to her. "It's several things. My husband was recently laid off. His company had ties to your uncle. They knew nothing of what was going on behind the scenes, but they lost the contracts and people lost their jobs. The country is better off now, we both know this and are glad, but it has hurt our personal economy." She wrung her hands together. "It hasn't been easy but we're making it."

Christiana frowned. "What company did he work for?"

"Buccaneer Enterprises. It's a ship building company primarily."

She nodded. "I know of it. I know the owner." Quite well, though she would not tell anyone else that. "Perhaps I can talk to the owner about his job?"

"Oh no, ma'am. There were people there much longer than he was who would deserve it much more. We get by better than many of them will. It hasn't been that long. Most will find new jobs, I'd imagine."

Her opinion of this woman grew. She thought of others before herself. "Can you write down as many names and as much information as you can? I will not be able to do anything until after everything from this storm is sorted out, but I will see what I can do for all of them."

The woman's eyes grew wide before she bobbed a curtsy. "Thank you, Your Majesty. The victims of this storm must come first, but I cannot tell you how much I appreciate even the sentiment." Something else lurked behind the tears shining in her eyes.

"What else?"

"I'm sure you have much more important things." She shifted from foot to foot. "You've already done too much just by promising to see what you can do."

Christiana drew herself up to her full height. Not very intimidating, but she gave her best queen look. Also not very intimidating, but perhaps enough. "I would like to know."

The woman acquiesced as the tears began to fall. "I have family in Ravenz-Sea. I haven't heard from them since yesterday morning."

With a sympathetic nod, Christiana reached out to rest a hand on the woman's shoulder. "I understand. I grew up with Princess Anastasia, you know. She is missing at the moment, too."

"I know. We have been praying."

"What are you supposed to be doing right now?"

"I am headed to the south hearth room, ma'am. I'm to dust in there."

"Skip it. Go to my office, and ask for Alexander Bayfield. He has the list of everyone at the shelter at Ravenz-Sea."

"They won't be on it, ma'am. They own a small store and would have stayed to protect it from looters."

"Would they help others they came across? Or shoot them on sight?"

She looked shocked at the suggestion. "Help them, ma'am!"

Christiana smiled. "Good. Perhaps Princess Ana and her companions have found safety with your relatives."

Wide-eyed relief crossed her face. "Oh, that would be wonderful."

"Go to my office anyway. Relay the information to Alexander and he will check the list from the shelter anyway. Are you familiar with the area then?"

"Oh, yes, ma'am. I grew up there."

"Then tell him I said you may be able to assist with deciding where to send the search teams when we can get them in. If you have any down time, write down the information about your husband and his coworkers."

She shifted again, uneasiness visible in her movements. "I'm afraid I'll get in trouble for not doing my job, ma'am."

"Let me deal with that. Tell Alexander to notify your supervisor. If you have any troubles, come to my office and see me."

Her face brightened. "Oh, thank you, ma'am."

After saying good-bye, Christiana started for her apartment

again, before turning. "You know, I do not know your name."

The maid turned and smiled. "Jeshua, ma'am. My mother was convinced I would be a boy named Joshua."

Christiana tilted her head. "Does Joshua mean 'God saves'?"

"Yes, ma'am."

"Does Jeshua?"

"Yes, ma'am."

Peace washed over Christiana. "I have a feeling God is going to use you, or your family, to help save others today, Jeshua. Thank you."

Jeshua bobbed another curtsy. "I hope so ma'am."

"Me, too," Christiana whispered, watching Jeshua nearly run toward the offices. "Me, too."

Ana found herself shoved to the side as several more people tromped in. There was Mr. Friendly, the first man. The next two carrying Jonah, and three women carrying two children in their wake. With women and little ones, they could not be all bad could they?

The door swung shut and she turned to look at the leader. "What happened? Who are you?"

Mr. Friendly shoved the hood of his slicker back and pulled off a knit cap. "Ma'am, I'm Terry Klefstad and this here's my family. Your doc came to our store lookin' to break in and take supplies."

Ana put her hands on her hips and glared at him. "He would not break in if there was any other way. He was looking to take care of me."

"Oh, I know that, ma'am. He jest didn't need to break in, that's all." The two men carrying Jonah set him down gently. "We 'bout turned the shotgun butt on him, but he told us he was looking for supplies for a gal, a little girl, and a new mama dog." He bent down to ruffle Lexi-dog's fur. "I suppose this is the mama right here."

The coil of fear slowly began to unwind. "Yes, it is."

Mr. Friendly held out his hand. "It's a pleasure to meet ya, ma'am."

Ana shook it. "Likewise."

"We packed up supplies and headed this way with the family but Dr. Jonah there slipped and fell as we got to the bottom of the fire escape. He knocked his head, but we knew where we were headed by then."

Desire to know more warred with the need to take care of Stacy. "Do you have food?"

"Yes, ma'am." He turned to one of the women. "This is my wife, Penny. Her sister had diabetes when she was a kid and their dad has it now. She can help the girl." He looked around. "Where is she?"

Ana breathed a sigh of relief. "She went down the stairs until she knew you were not dangerous." Penny smiled at her and said hello as she headed down the stair well, a small child in her arms.

Terry tossed back his head and roared with laughter. "Aw, honey, I'm about the least awful man you'll ever meet. I'm just a good ol' boy from Louisiana."

"Loo-zee-anna?"

"Lou-wee-zee-an-na." He pronounced it much more carefully. "It's one of the southern states in the U.S."

"Right. Of course. Is that near Texas?" All of the men burst out laughing. She looked from one to the other. "What?"

"Oh nothin', missy. Louisiana and Texas are next door neighbors and rivals goin' back for 'bout ever."

"Oh. Dr. Jonah was raised in Texas."

Terry chuckled. "Oh, I know. But we'll help 'im anyway. My sister-in-law, Ms. Martha, she'll help him out."

She turned to see the other woman tending to Jonah.

Stress began to bleed off as she realized she was no longer alone. Someone else could help shoulder the load.

One of the other men opened his pack and handed her what seemed to be a prepackaged sandwich. "Ham and cheese," he told her.

Not her favorite but as she ripped it open, she knew nothing would ever taste quite so good. "Thank you," she muttered around her mouthful of food.

"This is my brother, Jayson." Joshua clapped the man on the back and nodded to the other man helping Ms. Martha with Jonah. "And that's my brother-in-law Jason."

She shook her head. "That is too many Jasons."

"It is." He took his slicker off and ran a hand over his head, droplets of water spraying everywhere. "Folks call me Terry and call my brother Thing One and the other Jason over there Thing Two."

Ana swallowed. "Oh goodness! I could not do that."

Terry chuckled again. "Why don't we go check on that little girl you got with you and leave these boys and Miss Martha to tend to the doc?"

They went down the stairs to find Penny talking with Stacy. The girl sat cross-legged with the puppies sheltered in her lap. Penny must have given her a sandwich because she happily munched on one.

"Look, Miss Ana! Food!" The girl's smile made Ana smile.

"I know. Mr. and Mrs. Klefstad are quite nice to bring us food, are they not?"

Penny looked up at Ana and gave a nod. "My sister works in the palace so I know a bit how all this works, ma'am, but I've never met royalty, especially not royalty from somewhere else. I'm still not quite sure how to address you."

Ana settled on the floor, her back against the wall by Stacy.

Lexi-dog climbed into her lap. "Ana is fine. You have brought food and supplies. There is no need for formality."

Terry studied the gate. "I think we can get through here with the crowbar. I left it outside, though. Didn't want to scare ya too much." He winked at her. "I'll be right back and hopefully we can get in."

Ana leaned her head back and blew out another breath as Terry took the stairs two at a time. True to his word, he reappeared almost immediately with one of the other men. Ana did not know which one. Several minutes after that, they had broken through the gate and into one of the rooms. Terry, big rugged mountain man though he appeared to be, picked the now-sleeping Stacy up with the utmost tenderness and carried her into the dorm room, laying her on one of the beds.

"Why don't you lay down for a bit too, Miss Ana? You look tuckered out."

"If that means exhausted, I am." She lay on the other bed watching as Lexi-dog jumped up next to Stacy, and Penny set the puppies down to nurse again. She closed her eyes, and this time the sleep sounded much nicer with the soft bed underneath.

"We can take care of everything here and get us set up to be rescued soon as they can get here."

"They are coming?"

"Of course, they are, ma'am. We have a battery radio with us and have been listening. Jonathan somthin' or other has been givin' updates. Sounds like both the queens are pretty frantic about ya."

Her mind refused to function properly. "Both queens?"

"Yes'm. Your sister and Queen Christiana are both wishin' ya were home safe. If I were a bettin' man, I'd bet there are troops or rescue personnel of some kind just waitin' for the storm to break. We'll fly some sheets so they can see us from the air or land."

"Thank you, Terry. You are mos..." Her words trailed off, and she could not make herself wake up enough to finish her sentence. Instead, she sunk into the dark and rested.

Pounding.

Pain.

Intense.

Soft.

All assaulted Jonah at once as he struggled to come to terms with his surroundings.

Names jolted him.

Ana.

Stacy.

Lexi-dog.

Terry. Penny.

Jayson? Jason? Martha? More children?

Who were they?

With a groan, he tried to sit up and only succeeded in making the throbbing worse.

"Hey, there, Mr. Doc. Don't try to get up just yet." The gruff voice was familiar but Jonah couldn't place it. Until he remembered the shotgun.

"Terry?" he whispered.

"Yes, sir."

Jonah blinked his eyes open. "What happened? Where are we?"

"You fell about the time we got to the fire escape. We got into the dorm rooms. You're sleepin' in one now."

"Ana? Stacy?" He made himself sit up. "Her diabetes!"

"Are under control." He explained about his wife's experience with the disease. "All ya need to do is rest and recover from that bump on your head."

"What about the storm?"

"It's lessenin', but not enough for rescue just yet." Terry helped him take a few sips of water. "Why don't you just rest? We got this, doc."

It grated on him, but he had no choice. Not really. "Do we have any pain medicine?" Terry found some ibuprofen, and Jonah swallowed three before lying down on the bed. "Wake me up if you need me?"

Terry chuckled. "We won't, Tex. But sure. If we need you, we'll get ya."

"Thanks." Why had the other man called him Tex? Right. They were from Louisiana. Small world.

Jonah had no idea how long he hovered between awake and asleep, but he didn't drift off, not completely. He could hear the voices, a bit of laughter. Thunder, though not as intense as it had been during the night. It had to be near noon. Surely rescue would be here soon.

Finally, he could take no more and sat up. This time he was alone, but the pain had abated somewhat. He managed to get to his feet and followed the noise down two rooms to find Stacy playing jacks with two other girls. Ana sat on the bed talking with another woman. She seemed more put together than the last time he'd seen her, though it was obvious they'd all been through an ordeal.

Then he realized he'd heard a radio. "What're they saying?"

All the heads turned to him and Stacy jumped up. "Dr. Jonah! You're all right!"

He hugged the girl. "Of course I am."

"I'm so glad!"

"I'm so happy you're okay, too, sweet girl." He looked over at Terry. "What's the latest?"

"They expect the worst is over and the storm to be done

enough to launch rescue teams in the next few hours."

Jonah closed his eyes and sent his thanks heavenward. All of them sat around playing games or just talking as the storm began to obviously subside out the windows. The rain didn't beat down quite so hard. The windows didn't rattle quite as much. Soon.

They were safe and dry, but he wanted to get Ana out of there. He'd realized the reality some time earlier. *He* had gotten Ana into the situation, but *he* wouldn't be able to get her out. Someone else would do that. Terry and his family had gotten her to comfort. Paratroopers or helicopter rescue would get her out of here and back to the palace.

He couldn't do it. Others had and would.

And with that realization came the realization that he would never be enough. Never be good enough. Never be close to what she needed.

Something niggling in the back of his mind pushed its way to the forefront. "Terry, you told me Jayson owns the store, correct?" He turned to the other man.

"Yep. Sure does. We live about ninety minutes from here."

"I see." He turned to look at the other man. "So why were you here? Just to protect from looters?"

"Nah." Terry reached in the bag and pulled out an apple, handing it to Jonah who took it gratefully. "We saw Miss Ana there talkin' about how this area was gonna get hit real bad so we packed up and headed this way. We did some sandbaggin' near the middle school then crossed the bridge right before they stopped folks. Jay could've taken care of the shop by himself, but we figured there might be other folks over here and we could help a lot faster than rescue folks could. The shop is on high enough ground we weren't too worried 'bout it."

Terry shook his head as he pulled another apple out of the bag, snapping open a pocket knife at the same time. After slicing off a sliver, Terry looked at him. "Pretty amazin', ain't it? We came because of Princess Ana there askin' for folks to come help, and here we were able to help her and her friends out."

Crunching into the apple, Jonah turned that over in his head. He'd told Ana the time spent on television was a waste. That her time, everyone's time, was better spent *doing* something. "Terry?" He had to know.

"Yeah?"

"Would you have come if it had been some civil servant asking instead of a princess?"

Terry snorted. "Of course." Jonah knew it. "But..." Terry took another sliver of apple from his knife. "...the only reason Penny was watchin' the news was because she'd heard the princess was gonna be on and wanted to see why."

Right.

So the only reason the whole family was here, including Penny with her knowledge of diabetes, was because of Ana's appearance on the news.

Something to think about. And he would.

When the rhythmic thumping in his head died down.

Then it clicked.

The thumping wasn't in his head.

It was outside.

Lexi-dog jumped to attention and barked for all she was worth.

Ana looked at him. "Is that...?"

"Helicopters?" Jonah nodded and turned to see Terry had already left, the other men in his wake.

Stacy didn't look out the windows, but put the puppies in the purse and tried to encourage Lexi-dog into the satchel. The dog refused. Jonah wouldn't let Stacy leave without the black and white furball, though.

A slender man in Army green came through the door, helmet on his head. "Princess Anastasia?"

Ana had tears on her cheeks. "Yes."

Jonah closed his eyes and felt the stress bleed off as the man answered. "It's time to take you home, ma'am."

Chapter
Twenty-Five

*M*a'am?"

Christiana looked up to see an aide she knew, but could not name, with his head inside her office door. "Yes?"

"They have been recovered and should be here shortly."

If she had been standing, her knees would have given way. "Pardon?"

"The princess, Dr. Fontaine, and the girl are on their way here. That's all I know, ma'am."

She shot to her feet and stormed out of her office and down the hall to the conference room being used as headquarters. She pushed the door open and barged in. "Why was I not told?"

Alexander stood, his hands up. "We weren't sure they were going to be able to get there, yet, ma'am. We didn't want to tell you until we knew they could."

"When will they be here?"

"About twenty minutes. The press has been told where to be and when but not why. The speculation is that the princess will be returning. Jonathan will hold a press conference after we've had a chance to talk with them for a few minutes and get the bare details."

"They are all right?" She had to know. "Nothing is wrong?"

"Nothing serious."

Christiana sank into the chair next to her. "Thank God." She looked over at Alexander. "What about Jeshua's family?"

"I have not heard anything, ma'am. I do know they were with other people, but I don't know who."

"Can you try to find out please?"

"We'll ask as soon as they get here." Alexander gave her a look she did not know how to interpret. "It's almost over, ma'am."

"Thank God." She closed her eyes and sent a prayer heavenward. "But it is not. We will have a number of other people still trapped elsewhere. There will be property damage. How many other bridges need to be inspected? Can the funds be confiscated from Henry? He was lining his own pockets, was he not?"

"He was," Alexander confirmed. "We are tracking the money down and retrieving it."

"How much is his in his own right?"

"Not much. He had very little personal wealth when your parents died. He received a stipend and his living expenses were covered very well while he was regent. There was a fair amount likely accumulated legally, but the vast majority was not. What we can recover will be put into a fund to help pay for the things that have been neglected and to help the people who have suffered as a result."

She nodded. Before they could go on, word came that the helicopter would be arriving momentarily. Christiana followed Alexander to the portico on the side of the palace where it would land. She could see the press off to one side, under another awning set up to shield them from the rain. They shouted questions but she did not hear them well enough to answer. She would not have if she could.

The thump-wump of the rotor blades filled the air as the helicopter descended. It landed on the grass several yards away. The door slid open and a paratrooper in olive green jumped out then reached back to help Jonah then Ana out. The wind still whipped around though not nearly as strong as it had earlier. The paratrooper reached back in and brought out the little girl, handing her to Jonah. Jonah took Ana's hand and the three of them ducked their heads in the drizzle as they walked to the overhang where Christiana and Jonathan waited. As they reached it, Christiana and Jonathan turned and walked inside with them. Greetings could be done out of the public eye. Stewards waited with blankets and cups of hot chocolate. A doctor waited in the hearth room as did a roaring fire. As soon as they got there, Ana turned and Christiana gave her a big hug.

"I am so very grateful to see you, cousin."

Ana squeezed her back. "Thank you for sending the helicopter."

"Of course. I could do no less. Are you truly all right?"

"Yes. Tired, dirty, hungry, but otherwise no worse for the wear. Is my sister frantic?"

"Yes. I spoke with Charlie a few moments ago. They would like to video conference with you as soon as possible." Christiana could feel Ana shivering, and her clothing felt stiff.

Ana gave her another squeeze and turned when the doctor spoke to her. Christiana watched as Ana went to the other side of the room to where Jonah and Stacy sat with the physician. She caught some movement out of the corner of her eye and turned to see Jonathan watching the trio. With that, she knew - and she knew Jonathan knew - there was no future for him with Ana.

The hot water streamed over Ana, warming her to the core.

After washing her hair for the third time, she finally began to feel *clean*. She'd talked with her sister for a minute and would be leaving for Montevaro as soon as it could be arranged. First, she needed to talk to Jonathan, and they would hold a short press conference. Stacy would be kept out of the limelight, but she and Jonah would answer a few questions. With her hair pulled back into a low ponytail, she dressed in a warm sweater and slacks her mother would approve of.

She exited into the main living area of Christiana's apartment to find Jonathan waiting for her. He sat in one of the chairs with a tablet in one hand and making notes on a pad of paper with the other. He glanced up. "Do you feel better?"

"Much. Thank you."

He set the tablet and notepad on the table in front of him and stood. "I'm glad you're all right."

"Thank you for everything you did to find us."

"I didn't do much. Just kept the press updated mostly."

She dipped her head, unable to look him in the eye. "Still, thank you."

He blew a breath out. "There's no future for us, is there, Ana?"

Her eyes filled with tears at the pain and resignation in his voice. She shook her head. "No. I am sorry, Jonathan. I have fallen in love with Jonah, and even if he and I cannot work things out, I do not believe you and I will ever be anything more than friends."

"That's what I thought."

She finally looked up to see the sadness on his face. "I am sorry, Jonathan. The last thing I want is to hurt you."

"I know." He reached out and tucked his finger under her chin. "But I want you to be happy, and I'm sure you will be with Jonah." Leaning over, he brushed a kiss against her cheek. "But now they're waiting on us."

"Of course." She followed him out of the apartment and to

the press room. Jonah waited in the hallway just outside. He looked between her and Jonathan with an impassive look on his face.

Jonathan checked his watch. "We have about two minutes. We'll all walk in together. I'll make a short statement for the queen and then open the floor for questions. No more than fifteen minutes. The plane will be waiting for both of you when you're done."

"What about Stacy? Where is she?"

"She's taking a bath and being taken care of by Jeshua who is a relative of the family who helped you."

"What will happen to her?" An invisible hand squeezed Ana's heart at the thought of the little girl being left with strangers.

"I'm not sure." He tapped out a message on his phone. "By the time we're done here, I should have an answer for you."

"Her mother wanted to be buried in Montevaro. I want to make that happen, and I want Stacy to be there."

Jonathan tapped a bit more. "I'll have more information afterward." He checked the time again. "Let's go."

Ana gave Jonah a small smile, and they followed Jonathan into the press room. They stood to the side while Jonathan went straight to the podium.

The next twenty minutes were not the most pleasant of Ana's life, but she had been through much worse in the last few days. She and Jonah answered questions the best they could, thanking those who helped find them and prayed for their safe return.

When they made it back to the hallway, she turned to Jonathan. "Well?"

Before he could answer, Alexander joined them. "Your Highness, arrangements have been made for Stacy to return with you as well as for her mother's remains to be transported as soon as possible. I'm afraid the remains will not return to Montevaro with you today, but they will soon."

"Thank you."

"We have also made arrangements for Lexi-dog and the puppies to join you. I'm not sure about the quarantine requirements on the Montevaro side, but I'm sure your sister will figure something out." He told them the little dog had belonged to an older woman who was moving into an assisted living home in a few days anyway. She had worried about what would become of the little mama. When Alexander offered to pay her, she refused and said the dog was her gift to the little girl.

Ana made a mental note to do something to compensate the woman somehow. She could not help but give Alexander a hug. "Thank you," she whispered. She would not have guessed how attached she would have become to those little dogs. When she let go, Jonathan had disappeared. Alexander walked with her and Jonah to a side door where Stacy waited for them.

The little girl ran to her. "Miss Ana!"

Ana knelt on the floor and held out her arms. "Oh, Miss Stacy. I am so glad to see you."

"They said I get to go to Mon'varo with you?"

A sudden fear struck Ana. "Do you want to?"

The girl clung tighter to her neck. "Yes."

"Then you shall, and the dogs will get to go with us."

"Oh, thank you, Miss Ana!"

A car waited just outside and it took them to the airport. The Montevarian plane waited on the tarmac. By the time they left the ground, Stacy had fallen asleep snuggled against Ana. Ana brushed her hair off her forehead before looking over at Jonah. "How is your head?"

"It hurts some but the medicine is helping."

"I am glad."

Before she could go on, Jonah spoke.

Nothing like an apology to make a guy humble. "I need to

apologize, Ana." Jonah glanced up at her.

She tilted her head to the side. "Why?"

"For not believing what you do has value."

"Pardon?"

"I know I goaded you into this trip by saying your job as a spokesperson wasn't as important as actually getting out there and doing something. I can't tell you how sorry I am you were in danger or how wrong I was. The Klefstad family was only in Ravenz-Sea because of your spot on the news about needing volunteers. Without you on the news, they wouldn't have been there when we needed them." He still hadn't completely reconciled the thought, but he was getting there.

"I am glad they were there."

There was more to say, but this wasn't the time to say it. He could see Ana's eyelids starting to droop. "We don't have a long flight, but why don't you try to get some rest?"

Her eyes fluttered closed. "I think I will."

Jonah watched Ana sleep, Stacy snuggled in next to her. Purple smudges under her eyes told him how exhausted she was. Long sleeves covered her arms, though he knew there were scratches and scrapes all over them from their trek. A yip pulled his attention back to Lexi-dog who stayed in her crate at the insistence of the pilot. At least he hadn't required her to be in the small cargo hold. Jonah used the phone to check on Rachel, Louis, the other kids, and the rest of the team. Everyone was okay and glad to hear Jonah, Ana, Stacy, and the dogs were, too.

It didn't take long before the plane began its descent. As they walked down the stairs, he held a still-sleeping Stacy in his arms and followed Ana. In the distance, he could see reporters and well-wishers behind a chain-link fence on the other side of the tarmac. Ana waved at them as they walked to the waiting car.

No one else waited in the car. Carrie and Marty exited the plane behind them and climbed into one of their own.

"I need to make sure everyone knows it's not their fault,"

Ana muttered.

"Whose fault?"

"Carrie and Marty. I purposely misled them so I could sneak off. They are not to blame. Addie and Rick have both done the same from time to time without anything more than a lecture."

"They were never in such danger, though, Ana." He wanted to reach for her hand, to tell her the queen and her parents wouldn't be angry with her, but he doubted that would be the case.

"I know." She stared out the window as they drove toward the garrison. "I guess I am hoping that the fact we are all right and their relief will mitigate their anger."

"I hope so."

Stacy shifted against him as they reached the open doors of the garrison. Her eyes blinked open. "Where are we?"

Ana's face softened as she smiled at the little girl. "We are almost to the boat that will take us to the palace."

Her eyes went wide. "A boat?"

Jonah chuckled. "Yep. A boat will take us to the palace."

Stacy nodded, quite seriously. "I met the queen."

"Queen Christiana?" Ana asked her.

She nodded again.

"My sister is queen here in Montevaro."

Stacy shifted next to Jonah. "Will she like me?"

Ana leaned forward. "She's going to love you, just like I do."

Jonah suspected Stacy wanted to ask Ana if the princess could adopt her, but didn't dare. Good thing she didn't, because Ana would have to say no. The car rolled to a stop and the door opened from the outside. Ana stepped out then turned to help Stacy. The three of them walked to the boat, with Stacy clinging to Ana's hand.

Stacy pulled up and turned back toward the car. "Where's Lexi-dog?"

"She was in the car behind us. She'll be on the boat when we leave."

Stacy reluctantly turned and let Ana lead her toward the boat. Jonah followed them across the gangplank where the captain waited.

He bowed at the waist. "We are all so very thankful you are all right, miss."

Jonah could hear the smile in Ana's voice. "Thank you, Captain. I am very grateful to be this close to home."

The captain knelt down in front of Stacy. "Well, now, little missy, I'm told this is your first time on board a boat." Stacy nodded. "Would you like a tour? We have a few minutes."

The girl looked up at Ana and back at him. "Can I?"

Ana ran a hand over the top of her head. "Of course. But make sure you find us before we leave. I want to make sure you have the best seat in the house for the trip across the lake."

Stacy gave her a hug then ran off, hand-in-hand with the captain.

Jonah followed Ana into the interior of the boat. "She loves you, Ana."

Ana's arms hugged her stomach. "I know. I love her, too."

"You said something before about if you were married you could adopt her."

"Yes. I did." She looked out the window toward the garrison. "Some time ago, Jonathan and I discussed an arranged marriage of sorts."

Jonah felt sucker punched. She was going to marry Jonathan. She didn't love the man, but she was going to marry him anyway.

"But I told him before we left that there could be no future for us." She still didn't turn around.

Jonah barely let himself hope. "Oh?"

"I do not love him. It is possible that we could grow to love each other, but it is equally likely we would remain friends and little more for the entirety of the marriage. Given the desire of both of us to have children that would make for some awkwardness at best."

Jonah moved closer to her, the front of his shirt brushing against her arm. "Is that the only reason?"

For what seemed like an eternity, she didn't answer. "No," she finally whispered. "There were other reasons."

"Reasons? Several?"

Ana shook her head. "No. Just the one."

"Which one is that?" His heart thudded to a stop as he waited for her answer, praying the whole time he knew what it was.

"I am in love with another man."

Chapter
Twenty-Six

*A*na did not dare look up at Jonah. He stood so close.

"Oh, Ana," he breathed.

Before he could say anything else, their privacy was interrupted by staff members bringing supplies on board and Stacy running into the room.

"This boat is awesome, Miss Ana!" Ana turned to see the girl running toward her. She held open her arms and Stacy jumped into them. "I love it. Can I ride on it every day?"

She and Jonah both laughed. "I do not know about every day, sweetheart, but I will make sure you get to ride sometimes." Even after Stacy found her forever home, Ana would make sure the little girl got to visit from time to time. They went to the front of the boat, where Stacy could see the palace as it came into view. As expected, she oo'd and ah'd, jumping up and down and clapping.

Ana wondered at her energy. After the trauma of the last few days, all Ana wanted to do was sleep. Stacy seemed energized. Perhaps Charlie's daughter and her nanny would be around to spend some time with Stacy. Ana hugged her tighter.

"Sweetheart, when we get to the palace, I'm going to need to talk to my sister and my parents. It will be quite boring and I am certain you would rather do something else. I will make sure someone takes very good care of you, though."

"I want to stay with you." Stacy moved closer and rested her head on Ana.

"I know but Dr. Jonah and I have some people we need to talk to. I think you'll really like my niece. She's a very sweet girl and maybe she can show you some of the super special stuff about the palace."

Stacy's voice filled with awe. "She knows super special stuff?"

"Yes. In fact, she found a tunnel hidden in the walls of the palace. One that no one had been able to find for several hundred years."

"That's awesome!"

"I agree. I think you and Lindsey will get along well."

Ana hoped it was true. If Stacy and Lindsey did not get along, it could be problematic.

The boat slowed as it neared the dock on the island. They disembarked and were met by Danica, one of the many assistants to the royal family. She bobbed a curtsy. "It is so good to see you, Your Highness. We were all quite worried."

Ana wanted to hug the woman, but refrained. She had known Danica for many years, but there were too many people around and it would embarrass her. "I am very glad to be home."

"Your family is waiting in the blue room."

Ana held Stacy's hand and started down the hallway. "Is Lindsey there?"

"Yes, ma'am. Her nanny will be waiting for the young lady."

"Thank you."

They turned several corners before Stacy asked, "Are we there yet?"

Jonah laughed behind them, and Ana smiled. "Almost."

A minute later they walked into the blue room. Glad cries

came from all around as Ana's family descended on her. Hugs came from every side.

Addie and Charlie both gave her quick hugs. Rick's hug lasted a long time. "I'm so glad you're okay, sis."

She squeezed him back. "I know you are."

"We prayed hard."

"I know you did. We did, too."

After Rick, her parents both gave her very formal hugs, though her father clung a bit tighter.

Ana introduced Lindsey to Stacy, who was fascinated by the older girl. The two of them left with the nanny, and the rest of the group sat around the room. Ana sat on one of the couches, leaving plenty of room for Jonah. He chose to sit on a chair nearby.

Addie started the conversation. "Ana, we need to talk."

Ana nodded. "I know and I need to apologize to all of you. I tricked Marty and Carrie, leaving without their knowledge or consent. What happened is in no way their fault. Please know that."

Rick chuckled. "I can relate." He squeezed Ellie's shoulder. "I've put Dennis and Steve through more than they care to mention."

"And I met Charlie when I snuck away from Mark and Todd and got into an accident on an ice-covered road." Addie relaxed against her husband. "We have all been incredibly blessed to have nothing bad happen when we have gone against the wishes of our security teams. However, we cannot be sure that will always be the case. We all must make sure to listen to them. They have only our best interests at heart. We all know our security details have far more than their jobs in mind, but also our safety and well-being." She turned and looked at Ana. "Will you tell us what happened?"

Ana and Jonah spent the next few minutes taking turns telling the story.

As they finished her father stood, using his cane to make his way to Jonah's side. He held out his hand. "Thank you, sir, for taking care of my daughter."

Jonah stood and took her father's hand, but shook his head. "It's my fault she was in the situation in the first place, on several levels. You should know that your daughter is a remarkable woman. She fared far better than I expected and never complained. She never blamed me, though she could have." He turned to look at her. "On the flight back, I watched some of the footage of her as a spokeswoman in the hours before the storm hit and from when she spent time in the States. She is poised and confident and very good at what she does."

Ana felt her cheeks burn as she ducked her head.

Her father spoke next. "Yes. She is. I am very glad you can see the value in what she loves."

Jonah's voice was soft. "I haven't always, but I'm learning just how wrong I was."

Silence settled over the group. Ana yawned. Her mother would likely have something to say about it later, but she did it anyway. She could not help it.

Her father chuckled. "Go get some rest, Anastasia. We will have a late dinner together this evening." Even though Addie had taken over as queen, their father still reigned in the family dynamic.

"I need to find Stacy first."

Danica spoke up from the back of the room. "She is sound asleep in your apartment, ma'am."

That relieved Ana. The little girl needed her rest.

After a few minutes of goodbyes, Ana went to her bedroom in the apartment she shared with Rick until his Christmas Eve wedding to Ellie. The covers had thoughtfully been turned down for her. She changed into the pajamas left out and slid under the covers, sighing as she relaxed into the pillow. Pulling the covers up around her shoulders, she prayed for dreams of Jonah or possibly Stacy and not the nightmares she feared would come.

The royal family offered Jonah a place to sleep, but he politely refused. He needed to get home and check in with Louis and everyone still in Ravenz-Sea. He also needed to get back to the hospital. Sara was coming in for a follow-up appointment, and he wanted to be there. Instead of heading back to his apartment, he turned the borrowed car toward the hospital. Ana's comment about being in love with another man reverberated through his mind. Could she possibly mean him or was there another man in her life Jonah knew nothing about?

He parked in the garage attached to the hospital and put his business card on the dashboard since he didn't have a placard with him. A few minutes later, he walked onto the pediatric floor, hoping to slip to his office unnoticed.

But no such luck.

One of his favorite nurses, and grandmother to everyone on the floor, saw him and squealed. "Dr. Jonah! You're back!"

Jonah laughed and hugged her. "I am."

"We didn't expect you in today."

"I hadn't planned on it, but I heard Sara was going to be here." One more squeeze around her shoulders and he dropped his arm. "Are they here yet?"

Her face dropped. "Sorry, Dr. Jonah. They left a little while ago."

His disappointment was profound. "Anyone else around I need to see?"

"Nope. Everyone is being well taken care of and there's no one here you've seen before. You should head home and get some rest."

A wave of exhaustion hit him. "I think I will before anyone

else sees me." Jonah turned too quickly and his head began to throb. He needed to remember that he'd been through a trauma recently. By the time he made it home, the adrenaline had completely worn off. He took some pain medicine and collapsed into bed. Text messages had told him he didn't need to be at work for a couple of days. He'd sleep until he woke up. Eat. Then sleep some more.

And for thirty-six hours, he did just that. Slept. Ate. Repeat. When he woke up two days after returning, he finally took his phone off "Do Not Disturb." Certain calls and texts would have come through, but none had.

Including one from Princess Ana.

He had her set up on his preferred contact list, didn't he?

Flipping his finger upward on the screen, he scrolled through the messages. Most were friends checking on him. A few were unknowns. Listening to the voice mails let him know the press wanted to talk to him. But he didn't want to talk to any of them, not yet. Jonah wanted to call Ana, but they left things so uncertain between them. Would she welcome the contact? Had she done the same thing he had and slept the last two days away? And what about Stacy?

He checked his email rather than making a decision. *It's not avoidance*, he told himself.

But when he saw Ana's name pop up in his inbox, his heart skipped a beat. It was a short email, just saying she didn't want to bother him, but to call sometime. She included a picture of Stacy with Lindsey and freshly-painted fingernails. The little girl looked so happy. Jonah sighed. He knew Stacy wanted to live with Ana permanently, and it had nothing to do with her royal status.

A thought skittered across his mind. In one side and out the other. But as he went through the rest of his emails, the thought kept coming back, over and over, until the idea took root. He stared out the window and wondered if he could actually make it happen.

Because he had a feeling this could change his life.

Chapter Twenty-Seven

C hristmas Eve dawned bright and clear. Ana relished the last few moments in bed. It would be a busy day. In just a few hours, Rick would marry Ellie. The little chapel in the palace was perfect for the two of them. Just family and a few close friends, and, Christmas evening, they would take off to Greenland for a month-long honeymoon. Ana would be the maid of honor, a title offered when Ellie's best friend was unable to leave the Springfield, Missouri airport. A snowstorm had grounded flights through much of the Midwest. Ana knew Rick was glad his wedding had little of the fanfare Addie's had. Her father had to be glad, too. He would stand up with Rick.

A discreet knock on the door let her know it was time to get up and get ready for breakfast with the other women in both families. After a quick shower, she dressed in a pantsuit and low heels. She met Stacy in the little kitchen in her apartment.

"Hi, Miss Ana!" Stacy was way too chipper for this early in the morning. "Merry Christmas Eve!"

Ana gave the little girl a big hug. "Merry Christmas Eve." She held out their hands and looked at Stacy's clothes. "You look very nice today."

"These aren't my wedding clothes." The serious tone of her voice made it hard for Ana to contain her smile.

"I know. And you will look lovely in those clothes as well. Dr. Jonah will think you're the prettiest girl there."

Stacy giggled. "Dr. Jonah loves you, Miss Ana. He'll think you're prettiest."

Ana struggled with those words as they walked out of the apartment and toward the breakfast room. She had barely seen Jonah since their return. Between her schedule and his work at the hospital, and several other doctors taking sick as a stomach bug worked its way around, they had precious little time together. He came by most evenings to spend a little bit of time with her and Stacy, but there had been no chance to finish the conversation started on the boat after their return.

She and Stacy were the last two to arrive. Ellie looked nervous. Adeline looked pale. Their mother...well, she always looked a bit displeased if anything was not exactly the way she wanted it. And she had wanted another large church wedding with all the pomp and circumstance of Addie and Charlie's. Rick, for once, had put his foot down. He and Ellie wanted small and intimate. He had threatened to run off and elope if Mother did not "butt out."

Lindsey and the rest of the Brewer women were much more relaxed. Stacy took off to see the newly minted Duchess of Cassalonio. The title was Adeline's gift to her step-daughter. As queen, she was free to do as she pleased, but everyone seemed struck by the timing of it. Why had she waited rather than doing it after the coronation?

Ana had little time to think about it as the announcement came that breakfast was ready. She took her seat next to Stacy and tried to rebuild a bit of the protective shield around her heart. Even as she did, she knew it was too late. One day soon, probably after the first of the year, she would have to turn Stacy over to Family Services and a foster home until a permanent family could be found. Ana had gathered the courage to ask Addie if she could proclaim an exception to the "no single parents that are not immediate family" regulation, but Addie hesitated to do so. She had not come right out and said no, but Ana held out little hope.

Laughter filled the room, though Ellie continued to look both nervous and possibly a little scared. Ana would try to talk to her brother's fiancé before they separated to get ready. Ana, despite her maid of honor status, would not be one of the ones helping Ellie prepare. That honor went to her family members.

The rest of the morning passed quickly. Ana slipped on the silver dress she had planned to wear anyway. There had been no time to get a dress that matched the one the original maid of honor was supposed to wear.

The family stylist she worked with from time to time also helped Stacy get ready. The little girl really did look like a princess. Ana almost wished she had a toy tiara for her to wear, but no sense in getting everyone's hopes up. The hug from Stacy told her it was still too late, no matter how many times she had explained it. Family Services had agreed she was in excellent hands and would wait until after the first of the year to place her with a foster family. Ana and Jonah had decided, along with several others, to wait until after Christmas to have the memorial service for Stacy's mother. She would be buried in a few days, but until then, Stacy seemed to be doing better, and they had not wanted to risk sending her into a depression right before Christmas.

Before she knew it, she stood just outside the little chapel. Ellie would arrive in a few minutes but most of the guests were already seated. Jonah had not arrived, though his text message said he was on his way. Notice had come from security that he had passed through their checkpoint. He and the last few guests were on their way across the lake.

Her twin brother entered the ante room and tears filled her eyes. "You look so handsome," she whispered, holding her arms out for the hug she knew was coming. "But if you tell anyone I said that, I will deny it to my dying day."

Rick chuckled and squeezed her a bit tighter. "You look beautiful, Ana. If Jonah doesn't get his head screwed on straight soon, I'll do it for him."

"Leave him alone." She did not need or want her brother interfering. "If things progress between us, that is between us, without any help from you or anyone."

Rick kept his arm around her shoulder. "Not even a certain little girl?"

Her brother and his fiancé had fallen in love with Stacy as much as Ana had, to the point Ana almost feared he and Ellie would offer to be her foster, and then adoptive, parents. Ana did not think she could handle being so close and so far at the same time.

Stacy's cry of "Dr. Jonah!" told Ana the man in question had arrived.

"I think," Rick continued, "if she had half a brain, she'd be trying to get the two of you together and adopt you both." He winked at her and turned his attention to something behind her. "Told you," he whispered.

Ana turned to see Stacy dragging Jonah across the room. "Doesn't she look pretty, Dr. Jonah?"

Jonah's expression grew soft, and he had to clear his throat several times before he spoke. "She looks beautiful."

Rick moved back to talk to her father as Jonah and Stacy approached. He stopped just a few inches in front of her. "Hi."

Jonah found he had a hard time breathing. So close to Ana. Holding Stacy's hand. Life's perfection within his reach.

"Hi," Ana whispered softly.

Noise from behind him let Jonah know it was time to be seated. "If you'll excuse us, I have a beautiful young lady to escort to a wedding.

Ana's smile lit up her face. "I am certain she'll love it."

He leaned closer. "Save me a dance?"

She nodded.

"Or all of them?"

Her eyes blinked a few times and he chuckled. "If not all of them, at least more than any other man?"

"Of course." Another whisper.

Jonah smiled at her and led Stacy into the chapel. The little girl insisted on sitting on his lap and being held as they stood to watch Ellie walk down the aisle. The wedding didn't last long, but Jonah couldn't pay much attention anyway. He was too busy watching Ana. It amused him to think the nearly two hundred guests were considered "small." All two hundred left the chapel and headed to the ballroom. Though the wedding had been small by royal standards, the ball afterward boasted a much larger guest list. Combining it with the annual Royal Christmas Eve Ball accounted for much of the guest list.

Stacy stayed with him, though she would sit at the children's table for dinner. He'd been asked to sit at the head table with Ana. Much of the younger generation of royalty had been at Addie's wedding, but only those from Mevendia and Ravenzario were at this one. Because Rick wasn't about to be crowned? Or because it was Christmas Eve and they had family things of their own to do?

Stacy pointed out the fancy dresses worn by many of the guests and told him how much she wanted a dress like one or the other. His girl certainly was a girlie girl.

His girl?

Stop it! He couldn't let himself think like that. He didn't even know if Ana loved him like he loved her. If she didn't, there was no chance Ana or Stacy would ever be "his girl."

Lindsey's nanny approached and took Stacy to the bathroom along with several other young children in her care for the evening.

"There you are."

He turned to see Ana, her shimmery silver dress hugging her curves until it flared at her waist. He rested his hands on her hips. "You look beautiful."

"Thank you." She tweaked his bow tie. "And you look quite handsome."

Before they could talk any further, the dinner was announced. Jonah hid his smile as he caught a glimpse of Rick and Ellie kissing just outside a hidden entryway. When everyone had been seated, a voice filled the room announcing the arrival of Prince Richard and his bride. Jonah saw the two of them break apart, sheepish grins covering both faces when they noticed his attention. He winked, and that seemed to put them at ease.

Dinner went quickly and before he knew it, the couple was dancing their first dance.

He leaned to Ana. "May I have the next dance?"

She smiled and nodded, hurrying to finish her conversation with her older sister. Addie looked a bit peaked. Jonah would have to talk to her about it later. Before he had time to mention it, Charlie stood and reached for Addie's hand. Jonah took that as his signal to do the same with Ana and, in seconds, she was in his arms on the dance floor.

He stared down into her beautiful eyes. "When can we talk?"

"After the ball?" He could see the unasked questions.

"Could we sneak out sooner than that? Just for a few minutes even?"

Ana glanced around. "I suppose so. In a little bit."

Three dances later, he took her hand, and they snuck out the side door. Jonah shrugged out of his tuxedo jacket and settled it around Ana's shoulders.

"Thank you."

"Don't want you to be cold." They came to stand next to the stone railing overlooking the lake. He turned to face her. "I want you to know how much you mean to me." He trailed his finger down the side of her face. "You are an incredible woman. And..." He took a deep breath. "I've said it twice before and I thought I meant it. Now, I know for sure. I've fallen in love with you, Ana."

Her sharp intake of air let him know he'd surprised her. "Do you mean that?"

He nodded. "I do. I love you, Ana."

Her hands came to rest on both sides of his face. "Oh, Jonah. I love you, too." She raised up on her tiptoes and pressed her lips to his.

Jonah slid his arms around her waist and pulled her closer, letting the intensity of the kiss build until they were both breathless. She lowered herself until she was flat on the ground, but he held her close. "Ana, you are an incredible woman. I know I said that once already, but it's true. You're kind and gentle, but tough when you need to be. I can't imagine most women being able to go through what we did a few weeks ago and being as strong as you were. I can't imagine *men*, tough outdoorsy men, doing as well as you did."

She rested her head against his chest. "Rick would have done better."

"Rick would have done my part a lot better, but taking care of Stacy and the dogs? No way." He kissed her forehead. "I am so sorry for thinking what you did with your spokesperson role was of no value. I'm sorry for trying to make you feel obligated to step outside of what you do so well because it wasn't good enough."

Ana sighed. "Oh, Jonah. I am so glad I went with you. I never would have met Stacy or the other children or seen first-hand what it is like in Ravenz-sea. I hope Christiana would have realized just how bad things had become with those bridges even if I was not trapped on the other side, but given everything that happened, she is very obviously aware. Changes are being made for the better. I am glad to be a part of that."

Jonah's guilt started to ebb away, just a bit. "I'm still so sorry I put you at risk. I can't believe your family is still willing to put up with me being around." *Thank you, God. I know I don't deserve that.*

She looked up at him and smiled. "Oh, Jonah. They do not have a choice. I love you."

He bent down and kissed her again, pouring his heart and soul into it. Jonah could feel her pouring herself back into him. Clapping from the other room made them break apart.

"That is not for us, is it?" Ana whispered.

Jonah glanced back toward the ballroom. "No. But I think we better get back. You're the maid of honor after all."

After shrugging back into his jacket, Jonah rested his hand on the small of her back. Contentment settled over him and the guilt disappeared completely. They walked into the ballroom, and Addie caught his eye. She winked, and Jonah's grin widened. He gave a slight nod, and she smiled in return. The orchestra started another song, and Jonah leaned in toward Ana. "May I have this dance, love?"

She smiled over her shoulder. "You do not even need to ask." When she was in his arms, Ana looked up at him. "Any dance, any time," she whispered. "It is yours."

"I couldn't ask for anything more."

Epilogue

Christmas Day

*A*na sat on the floor near the Christmas tree in a place she seldom visited anymore. The apartment where she and her siblings had lived growing up. Technically, as the monarch, Addie could demand the apartment for herself and Charlie, but she would never do such a thing. In fact, it would not surprise Ana to learn Addie never planned to move in, but to use the apartment she had lived in whenever she was home after she turned eighteen.

Stacy sat on Ana's lap as laughter flowed around them. The door opened and Stacy's squeal echoed Ana's internal desire. Jonah swung the little girl into his arms and gave her a big hug. He winked at her, and she ducked her head. After greeting everyone, he took a seat in the chair behind her, Stacy seated in his lap. The whole family and Jonah were there. Rick and Ellie snuggled together in a chair barely big enough for both of them, but the newlyweds would not be separated. They would leave for their honeymoon after the afternoon's visit to an orphanage concluded. Ellie's parents, brother, and sister-in-law were all there, as were Charlie's parents, the Marquis and Marchioness of

Montago.

Her father called for attention. "I know tradition calls for me to read the Christmas story, but I feel it is time to pass the honor on. I spoke with Adeline several weeks ago, and she agreed with me." He held the large family Bible - not the ancient one preserved under glass in the Hall of Kings and Queens, but the one "only" a hundred years or so old. Papa walked to where Adeline sat next to Charlie and handed it not to her, but to the Prince Consort. "Charlie, if you will accept, the honor is yours."

Ana saw her brother-in-law swallow several times and seemed to be blinking back moisture in his eyes. Growing up, Addie had told Ana many times that she wanted to marry a man who would let her be queen while still being head of their household. This was one more indication she had found the right man.

Charlie reached out and took the heavy book. "It would be my honor." The spot was marked and he opened the book. Once everyone was seated, he began to read. "'And it came to pass in those days, that there went out a decree from Caesar Augustus that all the world should be taxed...'."

Ana rested the side of her head against Jonah's thigh as they listened to Charlie read. When he finished he led the extended family in a prayer of thanksgiving. He thanked God not only for the salvation made possible through the birth of the Christ child, but for many of the changes the year had brought. It had not yet been a year since he crashed into Addie's car and even less since Rick and Ellie first met. Charlie also thanked God for Stacy and Jonah, warming Ana's heart while reminding her this would likely be Stacy's only Christmas with them.

After the prayer ended, Charlie took over another job for the head of the household - passing out the gifts. Laughter and love filled the room as they opened them. Jonah set Stacy on the ground next to Ana and whispered he would be right back. A minute later, he returned with a large box.

He set it on the floor in front of Stacy. "This one is for you, sweet girl."

Stacy glanced up at Ana then reached to take the lid off the box. Before it was off, a furry nose peeked out and Stacy squealed again. "Lexi-dog!" She pulled the dog out of the box. Lexi-dog wiggled and yipped in recognition, licking Stacy's face between kisses. After a minute of laughter, Stacy handed Lexi-dog to Ana, looking back in the box. "And the puppies!"

Jonah chuckled. "Of course. They're far too young to be away from their mama. Do you think you can be responsible for them?"

Stacy nodded seriously. "Yes. But will my new foster family let me?"

Ana's heart ached not only at the question, but the matter-of-factness of it.

Jonah hesitated then nodded. "I'll make sure of it."

Ana kissed the side of the little girl's head. "If they cannot for any reason, they can stay with me and you can visit any time you like."

"Well, that won't be necessary." Jonah seemed quite sure. "I promise."

The rest of the family started to gather up the wrapping paper, but Addie asked them to stay. "Before you go, there's something else." She glanced at Charlie, and Ana sucked in a breath. "Rick will be especially glad to hear, Charlie and I are expecting a child."

This time Ana squealed, along with many other members of her family. She could not get to her sister through the crush of grandparents-to-be. Instead she looked over at her brother who was grinning from ear to ear.

Both of his arms shot in the air, as he mouthed the words, "Everest, baby!"

Ana laughed. Her brother had longed to climb the mountain for as long as she could remember. Once the baby arrived, he would no longer be the heir and might be able to convince Addie to let him. Ellie rolled her eyes. His new wife would probably be right by his side as he trekked through the Himalayas. Ana did not want to burst his bubble, but he would be "the spare" again until the birth of Addie's second child. As second in line to the throne, he very likely would still not be allowed. The accident that killed all of Christiana's family and should have taken her as well remained too fresh in the minds of security personnel.

Finally, the crowd cleared a bit, and Ana was able to congratulate her sister and brother-in-law. Everyone started to disperse again, but this time it was Jonah who called everyone to attention.

He came to stand directly in front of her. "Ana, I have one more thing for you. Charlie thanked God for the many blessings our families have experienced this year, and you are the biggest blessing in my life." Her heart thudded in her chest. "You are an incredible woman and so much more than a princess. You are a beautiful woman of God and truly successful at anything you put your mind to." Ana clutched her stomach as Jonah dropped to one knee, pulling a box out of his pocket. "Anastasia, will you do me the honor of marrying me?"

The diamond glittered up at her, and she recognized it as a family heirloom. Her father had approved. Tears filled her eyes as she nodded. "Yes. Of course."

Jonah slipped the ring on her finger and pulled her into his arms, kissing her repeatedly, but she remained aware of her family cheering in the background.

He held her securely in his arms as he pressed another kiss to her forehead. "I talked with your father and Addie," he told her, quietly enough the rest of the room could not hear. "Addie will push for a waiver to allow you to be Stacy's foster mother until the wedding, and we can adopt her." Uncertainty filled his eyes. "If that's what you want."

More tears fell. Happy tears. "That would be perfect."

He kissed her again, and she felt her heart swell. Ana would always be a princess, not just by birth but by rebirth as a Child of the King of Kings. Now, she would be more. She would become a wife and a mother and fulfill the calling she had felt God put on her life for many years.

And she could not be happier.

Dear Reader,

Thank you for joining Princess Anastasia and Jonah in *More Than a Princess*! I appreciate you and hope you enjoyed it! This is the third book in The Montevaro Monarchy series - and concludes the stories for this family! But wait! (Goodness, I sound like an infomercial!) The stories of the royal families of Mevendia and Ravenzario will be told this year - in the series *The Brides of Bellas Montagnes*! Book 1, *Hand-Me-Down Princess,* should release early this summer with the other two books to follow shortly thereafter. After the acknowledgments, you will find a preview of Prince Malachi's story as well as chapter 1 of *Finding Mr. Write*, book 1 in the CANDID Romance series - available now!

I see a meme floating around Facebook from time to time that tells readers what they can do to help their favorite authors. Buying their next book or giving a copy away is kind of a no-brainer, but the biggest thing you can do is write a review. If you enjoyed *Along Came a Prince* would you consider doing just that? You can do so by going to the Amazon page and scrolling down until you get to the button that asks if you'd like to write a review of your own.

I would LOVE to hear from you! My email address is carolmoncadobooks@gmail.com. You can find my website and blog at www.carolmoncado.com. I blog most Sundays and about once more each month at www.InspyRomance.com. And, of course, there's Facebook and my Facebook profile, Author Carol Moncado. If you recently liked my Facebook *page* (Carol Moncado Books)...I hope you'll "follow" the profile as well. Facebook recently changed the rules again which means very few people (often 1-5% of "likes") will see anything I post there. Following the profile will show you my book updates, updates about books from authors I love, funny cat (or dog or dinosaur!) memes, inspirational quotes, and all sorts of fun stuff!! I hope to see you there soon!

Thanks again!

Until
next time,
Carol

Acknowledgments

They say writing is a solitary endeavor and it absolutely can be. Sitting in front of the computer for hours on end, talking to imaginary people.

And having them talk back ;).

But the reality is no one walks alone. Since I began this writing journey five and a half years ago, I can't begin to name all of those who've helped me along the way. From my husband, Matt, who has always, *always* believed in me and my best friend, Penny, who has brainstormed and critiqued and made me stop using passive voice more times than I can count. Others like Becki, Allen, Tina, Bobbie, Candice, the fitting room attendant at my local Wal-Mart, and so many others who encouraged, cheered, and cried with me. My mother-in-love, Andrea, who has prayed over us for years. All of the rest of my family and in-loves who never once looked at me like I was nuts for wanting to be a writer, including Gloria, my avid-reader sister, who has watched my kids countless times so I could work. Jan Christiansen (my "other mother") has always believed in me and Stacy Christiansen Spangler who has been my dearest friend for longer than I can remember.

Then there's my writer friends. My NovelSistas, Jessica Keller Koschnitzky and Kristy Cambron, both sisters of my heart. They're part of my BritCrit gals. Joanna Politano (who has talked me down off more virtual ledges than anyone), Jen Cvelvar (the best case of misidentification *ever*), and Stacey Zink (who never, ever fails to have a fabulous encouraging word) are BritCritters, too. We do a lot more living than we do critting, and I wouldn't have it any other way. All five of them are beyond gifted as writers and I thank God they're in my life. There's my MozArks ACFW peeps who laugh with me, critique, and encourage to no end. And Melanie Dickerson. What would I do without you?

Then there's the Seekers, the AlleyCats, the InspyRomance

crew, the CIA, my TSG peeps (you know who you are!), and all of the others who've helped me along on this journey.

I could go on for days about beloved mentors like Janice Thompson who has poured her time and energy into this newbie, going above and beyond for me. People like one of my spiciest friends, Pepper Basham, who inspires me daily, or Julie Lessman, who has prayed me to this point. People like Jeane Wynn (*the* top publicist in the business) and Kathleen Y'Barbo (one of the top authors) who take me along on late night Wal-Mart runs and kidnap me to Chili's so I'm writing on a full stomach. All of these and so many more are not only mentors, but *friends* - I am beyond blessed! And, of course, there's Tamela Hancock Murray, agent extraordinaire, who believed in me enough to want to be my agent.

Super special thanks go to everyone who helped it get *More Than a Princess* to this point - I know I could never name all of you! But especially to Pam J. and to Ginger V. who read this before it was even finished, and Ginger Solomon (have you read her books?! She ROCKS!), Jerenda F., and Emily N. who helped proofread.

I said I could go on for days, and I could keep going. On and on. I know I've forgotten many people and I hate that. But you, dear reader, would quickly get bored.

So THANK YOU to all of those who have helped me along the way. I couldn't have done this without you and you have my eternal gratitude.

And, of course, last but never, *ever*, least, to Jesus Christ, without whom none of this would be possible - or worth it.

Hand-Me-Down

Princess

COMING SOON!

Nothing like being a hand-me-down Princess.

The words mocked Jessabelle over and over as she stared at her reflection in the mirror.

Hand-me-down.

Passed over.

Rejected.

Unwanted.

In less than an hour she would become Princess Jessabelle of Mevendia, wife of Prince Malachi, second in line for the throne.

Not because he wanted to marry her, but because Crown Prince William had rejected her.

Twice.

Prince Malachi only upheld his family's end of the marriage contract because her father had saved King Antonio's life when they were teens.

Under no circumstances would Prince Malachi ever have chosen plain, mousy Jessabelle on his own. It was probably just as well the Crown Prince refused to marry her. She wouldn't have to be queen. Every little girl dreamed of being a princess, right? And most girls wouldn't be sitting in a bedroom in a house provided for her family by the groom wondering if she could take off out the window. Would anyone notice? Guards had been posted on the grounds to protect the future princess, but she doubted anyone cared enough to sneak in and try to get pictures of her or kidnap her. Why would they? No one even knew who she was. But would any of them care if she snuck out? Would anyone even realize it was her if it weren't for the wedding gown?

When the engagement had been announced two weeks earlier, she'd been too busy throwing up to stand next to her fiancé at the press gathering. They'd told those assembled she'd taken ill suddenly, and the press had to find their own pictures of her. They hadn't found any where she was the primary focus. Instead, blurry background photos were the best they had.

She'd streamed the press gathering on her tablet later and wondered how anyone could believe Prince Malachi had any desire to marry her whatsoever. His comments about her were very general and could have been said about anyone, no matter how much he disliked them.

The twinkle of the massive diamond on her ring finger caught her eye as she stopped a teardrop from escaping with the tip of one manicured figure. Her fiancé was supposed to have given her the ring himself right before the press gathering, but since she'd been sick, her father had left it on her dresser with a note to put it on and not ever take it off. A glance at the clock told her she had less than five minutes to wait before her father would whisk her away.

With a deep, fortifying breath, she stared at her reflection, willing it to improve. The limp, light brown hair hung straight, just past her shoulders no matter what the hairdresser from the palace tried to do with it. Finally, the woman had given up and let it be. The veil would cover it and her face so no one would see her until the walk back up the aisle.

Even her groom would have a hard time seeing her.

Two minutes earlier than she expected, the knock came at the door.

Another deep breath. "Come in."

Her father, leaning heavily on his cane, entered. She could see the tears in his eyes and wouldn't do anything to let him believe she was anything else than ecstatic about the wedding. She'd never been demonstrative, but she couldn't let him know about the pit of dread in her belly. Not just about the wedding itself, but becoming a princess and living with someone she didn't know and the wedding night and the honeymoon and becoming not just the prince's bride but his wife.

With her father's health failing, she wouldn't do anything to hurt him. Not after he'd been both mother and father to her for so many years. In some ways, she'd hoped this day wouldn't come before he took his last breath. That he'd believe to his dying day that she would be taken care of by the royal family, but once he left her, she'd be able to put the family off for a time of grieving and then disappear. Perhaps to the States.

He came to a stop in front of her. "Oh, sweet, Jessabelle. You look as lovely as your mother did on the day we married." Tears trickled down his cheeks.

His eyesight was obviously going.

"Thank you, Papa." Best to tell him what he wanted to hear.

"Come, darling. Your carriage awaits."

Right. Because a real carriage with horses and everything was waiting outside to take her to the largest cathedral in Mevendia. At least she wouldn't have to suffer the humiliation of a wedding on the huge balcony in the palace courtyard like the unlucky lady who married the Crown Prince would.

The carriage waited inside massive stone walls separating the small courtyard from the street. A footman, decked out like footmen of old, held the door as Jessabelle helped her father in then followed. As the door swung shut, the driver clicked, and the four white horses started forward. The large gates opened as though by magic to allow them through.

Shouts and flashes greeted them. She paid attention to none of it, choosing to stare at her hands where they rested amid the satin, lace, and tulle of her dress and veil. The diamond mocked her with its silent testament to what time and intense pressure could create. She wouldn't be so lucky. Time and intense pressure wouldn't turn her into a diamond but rather into a crumpled mass of coal. Unwanted and unuseful for anything except destruction.

The roar of the crowd followed them through the streets. Several members of the royal mounted guard rode in front and behind the carriage. She should wave, soak in the memories, but all she could do was stare at the ring.

Jessabelle had never even spoken to her groom, but in thirty minutes, she'd be his wife.

*

* * *

Prince Malachi Jedidiah Jonathan Louis of Mevendia stood in the anteroom near the front of the cathedral. Twenty-one-years-old, second in line for the throne - a throne he didn't want - and about to marry a woman he'd never met, never even seen.

All because of the stupid, ancient laws no one ever got around to changing.

Why would they when they always seemed to work out so well? The mocking tone he'd used with his father reverberated through his head. He looked to see his mother fussing over Yvette's dress and hair one last time. His father and older brother, Crown Prince William, talked quietly about something serious. He had no idea what. They never included him in the serious conversations. After all, he'd never be king. Oh, someday he'd probably be the Regulator Maire of Erres. Something of a cross between a mayor and governor of Mevendia's capital city, that day wouldn't come until William wore the crown.

The bishop, complete with flowing white and gold robes and funny hat, entered the room. First, he said something to the queen then to Malachi's brother and father. The king turned to Malachi, looking him up and down.

He'd be found lacking somewhere. He always was.

Sure enough, the king approached, tugged on the red vest under his black uniform jacket, and walked around making a few more tweaks to Malachi's appearance. The intricate gold crown had already been placed on his head by someone else. He didn't remember who. The entire time he'd had help getting ready, he'd stayed in his stupor. Malachi didn't want this anymore than... Well, to be fair, he had no idea if his bride wanted this marriage to happen or not. Most girls in Mevendia would give their eye teeth to have his father insisting that one of his sons marry her.

By the time the king finished brushing off Malachi's shoulders and straightening his sword, the room had emptied, leaving just the two of them. His father came around to stand in front of him, clasping him on the shoulders.

"I know this isn't how you thought this day would come about, Mal, but I did what I thought was best."

Malachi simply nodded, knowing his objections to the ancient laws requiring arranged marriages for members of the monarch's family had been raised repeatedly. And shot down. Repeatedly. Out of the three sister countries that made up The Royal

Commonwealth of Bellas Montagnes, all descended from the same family line, Mevendia was the first to allow the firstborn to take the throne regardless of gender. It was also the only one that still required marriage contracts and assorted other antiquated ideals regarding the family's relationships.

And then he was alone. His brother would be standing on the stage waiting for him to emerge when the trumpets sounded the next time. His sister would lead the processional, acting as maid of honor for a woman she also had never met.

What a farce.

A farce that would lead to either a long, happy life or, more likely, long, lonely years stretching into eternity.

The blast of the trumpets signaled time for his entrance. The doors in front of him opened, though he didn't know who opened them. He took careful, measured steps in time to the beat of the music so he wouldn't arrive at his destination too early. A sigh escaped him when he saw his soon-to-be father-in-law appear seconds before all three of them reached their assigned spots.

The music reached its crescendo and stopped with a crashing of cymbals somewhere unseen.

The bishop took a step forward, the extraordinarily large Bible in his hands. "Hear ye! Hear ye! His Royal Highness Prince Malachi Jedidiah Jonathan Louis of Mevendia takes a wife! Let any who object speak now!"

There would be no objections, but he could hear the skirt of his bride rustling on the other side of her father. Was she hoping for an objection? Or praying there wouldn't be one?

After several heartbeats, the bishop continued, bellowing to be heard despite the microphone clipped to his lapel. "As there are no objections, His Royal Highness shall pledge his honor to Jessabelle Keller! Jessabelle Keller will pledge her loyalty, fidelity, and obedience to His Royal Highness!"

Something about the differences in what the two of them

would be expected to pledge to each other struck Malachi, but he had no time to turn it over in his head.

"Who gives Jessabelle Keller to the prince?"

The gentleman next to Malachi took a deep breath and spoke, though without the volume of the bishop. "On behalf of her late mother and the adoring nation, as her father, I do." He turned to give his daughter a hug and Malachi saw part of her for the first time. Her hands clasped her father's shoulders, the excessively large diamond ring twinkling at him under the lights.

"I will be fine, Papa," he heard her whisper.

And then her hand had been placed in his.

Malachi's fingers curled around hers without being told. Together, they took three steps forward until they reached the base of the stairs. He started to go on, but she didn't move.

With skill borne of years of practice, he kept a furrow from appearing on his brow. Her other hand, the one holding a bouquet of white calla lilies, seemed to be trying to grasp her skirt and he understood the problem. He switched her right hand from his left into his right and rested his left hand on her lower back for support.

"One step at a time, slowly," he whispered. "You'll make it."

His fingers might not. They could fall off from lack of circulation given how tightly she grasped them, but after another moment they stood at the top of the stairs.

The bishop glared at their hands until Malachi switched back. What difference did it make which hand he held? Who knew, but he did know every moment of the royal wedding was steeped in traditions, some dating back to the brothers who split the kingdom into three separate nations during the time of Charlemagne.

The bishop had begun speaking again. There was no "dearly beloved" or speech about the sanctity of marriage, or how the marriage of a man and woman showed a picture of Christ's love for His bride, the church. Malachi had been to enough "regular" weddings to know things were different.

In mere seconds, Miss Keller was reciting her vows, pledging herself to him before he would be required to do the same. No chance in risking a royal pledging himself to someone only to have them not reciprocate. Apparently, it had happened somewhere in the past.

"I pledge my loyalty to His Royal Highness, Prince Malachi, and to the crown of Mevendia," she repeated, though Malachi had to strain to hear. A microphone hidden somewhere picked up the sound for the rest of those gathered. "I pledge my fidelity, all of who I am, to His Royal Highness alone. I swear to my Maker I will obey Prince Malachi in all matters in which he gives instructions. I endow upon the prince all my worldly possessions." Like his family needed the worldly possessions of another family. "I give all I have to the prince. My purity. My honor. Even my life. Upon punishment of death should I break my word, I willingly make this vow. Until the time of my death, I belong to none but the prince."

The bishop turned to Malachi. Instead of looking his bride in the eyes and pledging to love, honor, and cherish as most men did, Malachi stared at the tassel on the bishop's forehead.

"I, His Royal Highness Prince Malachi Jedidiah Jonathan Louis of Mevendia..." Why was his name so long and pretentious? "...do swear before God and these witnesses that I have chosen as my bride Miss Jessabelle Keller." Or she'd been chosen for him. But whatever. "Until the time of her death or betrayal, I pledge to her the covering of my name and my country." How much more unromantic could these vows be? And chauvinistic?! His mother had gone along with this all those years ago? Really? "Upon my honor as a member of the Van Rensselaer family, rulers of Mevendia, I will protect her with all that I am."

Malachi's mind whirred at the speed of sound. Why hadn't he looked at the vows more carefully? Not that he wanted to marry this woman, but the one-sidedness struck him. He would have to reassure her in private that he had no intention of being anything but loyal. His vows were worded as they were because the princes and kings of old had often taken several wives or concubines and wouldn't dream of pledging their fidelity to one woman.

Once William became king, Malachi would convince him to change the law.

On auto-pilot, he slipped the wedding band given him by the bishop onto her finger, repeating something inane about a symbol of his protection. She slid a band onto his finger, once again promising her fidelity unto death.

And then it was time.

The bishop led them to a kneeling bench further back on the stage. Malachi's bride knelt as he stood at her side. The bishop bellowed a few more things about how lucky she was her stars had aligned or some such nonsense.

"As her husband, Prince Malachi shall remove the covering of her father."

Right. Take off her veil. He'd been told it would be simple, but his large hands fumbled with the clasp attaching the veil to her head. Wasn't it just supposed to slide out? But when he removed the clip, her hair fell forward, leaving the veil in place. Then he saw it begin to slip and realized his error. Removing the comb attached to the veil from her hair was simple.

The bishop moved to the side allowing Malachi to stand before his bride. A circle of intricate silver leaves embedded with jewels rested on a pillow being held by the bishop. He took it and held it high, praying he could remember his line. It had sounded corny before and nearly humiliating for this woman now. "I, Prince Malachi of Mevendia," Hopefully it was still valid if he didn't use the whole moniker. "With this crown declare this woman is no longer Miss Jessabelle Keller, but Her Royal Highness, Jessabelle, Princess of Mevendia and my wife!" He set the delicate crown on her head and prayed it would stay in place, at least long enough for them to disappear into the another anteroom for the signing of the documents. At least one member of the staff would be there to help secure it, or so he'd been told.

As he tucked her hand into the crook of his arm and led her to the doorway, Malachi realized he had yet to see the face of his bride.

* * *

Hand-Me-Down
Princess

Prince Malachi Van Renssalaer of Mevendia is getting married. The problem? He's never even met his bride. His father arranged everything, right down to the marriage contract. Malachi swears to himself that he will be nothing like his father in the ways that count - including his fidelity to his wife.

Jessabelle Keller would happily spend her entire life in obscurity, but her father once saved the life of a future king. Before he dies, her father is committed to seeing that king make good on his promise to have one of his sons marry her so she would be taken care of for life.

No sooner than Prince Malachi and Jessabelle return from their honeymoon, they find themselves dealing with both private trauma and the very public drama of groundless accusations from the press. Just as they begin to weave their fragile trust back together, a ghost from the king's past arrives and threatens everything they've ever held dear.

Secrets have a funny way of coming out and this one could rip the faith of the country in their leaders to shreds. Malachi is determined to protect Jessabelle no matter what it takes, but will it ever be enough for her to not feel like a Hand-Me-Down Princess?

* * *

To be among the first to know when
Hand-Me-Down Princess

is available for pre-order at a special price, sign up for the newsletter!

Previews may not be in their final form and are subject to change.

Finding
Mr.
Write

Available NOW!

Local Woman Arrested For Stalking Favorite Author

Dorrie Miller could see the headline now. She held the phone between her ear and shoulder as she shoved a pair of jeans in the drawer. "Did you really buy night vision goggles?"

"What do you think?" Sarcasm deepened the Appalachian accent until Dorrie could barely understand Anise.

Of course she had.

Anise had bought the night vision goggles and the ear wig thingies, the ones that looked like hearing aids, and heaven only knew what else.

Within two days of being at their first major national conference for writers, they'd be cooling their heels in a jail cell, hoping no one would use their escapades for story fodder. CANDID stood for Christian Author's Network, Dedicated to Inspirational Distinction, not detention.

"We're really going to stalk this woman? I know you want to meet her. I do, too. But stalking? That's a felony." Or a serious misdemeanor. Whichever. It wouldn't be good. "We'll have restraining orders and never be able to show our face at CANDID again." Dorrie checked her appearance in the mirror once more. Passable. "And how do you know MEL is going to be at conference, anyway?"

As administrator of the Mya Elizabeth Linscott Facebook page, Dorrie should know when the author had appearances scheduled. Dorrie had read all of MEL's books so many times she could quote large sections of them. Her collection would be complete with autographs, but the only way to get signed copies was to get them off MEL's website for twice the cover price. Sure, the extra money went to charity but Dorrie still didn't have that kind of cash. Instead, she had a standing order with the local Christian bookstore to get the latest book as soon as it released.

She'd even emailed with MEL a few times. Okay. MEL's assistant, but still.

How did she not know MEL would be making her first public appearance ever?

Anise hemmed and hawed for a second or two. "Well, I don't know for sure MEL's coming. But the bookstore coordinator sent me a list of authors who are going to have books and she's on it."

"One of her books is up for a CANDID Award," Dorrie pointed out. "Those are automatically stocked. She's up for an award every year. Those books are always there." Not that Dorrie had been at the other conferences, but she knew people and heard all about it.

"I know that. But she has 'five books' in parentheses next to her name. She'd only have one if it was just the book up for a CANDID Award."

Anise had a point. "Okay. She might be there."

"Let's plan how we're going to make sure we get to meet her. And bring your copies because they have a place where you can put them to be signed."

"You really think she'll sign them for free? Everyone else does, but she never has. She gives away ten free signed copies of each book when it comes out, but that's it." Dorrie had never won, no matter how hard she tried.

"You never know."

A glance at the clock showed Dorrie she had ten minutes before it was time to leave for her fourth ever local CANDID meeting. The one she was in charge of. What had she been thinking when she volunteered to be the coordinator? Dorrie half-listened to Anise prattle on as doubts assailed her once again.

Visions of George Costanza danced in her head to a Brad Paisley soundtrack as a dull ache began to seep into the edges of her brain. So much cooler in the online world. She should stay home where no one would discover she didn't belong with the cool kids.

Online, Dorrie knew she was a blast. Always fun. Always up for something. Or pretend something anyway. There weren't any real consequences to plotting with other readers to cyber-steal a flash drive with a manuscript on it from a favorite author when nothing actually changed hands. Or to resort to bribery with her peanut butter cookies. Dorrie had been known to send a box or two. Not that it had gotten her anywhere.

Another look toward the bookcase where her first edition Mya Elizabeth Linscott novels sat, unsigned, spurred her onward. She had to go. She had to follow her dream of becoming an author. No matter what anyone, especially her dad, said about it. In two and a half months, Dorrie could finally have a chance to meet her writing hero. If she was really lucky, have two, maybe even three, minutes to pick MEL's brain about the publishing world.

"Dorrie!" Anise's voice jolted her back to the present. "Can you get the walkie talkies?"

With a sigh, Dorrie turned to the conversation at hand. "Yes, I have walkies. I fail to see why we need them if we're using earwigs."

"Back-up. You know that. Back-up your back-ups. It holds true for manuscripts and trying to meet your favorite authors."

Anise was even more obsessed with back-ups than Dorrie had ever been. The advent of "the cloud" and "cloud storage" helped, but one could never be sure it was enough. The loss of a Publisher file with hours worth of tweaks to a floor plan for her character's house proved that.

Dorrie heard something in the background. A dog barking. Dishes crashing. Followed by, "I gotta run, darlin', and I know you've got your meeting. I'll talk to you soon. Knock 'em dead."

"Ha! Love you, Licorice."

"I'm not licorice. I'm Anise."

"Pa-tay-to, pa-tah-to. Same thing." The spice, anise, had a licorice flavor to it. Dorrie rarely let an opportunity to mention it pass her by. Of course, the spice was pronounced an-iss, but her friend hailed from Appalachia and said her name uh-nese.

"Love you, too. I think. See you in a few weeks!"

They hung up. Dorrie headed from her hometown of Serenity Landing, Missouri to Springfield and her first CANDID meeting with a for-real published author as the guest.

She just prayed she wouldn't make a fool of herself.

Dorrie sat at a table in Panera Bread wiping her hands on her dress slacks. The nice ones. The ones that made her feel a little more professional than jeans or her usual scrubs. It was only the fourth meeting but who was she to think she should be the one running a group like this? At twenty-three, Dorrie felt woefully unprepared to run the local meeting of the country's premiere group for Christian writers. Unpublished. Unagented. Uneverything. And inadequate.

And with a line-up of such prestigious guest speakers coming? Why her? Right. No one else volunteered to do it.

And just one guest speaker for now, .but Dorrie had to introduce her to everyone.

So what if "everyone" meant seven people?

Kathleen Watson really was very nice. Dorrie knew because they'd been talking on Facebook for months.

Dorrie took a deep breath and jumped in. "Okay, everyone!" Her voice echoed in the almost empty room as her nerves took a beating. "I think everybody's got their food, so it's time for the Springfield Area Christian Authors' Network, Dedicated to Inspiration Distinction group to welcome best-selling, award winning author, Kathleen Watson." What a mouthful! It made her even more grateful everyone just called the organization CANDID.

The half dozen or so writers gave a polite smattering of applause as Kathleen moved to sit on the table at the front of the meeting room. "Thanks so much for having me today. I was thinking I'd tell you a bit about me, my journey to publication, and life since then. Afterwards, we'll open it up for questions."

The door opened and in walked Prince Caspian – fresh off his voyage through the Seven Seas on the Dawn Treader. Dorrie's logical side knew it couldn't be the Narnian king, but had to be his doppelganger. Her romantic side didn't care. He was, after all, about six feet tall with longish chestnut colored hair that looked silky enough for every girl in the room to be jealous, and eyes the color of Hershey's chocolate.

"Is this the CANDID meeting?" His voice, smooth as velvet, melted Dorrie's insides.

"Um, yes," she managed to stammer. "Have a seat. We're just getting started."

He smiled, though Dorrie had the impression his full grin was much more drool-worthy.

Before she realized what he was doing, he slid into the chair next to her. If he got any closer Dorrie would be wearing his cologne. Very nice smelling cologne, too. Not at all like she expected from someone who spent most of his time on a boat with a giant talking mouse.

How was she supposed to concentrate? Ask insightful questions? Keep everyone on task during the Q and A if she spent the next two hours wondering if he'd take her back to Narnia with him?

Somehow, Dorrie managed to focus on Kathleen. She talked about what the industry had been like twenty years earlier when she first broke into publishing and how it differed now.

After about thirty minutes, Kathleen looked at Dorrie. "You know what? Why don't we skip straight to questions? You guys ask me what you want to know about life as an author. I don't know all of you so why don't we do introductions, then questions?" The look she gave left it up to Dorrie.

Dorrie moved to the front of the room to direct the conversation and told them a bit about herself when one of the other gals interrupted.

"Did I see your name on the New Beginnings list?"

Heat rose in Dorrie's cheeks. "I had two manuscripts final in different categories."

"New Beginnings is the CANDID contest for unpublished authors, right?" The question came from the other new member. Dorrie didn't think she'd heard the lady's name yet.

With a nod, Dorrie confirmed the statement but turned to the next person. All but two of the other seven people she'd met several times and halfway tuned them out. The newbie who'd asked about the contest introduced herself as Julie Harders. And then they got to Prince Caspian.

"I'm Jeremiah Jacobs. I've been writing for years, but decided to switch genres to political thrillers."

"What did you write before?" Kathleen asked.

He shrugged and looked uncomfortable. "A bit of everything

trying to find the elusive voice. I think I've found it writing political thrillers."

"Good." Kathleen turned to Dorrie. "Do you want to handle the Q and A?"

Dorrie gave a half-shrug. "Up to you."

They spent the next hour asking Kathleen questions about how she came up with new ideas year after year, about what life was like on deadline, how to avoid the deadline crunch, and on and on. Two hours after the meeting began, they wrapped up, chatting a bit in little groups until an employee stuck her head in and said another group was coming in a few minutes.

Grabbing her laptop bag, Dorrie thanked Julie for coming and asked her to come again. She needed to do the same with Jeremiah. If only she'd out-grown the high school "stammer-when-I-talk-to-cute-boys" phase.

"Jeremiah?" Here went nothing.

He looked up from where he was gathering his trash. Don't look him in the eyes. You'll drown in pools of chocolate that would make Willy Wonka jealous. The glimpse or two she'd gotten had been more than enough to realize drowning would be a marvelous way to go.

His voice jolted her back to Panera. And there were those eyes. Could he be smiling at her? "Thank you for letting me join you today."

"Of course. Are you new to CANDID?" She'd been told someone would send her an email telling her when a new member from the area joined, but she hadn't gotten one yet.

He shook his head. "No. I'm here for a few months trying to decide if this is where I want to move." At her puzzled look, he went on. "I work from home so it doesn't matter where I am and I'm tired of Chicago. I thought I'd try out a few other places before making a decision."

"That's smart. How do you like the Ozarks so far?"

"I've only been here ten days, but one of the things I looked at when deciding where to go was a CANDID group. It's not a requirement for wherever I settle, but it would be nice."

"Well, we're glad to have you for as long as you're here." Dorrie told him when the next meeting would be and got his email address so she could put him on the mailing list.

Dorrie went to take a sip of her soda, but the condensation on the plastic made it more slippery than she realized.

Like one of those slow motion scenes from the Matrix movies, every drop became individually visible from every other as the dark liquid first flew upward then plummeted down to Jeremiah's laptop bag. Dorrie could see his eyes widen as they both followed the trajectory of the cup downward. He grabbed for his bag, but it was too late. The sloshing brought everything back to real speed. At least it seemed to be in the non-laptop portion of the bag.

"I'm so sorry." Dorrie reached for the napkins sitting on the table next to her, frantically blotting at the papers inside.

Jeremiah pulled them out, spreading them on the table as he muttered something that sounded a lot like, "No, no, no, no, no."

Dorrie continued to blot at the papers. When she moved one of the file folders, papers and photos fell out – a sticky, wet mess.

Dropping to the floor to pick them up, tears filled her eyes. Just what she needed to make a good first impression on this guy. Not that she really thought he'd be interested in her of all people, but this ensured he would not. Especially if she ruined his photos.

She flipped one over and gaped.

He reached for it, but Dorrie sat back on her heels and stared. "Why do you have this?" The words escaped before she could stop them.

"Give it to me."

"This is the cover for the new Mya Elizabeth Linscott Cambridge Family Saga book. Not the one coming out in a couple months but the one that comes out in January. The title hasn't even been announced yet." Of course, after seeing the picture Dorrie knew, but the official announcement wouldn't come until the day before MEL's August book released. MEL would send out a newsletter with information on upcoming promotions, like when her eBooks would be discounted, and at the end, she'd announce the title and preview the cover of her next book.

Dorrie looked up at him. His face was an unreadable mask. She had to know. "How'd you get this?"

AVAILABLE NOW!

Jeremiah Jacobs moved to the Ozarks for a fresh start. He knows no one and has no plans to get romantically involved with anyone. Ever. He's already had his heart ripped out once and once is enough. Besides he has contractual obligations that prevent him from talking about work - and what woman would want to be involved with a man who has to keep his job a secret? When he attends his first local writers' group meeting, he finds the leader so intriguing, his instant attraction to her threatens to complicate his currently uncomplicated life.

Dorrie Miller has never been good enough. Not for her father or any of the guys she's dated in the past. She's pushed beyond her father's disapproval to have a good career while pursuing her dream of becoming a published novelist. The Christian Authors Network – Dedicated to Inspirational Distinction, or CANDID, is hosting their annual conference in Indianapolis and who's rumored to be in attendance? The super reclusive, super-star author, Mya Elizabeth Linscott.

The hunky new member of her local CANDID group, Jeremiah, wants to carpool to Indy. Dorrie can handle not making a fool of herself for eight hours each way. Right? But she never imagined doing a favor for someone during the conference would leave her accidentally married to the gorgeous guy she barely knows. How will she get out of this mess, married to a near stranger? Does she want to? Will her insecurities and Jeremiah's secrets tear them apart? Or can she trust that, all along, God's been helping her with Finding Mr. Write?

Finding Mr. Write is a mega-romantic story with amazing chemistry between the two characters, and Jeremiah is one of the most memorable and loveable heroes I've read in a long time. Carol Moncado's writing reeled me in and hooked me, and I was eager to see how Dorrie and Jeremiah would overcome their secrets and unusual circumstances to find true love. I loved this story! ~ Melanie Dickerson, award winning author of The Healer's Apprentice

Previews may not be in their final form and are subject to change.

When she's not writing about her imaginary friends, Carol Moncado is hanging out with her husband, four kids, and a dog who weighs less than most hard cover books. She prefers watching *NCIS* to just about anything, except maybe watching *Castle*, or possibly *Girl Meets World* with her kids. She believes peanut butter M&Ms are the perfect food and Dr. Pepper should come in an IV. When not watching her kids - and the dog - race around her big backyard in Southwest Missouri, she's teaching American Government at a local community college. She's a founding member and President of MozArks ACFW, category coordinator for First Impressions, blogger at InspyRomance, and represented by Tamela Hancock Murray of The Steve Laube Agency.

CANDID
Romance

Finding Mr. Write

Available NOW!

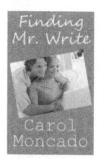

Finally Mr. Write

Available NOW!

Falling for Mr. Write

Available NOW!

The Montevaro Monarchy

Good Enough for a Princess
Preorder now!
Available NOW!

Along Came a Prince

Available NOW!

More Than a Princess

Available NOW!

The Brides of Bellas Montagnes

Coming Summer 2015

The royal families of Mevendia and Ravenzario
are no different than the rest of us. They
just want to find someone to love, and now
that their Montevaran cousins are settling
down, the pressure is on.

Hand-me-down Princess

Prince Malachi of Mevendia has no
intention of getting married.
His father has a different plan.

Queen of His Heart

Ravenzario's Queen Christiana's
life has been turned upside down.
The wedding to the man of her
dreams will fix that, won't it?

Prince from her Past

Princess Yvette of Mevendia has
been betrothed since before her
first birthday. Her intended groom
disappeared not long after. The
wedding is supposed to be next
week. Now what?

44345170R00190

Made in the USA
Charleston, SC
20 July 2015